W0027741

Delicious Vermin!

By Rosie Barham

OED definition of vermin: mammals and birds injurious to crops, game, or farm animals.
Rosie's definition: Some of it is edible! Low-calorie, cholesterol-free, and yummy.

Vintage vermin-eaters. My gt. gt. grandfather (centre) and his mates knew it was delicious way back in the 1850s.

First published in July 2014

ISBN number: 987-0-9926062-4-4

Designed and published by mpress (Media) LTD.

Unit Four, Ashton Gate, Harold Hill, Romford, RM3 8UF

Dedication and Acknowledgments

This book is for my family, both real and surrogate; they know who they are.

A huge thank you to:
Mike and Michelle Sully, who offer constant moral and practical support for anything I do, and particularly to Michelle for the entire Simple Puds section.
Terry Doe, editor of Airgun World, for allowing me the opportunity to inflict my passion for cookery on the general public; for the stunning scenic photographs, for writing the foreword, and together with Matt Clark, and Phill Price for invaluable advice regarding anything airgun-related that I needed to know.
Naidre Werner, friend and colleague, for her help and support.
Cliff Moulder, and Paul Moulder for their guidance and expertise.
Dan Green, for putting up with my procrastination in the illustration department and supplying at short notice.

Dave Barham who inadvertently supplied the inspiration behind the very first shooting article way back in 1989, and who continues to inspire me to this day.
Simon Barham for his unfailing support and encouragement in all things - and for making me laugh.
... and my surrogate son, Elton Murphy, for just being 'Murph'.

Special thanks to: Norrie and Shiona Southam and Eddie Jones for sending gifts of food by post, and Rob Collins for allowing me to tweak one of his recipes.

Foreword

Great title, isn't it? 'Delicious Vermin'; that's bound to catch an eye or two, no doubt about it. As intriguing as it is, that title won't work at all unless it's justified by the content of the book. I'm here to assure you that this is entirely the case and that the author has nothing to fear from the custodians of the Trades Descriptions Act. This book is, indeed, stuffed with vermin made delicious by the talent of Rosie Barham. Better still, her gift for instruction joins the pure enthusiasm for her subject, to make successful chefs of us all.

I've been eating vermin since I was a toddler, although I didn't know it was called vermin in those days. The rabbits, pigeons and collared doves my father brought home from his shooting trips on the Buckinghamshire farmland where I was born and raised were important food items to our family. For reasons that continue to escape me, we didn't eat squirrel back then but I've done my level best to make up for that sorry omission in the last ten years or so.

The happy fact is, edible pests can make great eating, especially if you have a skilled teacher like Rosie Barham to help you make the most of them. The meat of rabbit, squirrel, pigeon and dove is lean and tasty, and there are so many fine things you can do with it, if you know how. Thanks to this book, that know-how is ready and waiting for you to take tasty advantage of it.

Inside, you'll find scores of perfectly possible recipes, and you don't need to be a wiz in the kitchen to bring them to your table. This is a cook book for those who like to eat what has become known as 'proper food', free from preservative and pretension. The ingredients are there for the gathering, from your game dealer or your own game bag, and you'll need only the cookware found in most kitchens to turn vermin into something remarkable.

So, please read this excellent book, follow its plainspeak step-by-step guides, and as one who has done just that, I'm in the ideal position to assure you that your vermin will be truly delicious. Eat those pests with pride!

Terry Doe

Contents

Prologue

This collection of recipes and anecdotes is not a cookery book in the accepted sense. It was never intended to be a book at all, until some readers of my Airgun World column suggested it might be a good idea. I discussed it with colleagues and they agreed, so here it is.

Within these pages you will find the results of several culinary experiments that turned out okay, and a few that didn't, interspersed with the story of how it all began way back in the early '90s. There is some basic instruction for those just starting out as a cook, but I've kept that to a minimum. If you're not too familiar with herbs and spices, those chapters will be important to you. My reputation as a good cook is based on these two elements; everyone who has eaten my food thinks I'm brilliant, but I'm not – the herbs and spices are, though. The secret is to experiment until you find the combination of flavours you prefer.

The bulk of the recipes are for rabbit and pigeon, purely because I've always found it difficult to source squirrel – not because it is an inferior meat. Within the circle of friends who hunt with airguns, there are also shotgunners, so I'm sometimes given larger game as a gift, and I've shared my take on it with you.

Accompaniments and 'other stuff'; savoury rice, sauces, and so on, have a dedicated section, and Simple Puds are at the back of the book, in case you have a sweet tooth, or need to impress someone with your easy but 'expert' pudding prowess. I have Michelle Sully to thank for these; she provided both words and pictures, thank goodness! I can knock up a decent apple pie, but I'm not an imaginative pud cook.

The story of how to cope with the onset of airgun obsession - and it's not just youngsters who are seized by it - to deal with it and emerge relatively unscathed, runs through as a theme with the intention of entertaining those who have survived, and whose youngsters have grown into fine hunters, whilst reassuring those still going through it that they're not alone!

Rosie Barham 2014

In the Beginning: Perils and Pitfalls

My aptitude for cooking game came about by accident. It all started way back in 1988, when my boys were young teenagers and the eldest came home from school with an air pistol that he'd swapped for the Guns & Roses LP that I'd bought him for Christmas. What I imagined would be a passing interest developed into full-blown obsession and I began to write stuff down in an effort to make sense of the things that my eldest son, in particular, did in pursuit of his sport. Reproduced throughout this book are some of my meanderings from 1989/95 into the realms of everything junior-airgun-related, and I offer no apologies for rehashing them because it's for your own good. This is how it all starts and you should be told. Do not be alarmed, though; it all works out in your favour in the end. My sons are now grown and have families of their own, but I still receive the fruits of their huntin'/fishin' expeditions. It's a bit of a bonus.

Perils and Pitfalls

I've been the mother of a novice airgunner, and I feel that it's only fair to make you aware of the pitfalls that start to occur the minute you give permission for your youngsters to own an air rifle. Forewarned is forearmed, as the saying goes, and if your offspring is to be armed, I don't see any reason why you shouldn't be warned.

A decent air rifle is expensive. They won't settle for anything less than the best, particularly if they've got a Saturday job and think they own the world. My son, who exuded so much charm when it suited him that I began to cast about hastily for a bucket, shamelessly inveigled the use of my credit card with the immortal words, 'you're the best mum in the world, and I'll pay you back, honest.' They usually do pay it all back, but it takes them six months longer than promised, and meanwhile the credit card company is charging monthly interest on a loan that you didn't want to take out in the first place.

So, now we have the air rifle and you have to admit that it's pretty enough to be mounted above the fireplace in the sitting room, but this thing has to be fed and cared for with almost fanatical devotion. Pellets, gun oil, cleaning pellets and a soft, comfy case are vital to its present existence and to ensure that it lives until the loan has been repaid.

You must read the manual on aftercare that comes with the rifle, or you may find yourself, as I did, driving 15 miles through patchy fog to the nearest specialist gun shop to find out why the blessed thing is ailing. The guy behind the counter cocked it as directed in the manual and fired off the 'stuck' pellet into a safe container. The whole operation took 20 seconds and then there was the 15-mile drive home; the fog was thicker, and a huge car factory on the main road had knocked off for the day so there was a two-mile tail-back.

When things finally settle down and your offspring begins to enjoy his new hobby, keep an eye on him at all times. If you are in the habit of leaving pegs on the line after bringing in the washing, they may spontaneously combust, to lie in splintered heaps all over the garden. No one seems to know how this happens, but the hardware store proprietor will make a small fortune from your weekly visits for further supplies.

Keep a sharp eye on your wardrobe. Khaki, linen trousers will be 'borrowed' to go with the camouflage jacket he got for Christmas and will be returned covered in mud and gun oil, at the very least. I'm pretty tall but my son was above average height and the trousers were only regular length so the hems had to be ripped open to prevent them from looking like Bermudas. I handed over the khaki sweatshirt too; there was nothing to wear it with now, anyway.

Check the pockets of every item of clothing on washing days otherwise your washing machine will sound like one of those Victorian musical boxes. It can be pleasant to listen to and builds up to an interesting rhythm, but it's not so good when the bill comes in for picking out the pellets from the innards – not to mention the cups of tea dispensed to the repairman. You may be forced to witness several vacuum cleaners in their death throes, too; it can be quite distressing.

I made him join a gun club and it turned out to be one of the best things I could have done. They offered loads of practical advice along with much-needed emotional support to a nervous mother. One answer to the problem of an over-enthusiastic, teenaged air rifler, they said, was to build a special target area and insist, on pain of death - or even worse, confiscation - that this was the only bit he could shoot at.

We spent all day and my birthday money building a target area. Several paving slabs were propped against the back fence, ground was levelled off and gravelled, and we bought one of those target things that twizzles round when hit - and a new scope, which just happened to be on display in the gun shop near the target thing that twizzles.

Soon it was time to try it out with a few shots. Christmas cards were scrutinized for bright and visible targets which were taped to the slabs, and we were off, theoretically. A few minutes later, and before a shot had been fired, the local constabulary knocked on the door with a formal complaint from an elderly neighbour, some houses away from the back of our garden. Apparently, he'd spotted number one son checking out the new scope through the open bedroom window, before using the garden for target practice. The complainant had 'heard shots' shortly after his vision and imagined that innocent birds and mammals were being picked off from a great height - well, the first floor window, anyway.

The police were very reasonable about it, especially when they noticed the BASC badges and literature lying about, and realised that my son had a serious hobby and was not a budding terrorist. There was a downside, though. We were told not to use the target area anymore. Anymore?
"The old boy could hear a car back-firing and think it was a rifle shot," they said. "You'll have us round here all the time. If you must practise at home, fire from the bottom of the garden up toward the house – can't say I was too impressed with that one – or, better still, save it for the gun club."

Needless to say, the area was not used, and for some time it sat barren and expectant so I made it into a rockery. I was tempted to turn it into a nuclear power dump; let's give the old boy something to be nervous about, for goodness sake. Meanwhile, number two son, then nearly 14, was avidly reading the latest issue of Airgun World.
"Ma," he said, speculatively, "how old do I have to be before I can ..."

Ten Pointers Toward Being a Good Airgun Quarry Cook

1. There is no rule that says you need to have breasts in order to cook. Both my sons do all the cooking in their respective households and they're very good at it. You can do it, too!

2. Eat everything edible that you shoot. You have access to the finest, leanest, most natural meat going, and it's almost criminal not to do it justice.

3. Keep it simple. So many people think that to be a good cook, you need to use ingredients that no one's ever heard of; and plenty of them. Too many flavours muddle the result and the dish ends up tasting of nothing in particular.

4. Always have the basics in the store cupboard; rice, pasta, flour, tinned tomatoes, assorted tins of beans, lentils, barley, olive oil, vinegars, suet, and most importantly, herbs and spices.

5. Speaking of herbs and spices – don't go paying exorbitant amounts for piddling little jars of stuff in supermarkets. Find your nearest Asian grocer and browse for ten minutes. You'll find all your favourites, top quality, and for a quarter of the price.

6. When you thicken a sauce with flour, it's best to coat the 'dry' ingredients with it - i.e. browned meat and/or veg - before you add any liquid. Keep stirring until it thickens and then turn down to a simmer. That way, you'll never have lumpy gravy.

7. Invest in a decent saucepan, heavy-based frying pan or wok, and a reasonably sized stockpot that will hold a rabbit/squirrel stew and dumplings for as many people as you anticipate feeding. Plonk it in the middle of the table with some crusty bread and you'll have heaven on a plate!

8. One of my best kitchen friends is my slow cooker; you can't beat coming home after a long day to the aroma of something tasty that you didn't have to spend time preparing in the kitchen.

9. Oh, and knives! Carving, paring and filleting knives, and a small cleaver should cover most of your kitchen jobs. Make sure that they are the best quality you can afford, and keep them sharp - I sharpen mine every time I use them. Invest in a knife-sharpener; they're only a couple of quid and worth every penny if you can't get to grips with a steel.

10. Finally, enjoy it. Cooking should be a 'love' thing. The joy gained from preparing food for those you care about, and the pleasure given to them when it turns out okay (and the entertainment value when it doesn't!) cannot be measured. Opening a packet ready-meal just doesn't hack it.

Hardware Essentials

You don't need loads of fancy equipment to be a half-decent cook. As I've said, you can get by with a decent saucepan, or two, a heavy-gauge frying pan, maybe a wok, a sieve or colander, and a good-quality set of knives. Mind you, a few gadgets can make our lives a lot easier. They were not available when my mother was a young woman so I used to watch her in the kitchen, fascinated as she pushed things through sieves, mashed potatoes with a fork, or stood for hours, serene and unflustered, while peeling, chopping, mixing, and stirring. As a small child, before the advent of freezers and microwaves, I was dragged out to the shops in all weathers in order to buy provisions - maybe that's where my hatred of all things shopping-related stems from. Mum bought and cooked fresh, seasonal food every single day, in small quantities just enough for our needs, because in the '50s we had no means of keeping it from spoiling

Before beginning to write this section, I stood in the middle of my kitchen and looked around me at the amount of equipment that I have accumulated in a relatively short time. When my marriage disintegrated 15 years ago, I walked away with virtually nothing; all my beloved pots and pans, some inherited from my grandmother, my Kenwood mixers, stock pots, mixing bowls, copper jelly moulds, espresso coffee maker … all left behind, and I won't bore you with the details, but I'll just tell you that by the time I realised that I hadn't got them, it was too late. So, I remembered a verse from the poem hanging on my bathroom wall, metaphorically turned the page, and started again.

'If you can bear to hear the truth you've spoken
Twisted by knaves to make a trap for fools,
Or watch the things you gave your life to broken,
And stoop and build 'em up with worn-out tools.'
Rudyard Kipling

Fifteen years on, surrounded by relative luxury, I asked myself which implements I couldn't possibly do without, and came up with the following:

A food processor, and a Kenwood Chef mixer: You may think that they do the same jobs, but that's not so. I can make bread, whisk meringue and make huge cakes with the Kenwood; the food processor slices, grates, chops … so I have the best of both worlds.

An aluminium wok for stir-frying: I did have a heavier-gauge one but it didn't give me the versatility of the lighter metal. Tossing sliced vegetables or a handful of prawns in a sauce is so much easier if you can actually lift the pan.

A large saucepan: Used for family-sized amounts of pasta or potatoes; blanching a glut of summer vegetables to freeze in bulk.

Stock-pots: I have two; one is used for hearty stews and soup, or boiling a ham or a steak and kidney pudding, and the other for making jam and chutney.

Steamer: This is invaluable for cooking half a dozen vegetables at once, and it retains all of the flavour and vitamins. You're not throwing out any of the nutrients in the water – which I use for gravy more often than not, incidentally.

Slow-cooker: I love coming home on a dark and cold winter night to the smell of a stew or curry emanating from my slow-cooker; instant comforting food involving very little effort.

A selection of knives: It's worth investing in some decent steel, and a few knives of varying sizes won't break the bank. A good-quality carver, a cleaver, a paring knife, one for filleting and a bread knife should cover all your kitchen needs – and don't forget the knife sharpener.

Zester/grater: I know that a food processor grates cheese and slices vegetables, but I've yet to find one that will zest a lemon. A pinch of citrus peel will add a zing to many dishes – you'd be surprised.

So, these are the basic items of kitchen equipment. You'll also need mixing bowls, oven-proof dishes, wooden spoons, a tin-opener, and so on, but the bog-standard kit is simple.

There are a few things in my own kitchen that I could do without, and did so for many years, but don't want to ever again: a freezer, microwave, refrigerator, dishwasher, toaster, electric kettle and coffee maker. All of these things are mostly taken for granted, these days, and the youngsters I know marvel at the fact that some of us just didn't have access to them, either for financial reasons, or because they simply hadn't been made commercially available. I wouldn't want to go back to 'the good old days', though – I'm quite happy with all mod cons, thank you very much.

Like I said, there really is no need to spend small fortunes on gadgetry. On more than one occasion, I've fed a group of lads beside a lake in France for a week – three meals a day – using just one heat source and a wok. It took a bit of inventive thinking, but I did it, and no one complained. There really is no excuse for not cooking decent grub, wherever you are and whatever your resources. One last thing to end the lecture: always buy the best-quality basic utensils that you can afford. It really is false economy to buy cheap saucepans that will need replacing after six months.

Store Cupboard

Years ago, when my boys were teenagers, their friends had a habit of either dropping in around mealtimes, or turning up early and staying until it was time to eat. Their father also used to bring virtual strangers home from the pub and insist that I feed them. 'It'll be fine,' he'd tell them when they questioned the wisdom of arriving uninvited at mealtimes. 'Of course, there will be enough food to go round. I'll tell the wife to throw in a few more potatoes'.

I gave up my own dinner a couple of times, ate quite a few meals consisting solely of potatoes, and then began to stock up on staples like flour, suet, rice, and pasta, so that if unexpected, and sometimes unwelcome guests were thrust upon me, I could add to the menu with relative ease. You'd be surprised how much further a small joint of beef will go if include some mushrooms and shove pastry around it. Lamb chops can be cooked in a 'toad in the hole' stylie, and chicken portions, stripped of meat and mixed into paella rice with a few frozen vegetables will feed half as many people again as plain chicken and spuds.

Of course, there are less extreme reasons for keeping a supply of basic ingredients in your kitchen. In bad weather, it's so much more convenient if you don't have to traipse to the shops in order to get something that will keep for months in a cool, dark place, and I love the idea of being able to create something tasty from very little, and that can be done easily given a decent store cupboard and a little inspiration.

These items are in my kitchen now:

Flours:
Self-raising: for dumplings, cakes.
Plain: for Yorkshire puds, crumbles, biscuits, pastry.
Strong white: for breads, buns.
Wholemeal: I usually mix this with white flour 40-60% because it can be a bit heavy on its own.
Cornflour: for thickening sauces.

Grains and pulses:
Red lentils, split peas, and barley - for stews.
Semolina – I use this instead of breadcrumbs for 'egg and breadcrumb' coating.
Porridge oats can be used in the same way, or to add bulk and thicken a stew.

Tinned Beans:
Cannellini, haricot, broad, red kidney, black-eyed, borlotti, mixed bean salad …

Rice:
Bomba: for paella-type dishes.
Basmati: for accompaniment to curries.
Arborio: for risotto.
Short grain: for sweet rice dishes.

Pasta:
Spaghetti lunghi: long spaghetti because it's somehow nicer than the short stuff, although I don't know why it should be.
Rigatoni: for when I can't be bothered to twiddle a fork.
Macaroni: for macaroni cheese – with or without pigeon, or for a sweet macaroni milk pudding.
Lasagne sheets and cannelloni tubes.

I always keep a variety of tinned items: stock cubes of all varieties; condensed chicken or mushroom soups, which I use as a sauce sometimes; vinegars and oils for cooking or salad dressing; tomatoes, tomato puree; sweetcorn, beans – which are great for padding out dishes that contain little meat - and jars of olives, chargrilled peppers, artichokes, anchovies, capers and cornichons, for adding that little extra something.

Don't forget the freezer. A stash of frozen fruit and vegetables can be a godsend when you're caught out by unexpected guests. You can knock up a crumble easily with a pack of frozen berries, or rhubarb, and to have a pack or two of frozen pastry in reserve isn't a sin; it defrosts fairly quickly, so pies are a doddle, too. I don't buy ready-meals, ever, but frozen fruit and veg retain all the nutrients of the fresh stuff, and are rarely chemically enhanced. I always read the labels before I buy.

Always have a supply of fresh eggs, butter or substitute, cheeses and bacon on hand, and of course, the indispensible garlic, spice and herb department, and you'll be prepared for any challenge in the kitchen.

Emergency rations.

Herbs Make All the Difference

I have a reputation for being an excellent cook, but the 'producer of fine food' label is not strictly accurate, and I'm about to admit it. I'm not a brilliant cook, no better than anyone else, but I have a secret or two that make people think so, and I'm prepared to reveal all, provided you don't tell.

Many of my concoctions are unique, but only because I rarely remember what I've put in them, and they never taste exactly the same twice running. When asked to reproduce a particular version of something, or give out a recipe, I have to refuse because I simply cannot recall all of the ingredients. The secret of unique flavour, though, is fresh herbs. Herbs and spices are what it's all about, people - coupled with the best-quality ingredients that I can find. These two factors are what make it all happen, and are essential to any recipe that I produce.

I much prefer to grow my own herbs, rather than resort to the dried variety, but the dried ones will do, and there are rare occasions when the more intense flavour of a dried herb is preferable; dried chamomile, bergamot and mint infused in teas, for example. Dried herbs are more pungent than fresh and they're all passable alternatives if you're unable to source the fresh ones. I use dried basil when my windowsill plants are not growing as fast as I'd like, but in my opinion, if you're going to throw any ingredient into your food, then the fresher it is the better.

Try a handful of chopped coriander stirred into a pigeon chilli, just before serving, for a bit of a lift, and curries will benefit from the same treatment. They just don't have that certain something without fresh coriander strewn over them, and even if you must use instant curry sauce from a jar, the improvement can quite remarkable.

Stab a rabbit a few times and insert rosemary and garlic into wounds before wrapping the whole thing in a big foil envelope, with a little red wine and a couple of chopped shallots. Unwrap it after about an hour and a half, add a spoonful of crème fraîche, rewrap, then cook for a further ten minutes and everyone will think that you've had lessons from that bloke, Gordon Bleu.

Mint can be thrown over new potatoes, peas, carrots ... floated on the top of homemade lemonade, or Pimms - especially Pimms - or mixed with olive oil and white wine as a marinade. Make your own mint sauce with cider vinegar and a little honey for sweetness. You can 'frost' mint leaves with egg white and caster sugar to top a fruit salad, or hang a sprig on the side of a cocktail glass, purely for effect.

Whenever you're within spitting distance of a tomato, think basil. You can use it for the obvious tricolore salad, traditionally served as a starter in Italian households – that's sliced mozzarella, tomatoes and basil leaves, for those who don't know any traditional Italians. Toast a pitta (or two – it's more-ish), drizzle a teaspoonful of olive oil inside it and then add extra-mature Cheddar, sliced, still-on-the-vine-tomato, and half a dozen basil leaves. My late mum-in-law used to serve this as a delicious light lunch to me and my boys when they were little, and it's still a favourite. Forget about sage and onion stuffing mixes in packets. It takes seconds to zizz a few breadcrumbs in a blender – you can pop in a quartered onion at the same time. Add a couple of chopped sage leaves, black pepper, a little salt, bind it with an egg and bake for about 15 minutes. There's nothing like it, really there isn't, and it takes just about as long as opening a packet and waiting for a kettle to boil. Wrap a couple of pigeon breasts in foil with a sage leaf on top of each one, and a sprinkling of salt and pepper; great for barbecues. Sage leaves can be used to enhance oily or strong-flavoured fish, like mackerel, herring, hake … I place a sage leaf on top of a split herring or mackerel before I grill it, or chop a couple of leaves to add while pan-frying white fish.

Thyme is probably my favourite herb and I grow three varieties in my patio tubs – common, broad-leaved and golden creeping – for no other reason than they look pretty and I use it all the thyme (sorry), so one plant is never enough for my needs.

Try stuffing a whole young rabbit with dried apricots, thyme and a handful of breadcrumbs. Sew up the cavity and then roast it for an hour, basting frequently. Or, substitute the apricots for almonds and stuff a trout in the same way. Either dish is delightful for a winter evening meal, with creamy mashed potatoes and celeriac, and a green veg.

Herbs aplenty - and they make all the difference.

Parsley is best friends with fish, of course. A fillet of cod, or more likely pollack these days, a few prawns, mashed potato, a handful of parsley and an egg, seasoned, mixed well and fried as fishcakes is superb with a parsley sauce. You can do the same kind of thing with pigeon, or squirrel. Just cook the meat first before you chop it finely and add to the potato mixture. I cheat sometimes and use a packet of white sauce mix as a base for the sauce, and then add fresh parsley and black pepper. You can make a similar sauce with dill.

Omelettes knocked up with whatever you happen to have handy: grated cheese, ham, mushrooms, shrimp … whatever … always taste much better for a handful of chopped chives. They are great in salads, and new potatoes tossed in chive butter are wonderful. Baguettes spread with herb butter before filling are much more interesting, and a couple of pats melted on top of pan-fried pigeon or squirrel is amazing. (See page 206 for Herb Butter recipe)

Finally, in my herb collection is the dependable bay leaf. I have a small bay tree outside my front door in a huge pot, given to me by my friend, the late Barbara Sully, and I think of her at least once a week because I pick bay leaves so often. The dried variety is just as good, and I usually dry the pruned branches in late autumn, and store the leaves in airtight jars. They're often given away to friends who don't have bay tress of their own.

I know you can buy fresh herbs readily in supermarkets these days, and the ones they call 'growing herbs' will last you about a week, but nothing beats growing your own. It's so satisfying to have a few pots on a window sill so that you can harvest fresh, fragrant leaves as you cook. They can be cultivated outdoors in pots quite easily, but if you are lucky enough to have the space for a 'real' herb garden, there's nothing better on a warm, summer afternoon than sitting outside with a cuppa, running your hands through the leaves and inhaling the perfumes that waft upward.

Some people class garlic as a herb, and I suppose it is, although it is used more and more often these days as a vegetable, sweet and flavoursome roasted around a Sunday joint. If I could take only one seasoning to a desert island, garlic would be my choice; to me, few meals are complete without it. I've heard people (often my own dinner party guests) say that they 'can't stand garlic'. It stinks and just the thought of it makes them feel ill, and yet they have eaten and enjoyed my food, and gazed at me in disbelief when told that it contained garlic. I only mention it if they ask me for the recipe, of course. I don't say, 'Nar nar ne-nar nar, you've just eaten garlic!' and most of my diners go home replete, and happily in ignorance of the fact that they've just consumed their 'food nightmare'. Prejudice, in any shape or form is a terrible thing.

So, try the herb secret. I promise it'll work for you, and you'll be lauded and applauded whenever you cook for others.

A Word about Spices

I learned very early on in my cooking adventures that spices could make all the difference to an ordinary dish that would otherwise be mundane, and enhance a really good plate of food beyond all expectations, so I've always kept a varied supply to hand. I started off with the basics; pepper - black, red and white - cloves, cinnamon, ginger, nutmeg ... and as soon as I'd experimented successfully with those, added a few more to my collection. I have to say that I inflicted a few culinary disasters on my family before I got the quantities right, but I had teenaged boys with a lot of friends who were constantly hungry, and they'd eat anything, so nothing was ever wasted.

If you're not sure how much of a particular spice to add, just use a very little, taste, and add a bit more if the flavour isn't right. As the old saying goes, 'You can always put more in, put you can't take it out.' Always taste regularly as you cook, anyway. How else are you going to know if it is salty, sweet, sour, or tender enough?

This is a list of the spices that I have in my kitchen at any one time, and a brief description of what I do with them.

All Spice: Although this single spice has hints of clove, cinnamon and nutmeg, it is a spice berry in its own right. It gives you the best of three worlds and is especially good in anything that needs a subtle but warm flavour.

Caraway: I put a teaspoon of this into any kind of cabbage, which I always stir-fry with bacon and onion – and I make 'seedy' cake sometimes to remind me of my grandmother's Sunday afternoon teas.

Celery seed: Used for flavouring as a last resort if I've run out of celery and can't be bothered to go to the supermarket. Don't go mad with this, though. A few seeds are all that you'll need. It gives quite a concentrated celery flavour.

Chilli flakes or whole dried chilli: I found out about the whole dried chilli deal by accident one summer, when I'd been given some freshly-picked chillis by a friend. I took them out of the bag, got side-tracked by a phone call, or a Mars Bar, or something equally important, and instead of storing them in the salad tray, completely forgot about them. The weather was hot and dry, and by the time I'd remembered about them days later, wandered about the house for a bit - 'what the hell did I do with those chillis?' - and eventually found them on the kitchen windowsill, they had dried out nicely. Once in an airtight jar they kept for about a year, so I do it all the time now. I grow my own chillis indoors, harvest during a hot spell, and then dry naturally on kitchen paper.

Brown mustard seed: Used mainly as an ingredient in a home-produced curry powder. (See page 207) Also added to the water when boiling a gammon joint, along with a halved onion, a few chilli flakes, two cloves of garlic, a cinnamon stick, two cloves and a bay leaf or two. You must try this. The spices will give you a gammon of piquancy, quality and flavour that you cannot buy in any shop.

Cardamom pods: Curry powder/paste ingredient and also useful for stews, along with cumin.

Cloves: Use very sparingly. These have a strong fruity flavour and one or two in a dish will give you all the warmth that you need.

Coriander - whole seeds, and ground: A curry powder/paste ingredient, but the ground seeds are great when combined with ground cumin and nutmeg in a soup or broth.

Cumin: This is one of my favourite spices for pigeon because it's quite a strong flavour and imparts a kind of earthy edge.

Cinnamon: Many cooks consider this to be a sweet spice, but it can be used very successfully in savoury dishes. It's particularly good with rabbit.

Fenugreek seeds: Half a teaspoon of fenugreek in a stew will enhance it more than you would imagine. The seeds are extremely pungent, and belie the depth of flavour. They smell so unpleasant that you'd be tempted to throw them in the bin, if you didn't know better.

Fennel seeds: These have a kind of aniseed flavour and I use them in salads, rabbit recipes and a rub for roast belly pork.

Garam Masala: I buy this ready-made and sprinkle it on top of braised, stewed, or even on roasted meat as it cooks – and not just on game.

Garlic Powder: This is pure indulgence for when I want the taste of garlic but can't be bothered to squeeze a tube of puree, let alone peel and squash the real thing.

Ginger: Ginger with garlic and chilli, a classic, Indian-inspired flavour combination used for marinating. Also used for sticky ginger cake or muffins.

Mace: This is a vital ingredient for any kind of hot-water crust pie, particularly pork or game. It gives that 'pork pie on a summer afternoon by a river' taste.

Nutmeg: More usually associated with the top of a creamy, oven-baked rice pudding, but try it in a butternut squash soup, or a rabbit stew.

Paprika – hot, sweet, or smoked: Paprika is an underrated spice, in my opinion. I use it often, in all three of its incarnations; hot for when I want a warm, spicy effect, sweet when a gentle, peppery flavour is required, and smoked for savoury rice or a Hungarian goulash kind of deal.

Pepper: Black – ground or whole corns are strong and hot, but not fiery.

White – for mild pepper requirements.

Green, pickled in brine – I found these by accident in Aldi and they're great for a sauce to accompany seared pigeon breasts.

Pink – I bought some of these, but I had no idea what they were for until I got them home and looked them up on t'Internet. It turned out that they are not pepper at all, but a completely different plant. They're great used in salads or when combined with the black variety, though.

Red (cayenne) – Be careful! This is potent stuff and should be used very sparingly. Taste, and taste again, after each small pinch and don't rub your eyes - or anything else, come to that - until you have washed your hands a million times. Better still, use the edge of a teaspoon instead of finger and thumb.

Saffron: Great for adding colour to a dish, and its unique flavour. I'm addicted to it although I have heard others say that they can't taste it in a dish. It's expensive but, in my opinion, well worth it because it's not something that you'll use every day.

Star Anise: Reminiscent of Chinese five-spice powder, and fantastic in stir-fries, or used as a marinade ingredient. You can also grind it in a pestle, along with ginger and garlic, and use it as a rub for roast pork – or rabbit.

Sumac: A tangy, lemon taste and used in Morrocan-style dishes. No substitute for fresh lemon, though; it's quite a subtle flavour by comparison.

Turmeric: If you're after colour and an earthy taste that's cheaper than saffron - this is the one for you.

Vanilla pod: For sweet dishes, custard, and cakes.

Golden Rules

1. Make sure that rabbits are paunched as soon as possible after shooting. If this isn't done, the gut contents can taint the meat.

2. Learn to recognise the symptoms of myxymatosis, on the internal organs (light spots on the liver) as well as the outward signs. There is no scientific proof that eating the meat will make you ill, but no one wants to eat a rabbit with myxi.

3. Get your shot game into a cool container quickly, especially in the summer, before flies can get at them and lay their eggs.

4. Wash your hands every time you touch a different ingredient.

5. Don't use the same chopping board for meat and vegetables. It's a good idea to colour-code them; red for meat, green or white for veg., so you don't get them mixed up.

6. Keep your knives sharp and in a block, if possible, to prevent them rattling around in a drawer. Sharp knives mean fewer accidents.

7. Always dispose of any waste material immediately after the game prep – either in an incinerator, or triple-wrapped in a bin.

8. Scrub down work surfaces before and after preparing any meat. Use an anti-bacterial solution, if possible, but good old soap and hot water will so the job.

9. About three months is the maximum time to leave game in the freezer before you use it; meat toughens the longer you leave it on ice and freezer burn makes it inedible.

10. Always turn saucepan handles inward, away from the front of the cooker, so no one can bump into them.

PIGEON

- Spring -

PIGEON

Dinner Jackets

I found a few pigeon breasts lurking at the back of the freezer recently, and had no idea what to do with them, nothing that hadn't been done already, anyway, until a Facebook friend of mine, Tom Bettle, offered me a rabbit recipe suggestion. Yes, I know that doesn't make sense, because this is a pigeon dish, but it triggered a train of thought and I realised that I hadn't used a baked potato as a medium before, and it's about time I did. I have substituted the rabbit fillets in Tom's recipe for pigeon breasts, but it will work with either meat – maybe a tad less garlic with the rabbit - and I intend to try that version just as soon as I can get to a farmer's market to source some bunnies.

I have heard people complain about all the social media sites; bemoaning the lack of privacy, the perils of giving out personal information to strangers, the bombardment of trivia, and the never-ending photographs of what people had for their dinner, but I have to say a big 'thank you' to Facebook. Apart from putting me in touch with old friends, with whom I would otherwise have lost touch, it has provided me with several dozen new ones – most of whom have a culinary interest and so we swap ideas. Long may it continue.

Anyway, thanks to Tom, you can knock up this little gem within minutes if you have a microwave oven in which to cook the potato, so it's ideal après-pub food – and it's quicker than standing in the queue at the kebab shop, besides being much nicer to eat. For those of you who have never cooked a baked potato in this way, it's done like this: Grab a potato, make a cross incision on the top and bung it in the microwave for five minutes. If you want it brown and crispy, pop it into a hot, conventional oven for another ten, but if not, just turn it over and give it another couple of minutes.

Even if you don't have a microwave, or don't go to the pub, you can still cook this easy dish in a conventional oven and eat it for a light lunch, a half-time snack during the footy on TV, or a tasty main meal with a salad or a green vegetable. Please try it. It is simplicity itself, just about as healthy a meal as you can get, costs about 20p if you shoot your own pigeons, and is seriously delicious. If you haven't spent all night in the pub, this is wonderful with an ice-cold lager, or if you're slightly squiffy already, with a Diet Coke.

INGREDIENTS:

Pigeon breasts
Garlic
Butter (and olive oil for frying)
Basil – or you can use sage
Potatoes
Seasoned flour

METHOD:

Dust the fillets in well-seasoned flour and fresh, (or dried) finely chopped basil.
Crush a garlic clove or chop it really finely. Go for more garlic according to taste.
Add it to a blob of melted butter and a splash of olive oil in a frying pan and when sizzling hot add the pigeon.
Brown it all over and then turn down the heat and cook for 5 to 10 minutes.
Serve immediately, over a hot jacket potato. Pour the pigeon cooking juices over the opened and crushed potato. You can add more butter to the spud if you're as unhealthy as me.

You will need …

Cut a cross on top of potato.

Toss meat in seasoned flour.

Butter and olive oil in pan.

Fry gently until …

… it looks like this.

PIGEON

Jamaican Jerk Pigeon Pockets

I am often asked how I come up with recipe ideas month after month. I tell everyone that I'm just so talented they fall out of my brain on a regular basis, but the reality is that I'm always on the lookout. I study menus if I'm out for dinner in restaurants, leaf through cookery books in shops, jot down ideas from TV programmes and listen to my culinary friends as they speak about which ingredients they put with what to make something delicious.

A few weeks ago, I was sitting with a friend having a cuppa and we came up with this idea. I can't take much credit for it, really, because one friend was the initial inspiration and Michelle (Simple Puds) suggested some of the fine-tuning. All I did was cook and eat it, but it turned out so well that I shall do it again and inflict it upon family and friends.

As we sat and discussed the finer points, I was reminded of a West Indian party that I had attended when I was a teenager in the 70s. It was the first time that I'd sampled anything curried wrapped in pastry and I was so excited that I demanded the recipe from the host's mother – who had done all the catering herself – there and then, much to the bewilderment of the bloke I was with at the time. He was amazed that I could be interested in anything other than him and dumped me shortly after that. I didn't mind too much; I'd learned how to cook genuine Jamaican curried mutton patties and it was a matter of priorities.

Anyway, back to the plot. I decided that the mutton could be replaced with pigeon, a pack of Schwartz Jerk Chicken Mix would substitute for the myriad spices that I really should grind and roast, and I'd add potatoes for a bit of padding. It's amazing what you can create with a little imagination, and this is so simple to do, and takes so little time, that it has to be worth making a few when you have the oven on, if only to freeze for summer picnics.

INGREDIENTS:

Pigeon meat, cut into very small pieces
One onion, two cloves of garlic
A large, cooked potato and a couple of tomatoes, diced
One green pepper
Schwartz Jerk Chicken Mix
I've used two teaspoonsful, but it's a matter of taste and depends on how hot you want it to be
A handful of frozen peas
Half a slab of packet puff pastry
Oil for frying, beaten egg for egg-washing

METHOD:

Chop all the ingredients to roughly the same size, to ensure even cooking.
Place the onion, garlic, potato, and green pepper into a pan and fry gently for a few minutes, until the onions are softened.
Add the pigeon meat, spice mix, tomatoes, and peas.
Add two tablespoons of water, a chicken stock cube, then cook for a further five minutes, stirring every now and then. The mixture should be gloopy.
Season with salt to taste.
Remove from the heat and allow to cool to room temperature.
Roll the half slab of pastry into a square. Then cut this into 4 equal squares.
Spread the filling over the base of each square, brush the edges with beaten egg, fold over and seal with a fork.
Egg wash the tops and bake for about 20 minutes at 180° - that's a moderate to hot oven.

You will need ...

Onions, garlic, potato and pepper.

Add pigeon, spice, tomatoes and peas.

Add water and stock.

Spread filling, brush edges with egg.

Crimp edges, and egg wash.

PIGEON

Pigeon in the Hole

I was going through my mum's cookery books and found some hand-written recipes that I remember her cooking for me when I was a child. Times were hard in the 50s, some foods were still on ration and my mother was an expert at 'making do' – a talent that I've inherited, I'm pleased to say. There have been times in my life, too, when money just wasn't available to buy food, but I managed to feed myself, and my boys, on very little outlay, and still make tasty dishes and the occasional tea-time treat.

Anyway, that's all history. Mum used to make a variation of this recipe and double it up, so we ate it for 'afters' as well. She used to mince the remains of the Sunday roast, add minced onion, a couple of slices of stale bread, an Oxo cube, salt and pepper, and an egg to bind it all together and then shape the mixture into sausages. These were placed into a small roasting tin and covered with a Yorkshire Pudding batter.

Thyme also went into the YP batter. My father, ahead of his time, grew herbs in among a multitude of vegetables in our bomb-crater garden, so I grew up with knowing how to use them, and Mum traded her precious herbs for eggs with our next-door neighbour, who kept chickens. I used to steal her strawberries through the wire fence, and both she and my mother must have known, but neither chastised me. Mum probably gave her a few extra sage leaves, as compensation.

I've adapted the recipe and used pigeon meat, instead of leftover beef or pork, but you could use rabbit if you prefer.

The 'afters', incidentally, were smaller versions of the Yorkshire pudding, served warm with a dollop of jam in the middle; a wonderful treat at the time.

INGREDIENTS:

For the batter:
4oz plain flour
2 eggs
Half a pint of milk
Salt and pepper
Teaspoonful of dried thyme, or handful of fresh.
Pigeon meat, chopped
2 slices of bread, blitzed into crumbs.
Chopped onion
Couple of sage leaves
Small pinch of mace, if you have it, or a half teaspoon grated nutmeg.
1 egg

METHOD:

Preheat the oven to very hot. 220 C
Prepare the filling first: Place all ingredients in a bowl and mix until combined. Shape into sausages.
While you're making the batter, put a tablespoon of oil into a roasting tin and place in the hot oven.
Make the batter: Put the flour and seasoning into a large mixing bowl, make a well and add eggs.
Add the milk gradually, and whisk until the mixture reaches the consistency of double cream. You should be able to see air bubbles.
Be careful when you remove the tin from the oven. The oil should be smoking. Pour the batter mix on to the hot fat, quickly place the sausages into it and shove it back in the oven. Cook for about half an hour – in the middle, or it'll burn.
Serve with anything you like.

For the batter ...

For the 'sausages' ...

Combine meat mixture.

Whisk batter ingredients.

Pour batter over sausages.

Bake until golden.

PIGEON

Pigeon Pockets

There is a physiological reason behind the craving for doner kebabs, curries, or fat-laden fry-ups that many people find vital to their well-being after serious and lengthy exposure to alcohol. It isn't, as my sons and ex-husband always insisted, partly 'tradition' and partly because 'you don't understand, drinking makes you hungry.' These excuses offered because they were desperate to be driven to a fast food outlet of any description after I'd picked them up from the pub, and all I wanted to do was to get home and go back to sleep.

I had a serious accident, early on in my marriage; actually getting married in the first place was a bit of an accident, thinking about it. The injury occurred while cooking deep-fried prawns and chips demanded by a wayward and very drunk husband, at 3am. I had to make the batter, dip the prawns, and fry them for a few minutes in batches and was so tired (my eldest son was a baby at the time) that I did it while perched on a high kitchen stool in front of the hob. Inevitably, I dripped boiling oil on to my legs and sustained burns severe enough to warrant hospital visits for about a month. I refused thereafter to obey orders for home-cooked, deep-fried food in the middle of the night, and that's when the 'tradition' of buying fast food after the pub/club began.

Apparently, according to the experts who have, I'm sure, spent many happy hours researching the subject, the relatively large amounts of grease, salt and sugar contained in favoured midnight snacks has a beneficial effect by absorbing some of the excess alcohol and so allowing the liver to recover more quickly from the onslaught.

These pigeon doners, though, don't involve much cooking and are delicious, if you can wait for long enough to get home and heat up a frying pan. Trust me, they are much better for your health, if you're careful in the kitchen.

I marinade my pigeon breast strips in lemon juice, olive oil and garlic, but if you can't be bothered you can just bung 'em straight into a pan with some oil, salt and pepper and a few dried chilli flakes, fry for a few minutes and shove them into toasted pitta bread with the already sliced vegetables. You can't injure yourself too badly with a toaster.

METHOD:

Slice onions, pepper, tomatoes, cucumber into a bowl, cover with Clingfilm and place them in the fridge along with the pigeon breasts, which you have already cut into strips and marinated in lemon juice, garlic, and vegetable oil.
Go out and get slaughtered.
On your return, this is the order in which you should do things:
Cut large pittas in half, diagonally, and place in the toaster. Heat up a tablespoonful of oil in a pan, throw in the pigeon breasts – not the marinade, just the meat – and move it around a bit for three minutes. Open the toasted pittas carefully with a knife, and stuff them with the cooked pigeon. Throw the previously prepared salad on top, squirt on a generous amount of chilli sauce, eat every scrap, leave the mess for your mother/wife to clear up in the morning and pass out on the couch/stairs/spare bed. Jalapeño peppers can be bought in jars and munched alongside the pittas, if you think you're hard enough.

You will need ...

Marinate in oil, lemon and garlic.

Assorted salad vegetables.

Cover and refrigerate.

Fry for three minutes.

Post-pub provender!

Posh Pigeon

I don't do posh food. Way back in the late-'80s, when eating small amounts of exorbitantly-priced food became fashionable I spent the whole of one afternoon preparing a luxury six-course meal for the family. It would have cost a small fortune in a restaurant, but they thought I'd served up half a dozen starters and when they realised that they were waiting in vain for a man-sized portion of steak and chips to follow, the boys sauntered off to the local curry house and my then husband lost his temper and went to the pub for a week.

I visited several high-class establishments, but the way in which the food was presented pretty much guaranteed that it was lukewarm, and although the flavours were good, there just wasn't enough of it for me; plus, I can only pretend to be sophisticated for 20 minutes at a stretch so it was hard work all round.

Recently, I thought I'd have another go and raked through the kitchen cupboards and found my '80s tian rings – 25 years on. If you don't have them already, you can make them. A small tin of baked beans, or anything else of a similar shape, will do the job. Just remove the 'lids' from both ends of the tin and use the cylinder shape to stack your food.

This recipe looks complicated, but it isn't. It's very quick to make and surprisingly delicious. I say 'surprisingly' because I'm an advocate of long, slow cooking or marinating overnight before a quick blast of heat, but you can do the whole job in the time that it takes for the potatoes to boil. It's cheap and hardly sophisticated, but only you and I will know that, so if you want to impress, give it a go. Make sure you put flowers on the table, and invest in some gigantic plates – apparently, that's an essential part of 'the look'. I'd follow it up with a huge apple pie and custard, just in case your diners are still hungry.

INGREDIENTS:

Two pigeon breasts
Oil for frying, salt and pepper and a little dried thyme
Spinach, potato, parsnip
1 tbs crème fraîche
For the jus: 2 fl oz red wine and the same of water
1 chicken stock pod
Black pepper

METHOD:

Slice the breasts as thinly as you can and season with salt, pepper and dried thyme. Set aside.

Make the jus (gravy for the unsophisticated among us). Mix the wine, water, stock pod and black pepper in a small saucepan, bring to the boil and then turn down to a simmer. It should have reduced by half, by the time the spud mixture is cooked.

Boil potatoes and parsnip together until tender – about 15 minutes and then mash with a tablespoonful of crème fraîche until there are no lumps.

Wilt the spinach in a pan containing one tablespoon of salted water for about two minutes.

Flash fry the pigeon meat in a little oil for 30 seconds, turning once.

Place a greased tian (baked bean tin) off-centre on a large plate. Layer creamed veg, then spinach, and put the flash-fried pigeon breast on top. Slosh a little jus around it - resist the urge to make a moat – and serve with an asparagus spear or two.

You will need ...

Stock, wine and water.

Mash potatoes and parsnip

Flash-fry the pigeon.

Get ready for assembly.

Layer in the tian.

Pigeon Pizza

A few friends and I were wallowing in nostalgia for the 'good old days' recently and we agreed that our collective addiction to all things chocolate was due to the fact that we didn't have confectionery on tap when we were kids. We ate seasonal and mostly home-grown food for much of the '50s; 'we only had chicken at Christmas' veered toward the Monty Python sketch, 'we ate gravel and lived in a paper bag', and inevitably, the 'I ate my pet rabbit' story that everyone of a certain age seems to have experienced. There was much shuddering and 'how could you?' from a couple of the younger members of our group when I said that I still ate rabbit on a regular basis … and pigeon.

"If we were meant to eat pigeons," said one youngster, "they'd sell it in supermarkets."

I pointed out that there were loads of things sold in supermarkets that no one should ever eat, but she remained unconvinced.

"I'm going to feed the baby boys with pigeon when they come over at the weekend, anyway," I said, defiantly.

"I wouldn't allow my kids to eat pigeon," she said. "Disgusting!"

I explained, patiently, that we don't eat feral pigeons, or pet rabbits, and wild meat isn't pumped full of chemicals, hormones, water; it's lean, low-calorie, and the animals have had a life roaming free, they are not contained somewhere and being fed on pellets. She was still dubious, but did admit that she hadn't thought of it like that. "My kids wouldn't eat it, anyway," she said. "They're far too fussy."

My young grandsons live 120 miles away so when they come to Nanny Rosie's house, it's always a special occasion and this time I'd worked out a 'play in the kitchen' afternoon to coincide with the need to produce something for the magazine. It would be fun, and pizza seemed to be a good idea.

They couldn't wait to get stuck in. Lucy, stirred the tomato sauce; Thomas and William chopped the vegetables and flattened the bread dough while I flash-fried the pigeon and bacon, and Simon was in charge of the camera. It was a real family affair.

We were all surprised when the littl'uns stole bits of pigeon from the pan. They absolutely loved it and I had to stop them before they ate it all – so much for kids not liking it – and they even took the spare pizza home with them.

INGREDIENTS:

For the topping:
Tomato sauce (see page 209)
Pigeon breasts (diced)
Lardons, or diced bacon.
Any combination of mushrooms, tomatoes, peppers, sweetcorn, red onion, olives, ham, etc.
A packet of white bread mix.
Strong cheddar, or mozzarella.

METHOD:

Make up the bread dough (add warm water) and leave to prove.
Knock up the tomato sauce.
Slice vegetables and prepare meats for the topping.
Grate the cheese.
Flatten out the dough into pizza shapes.
Dress the pizza and then shove into a very hot oven for ten minutes.

You will need ...

Chop the mushrooms.

Real Play-doh!

Leave some for the pizza!

Place the toppings.

Add the cheese.

PIGEON

'Wood'pigeon al Fresco

I've always loved experimenting with food and flavours, which turned out to be a good thing because there was a time when I had very little money, and two small boys to feed. If it hadn't been for my knack of creating something tasty from few ingredients, they wouldn't have had such a varied diet. I have my mother and grandmother to thank for handing down recipes and for educating me food-wise. They taught me which ingredients went with what, how to season, and the use of herbs, long before herbs and spices were made popular by TV chefs.

So, for me, the use of unusual ingredients is exciting and the Ronnie Sunshines' foraging day (see page 237) that I attended was inspirational, and the highlight of the day was when one of the tour guides showed us how to strip the breast meat from a pigeon without using any kind of implement, just our hands. I was so proud that I did it.

Back at base camp at the end of the day, some of the party were sent off to forage and the team fried a bounty of beech nuts, chestnuts, mushrooms, wild sorrel and hedge garlic in a little oil, and then mixed it into a big pot of boiled rice, with some salt and pepper. The pigeon breasts were cut into small pieces and placed into a Dutch oven, over the open fire, and when they were almost cooked a few handfuls of bird cherries – also gleaned from the woods – were added to make a sauce. I've attempted to recreate our pigeon feast, and substituted ingredients that you can forage from your local greengrocer, or supermarket, in place of the wild stuff. It doesn't taste quite the same as when eaten in a glade surrounded by wood smoke, but it's tasty nevertheless.

Incidentally, my pigeons for this recipe were sent down from Scotland by some friends, Norrie and Shiona Southam, to whom I have to say a huge thank you. They sent me enough pigeon meat to last me for about six months - still cold when I received them, after being frozen overnight and posted first class - and they taste of kindness and friendship, a much better flavour than the farmers' market ones!

INGREDIENTS:

Two pigeon breasts
Oil and a knob of butter for frying, salt and pepper
1 cup long grain rice
Half a dozen mushrooms
Chopped onion
Handful of hazelnuts, chopped or crushed
Finely chopped cabbage, or mixed salad leaves
Chicken stock cube and two cups of water
Port wine sauce: See page 207.

METHOD:

Slice the pigeon breasts quite thinly and fry in the oil and butter for a few minutes, then season and remove from the pan. Add the rice to the juices and swish around a bit, then add all the other ingredients, bring to the boil, turn down, lid on and steam for ten minutes. No peeping or poking. When the rice is cooked – taste it to find out – fold in the pigeon meat and serve with the sauce.

You will need this ...

... and this.

Fry pigeon strips.

Add rice to hot oil.

Make a port wine sauce.

Boil rapidly, reduce by half.

Hospital Case

Number One son had been proper poorly. He suffers with chronic asthma and one summer he endured a particularly bad attack, ending up in an oxygen tent for three days with a tube poked up every orifice. The doctors couldn't understand why he was so ill. None of the usual reasons for severe asthma attacks seemed to account for it, but after several hours of cross-questioning, X-rays and the testing of most of his bodily functions, at last we came to a conclusion.

He'd been out rabbiting a couple of days previously, at the usual farm, and had tramped – or more likely crawled – for several miles over the fields to the farm's boundary. On the adjacent farm there were acres of jolly, bright, yellow oilseed rape fields, all in full bloom, and all waiting to trigger off the mammoth allergic reaction we were now privileged to witness.

"So, he's allergic to rape, as well," I said, miserably, "something else to keep him away from." He got 19 out of 24 in his allergy tests, far better marks than he ever got at school.
"Very sorry," said a doctor with a warped sense of humour. "It's just one of those things, but we'll have to make sure the nurses know he's allergic to rape – so they'll leave him alone."

"Ma," gasped the afflicted one with his almost dying breath. "Get me this month's Airgun World, and my pyjamas – and a bottle of lemonade, and my toothbrush – and make sure it's Airgun World, not the other one." He knows he's at death's door; he has knocked on it several times. Does he want to see his father, brother, grandmother? No, he has his priorities firmly in his mind.

I tried a newsagent near the hospital.
"Never heard of it," he said. "Don't exist."
"Of course it exists," I told him firmly. "It sells worldwide. My son usually gets it in London."
"Well, yes. You could get it in London then, but not down here."
"Make up your mind. You just said it didn't exist."
"Mmm ... well. We can order it for you," searching through the catalogue. "I can't think where to look in this index. S'not under cookery."
"Why on earth should you look for it in cookery?" I asked, not a little bewildered and showing signs of panic. I couldn't go back to the hospital without it. My child would have a relapse.
"Stands to reason, title like 'Egg and Whirl'. Has to be cookery, dunnit?"
He looked on in amazement as I told him to forget the whole thing and sniggered my way out of the shop. Fortunately, there was a much larger newsagent nearby and I bought the coveted magazine with no trouble at all.

Two days later, the patient was out of the oxygen tent and eyeing up the nurses. By now, he had shed the 'I am poorly' pyjamas in favour of a camo T-shirt and trousers. With his military-style haircut, and shooting mags arranged casually on the bedspread for the benefit of female passers-by, he looked like a squaddie, apart from his feet encased in Dennis the Menace slippers, which quite ruined the image.

He was in an NHS single room on the ground floor, with an ever-open window. He said it helped his breathing, but I know the way his mind works. It overlooked the lawns where all kinds of wildlife gathered at dusk, many species of fur and feather, mostly magpies and pigeons.
"Do you think they'd mind if you brought my rifle in?" he asked, innocently. "I'd love to show it to Dr. Livingstone."
I told young 'Stanley' I was quite sure that they'd mind a lot and he'd have to make do with photographs of his pride and joy. We had enough of those to mount an exhibition in the sluice room.

By the fifth day, he was well enough to invite half the gun club to his bedside. They arrived bearing gifts – a couple of tins of fresh, juicy pellets, ancient issues of Airgun World and Air Gunner, and a very large takeaway Vindaloo that promptly leaked yellow gravy all over the bed. I left them to it while they had a party with several nurses and the night sister.

At the end on the week, they discharged my junior airgunner to convalesce at home. He spent two days cleaning and polishing his rifle before venturing out to a new club, where there's an indoor target range. He'd just have to put up with it until the end of the pollen season. It's not ideal; not at all what he wanted to do, but it protected him from rape.

Beautiful to some - near-deadly to my boy.

PIGEON

- Summer -

Cou-velle Cuisine, or Posh Tarts

I've always been a rustic kind of a cook. Nouvelle cuisine chef-ery, and making food look 'classy' is pretentious nonsense, in my opinion. Food has to look half-decent, of course, no one wants to eat something that looks as if it's already been digested, but I can't see the point of making food look pretty just for the sake of it – or more accurately so restaurants can charge a small fortune for it. What's all that 'jus' business – it's gravy - and dropping garnish from a great height so that it lands naturally? Having a plate the size of Exmoor for a noisette of lamb on pureed cauliflower topped by a parsnip crisp, doesn't make for a satisfying plate of honest, hearty grub after a heavy day in the field, or even the office.

Having said that, though, there are occasions when small is actually quite nice. It depends on how hungry you are, and how much time you have spare for fiddling about making ingredients look elegant, rather than getting on with preparing a hearty meal for six. Small items of hand-held food are perfect for packed lunches, a light repast with a mate, or a snack while watching TV – so I came up with these little tarts. If you're a fan of the nouveau, you could always bung one on top of some disguised cauliflower on a huge white plate, and drizzle a little balsamic vinegar around the outside. There's nothing quite like a posh tart, as the bishop probably said to the actress.

INGREDIENTS:

Olive oil for greasing tin, and frying
Four pigeon breasts – thinly sliced
One onion – finely chopped
A bay leaf
Half a dozen mushrooms, finely chopped
Half a tablespoonful of flour
A beef stock pod in 4 fl oz water
A quarter of a bottle of ale
A tablespoonful of tomato puree, salt, and black pepper
Shortcrust pastry, and one egg

METHOD:

Grease the tin with some of the olive oil and set aside.
Fry the pigeon breasts and the onion in the rest of the oil, until the meat is browned and the onions are tender.
Add the mushrooms and bay leaf, and swish around for a minute or two.
Add the flour and incorporate into the 'dry' ingredients.
Then add the ale, stock, tomato puree, and seasoning.
Bring to the boil, stirring all the time, then turn down the heat to the lowest setting and simmer for five minutes.
Allow to cool while you line the bun tins.

Roll out the pastry, cut out bases and lids, line the tins, then egg wash the rims of the tart cases so that they will seal when you put the lids on.
Place a teaspoonful of the filling into each base, then place the lids and crimp, or seal with the tines of a fork.
Egg wash and pierce the tops to allow steam to escape.
Bake for about 20 minutes at 175°C, or until the pastry is golden brown.

You will need ...

Fry onions, meat and mushrooms.

Combine other ingredients.

Line the bun tin.

Cooled mixture in each.

Nice things, small packages.

PIGEON

Pigeon Pasties

I suppose it's an age thing but I find myself becoming more and more irritated by the number of ready-meals available these days, and by the people who rely on them. There are three whole aisles full of the things in my nearest supermarket and I know families who survive by just opening packets. The argument is that the ingredients are 'fresh' and of good quality. Maybe so, but they're still shoving chemicals into their bodies six nights out of seven. Processed food has to contain at least a preservative, otherwise the turnaround would have to be about 48 hours, and that's not commercially viable. Have a look at the label next time you have a convenience meal, you'll be surprised at the number of 'extras' involved.

Then there are the MacD/KFC brigades who eat take-aways several times a week. Oi! Compulsive fast food eaters! No! Take-away food should be a treat, maybe for a birthday celebration, job promotion, whatever - half a dozen times a year at most.

I had a conversation with a friend recently who told me that she found it too time-consuming to cook proper food, easier and cheaper to let someone else do the work and that my take on it all was due to my advanced age and fixed opinions, but she's only 24, bless her. She has three small children and 'hasn't the time to peel potatoes or muck about with cutting up meat. I can't afford it, anyway.' I was appalled given these revelations but tried not to show it.

I showed off instead. 'I can cook your family a tasty dinner for a fiver, using a couple of pigeon breasts, a pack of Jus Rol and some vegetables,' I told her. 'You can help.' She agreed and we decided that it might be a wise move not to specify the separate ingredients when asked by her boys 'What's in it?' They had enough trouble tolerating a new pizza topping, let alone a strange meat concoction.

You can serve this with anything you like and bearing the kids in mind and the hot summer sun, we chose chips and peas, but mashed potatoes, a green vegetable and some gravy makes this the ideal winter dish, too.

How did it go down? Er … not brilliantly, I'm afraid. What I hadn't allowed for was the fact that my friend's children, and her partner, are so used to ready-made food that my offering was completely alien to them and they wouldn't even taste it. Oh well, I tried. You can't win 'em all, and they did eat the chips. I'd left her to her own devices on the potato front and they were out of a packet.

INGREDIENTS:

Three pigeon breasts, diced
A medium-sized swede, diced
One large onion, finely chopped
Two small potatoes, diced

METHOD:

Make sure it is very finely diced, mix it all in a large bowl, add salt, pepper, crumbled stock cube and a tablespoon of water.
Roll out the pastry. Grab a round side plate and use it as a template to cut four circles.
Divide the meat and vegetable mixture into four and place one portion of it in the centre of one of the circles of pastry. Egg wash round the edge of the circle, fold the pastry over, and crimp it round the edge. It's now pasty-shaped. Repeat until you have four pasties.
Bake in a moderately hot oven, 170° Celsius, for about 45 minutes.

You will need …

Dice everything finely.

Mix it all thoroughly.

Use an inverted soup bowl.

Place mixture in the centre.

Crimp and eggwash.

PIGEON

Pigeon Bites

I've been told that my sausage rolls are a bit special. Certainly, they have often been the motive behind invitations to various functions and get-togethers – 'Do come along to thingy's barbecue/christening/birthday bash. It'd be great to see you and if you could bring some of your fantastic sausage rolls … but it's okay if you can't ...' I always do.

I came up with Pigeon Bites, although technically you can almost swallow them whole. It just sounds better than 'sausage rolls with bits of pigeon inserted'. You could, as I have done in the past when going through my 'kitchen goddess' phase, buy shoulder pork and mince it yourself but frankly, it's too much trouble. I soon gave up the idea of being the next Nigella and most supermarkets have it all ready minced and measured out for you in nice, square packets.

These morsels are absolutely delicious and this recipe will not be enough, I promise you. I once made four batches before I could salvage enough of them from the cooling stage to freeze. Mind you, at the time, I was living with thieving teenage mouths and their 'visiting on baking days' mates. You might get away with it, though.

You can make these Bites with any kind of meat you happen to have handy, although chicken doesn't quite cut it, I've found - that's better used in a pasty or a pie, with mushrooms. With a little imagination you can combine most ingredients and come out with something original and tasty; try minced lamb with a chopped onion and a carrot or two, with a couple of dollops of mint sauce from a jar; or pork and apple, with some sage. I tried the last one, substituted rabbit for the pork, and made about 80 rolls for a friend's daughter's christening; they'd all gone within half an hour and I was getting complaints that I hadn't made enough!

INGREDIENTS:

A pack of shortcrust pastry.
About 250gr of finely minced pork, or the meat from four good quality sausages.
A finely chopped onion, two squashed garlic cloves and a pinch of dried thyme.
Half a pack of any stuffing mix.
Two eggs: one for binding it all together and the other to glaze the pastry.
A couple of pigeon breasts, thinly sliced.
Black pepper.

METHOD:

In a large bowl, combine pork/sausage meat, onion, thyme and garlic.
Make up the stuffing mix with boiling water, add to the bowl. Stir it in.
Now fold in the egg and mix well to enable the ingredients to combine.
Flour a surface, cut the square of pastry in half and roll it until you have a long strip about four inches wide and as long as it will go.
Place the filling evenly along the pastry, and arrange the pigeon breast on top of it.
Fold up the lower edge over the filling and brush with beaten egg.
Pull the upper edge over so that it sticks.Egg wash the whole thing and cut into one-inch pieces.
Place on a baking tray in a moderately hot oven (170°C) for about 20 minutes.

You will need ...

Combine all ingredients.

Roll out pastry.

Top meat with pigeon strips.

Pull upper edge over.

Cut into bite-sized pieces.

Pigeon Tartlets

I avoid weddings these days, whenever possible, because I've always had to go to such ceremonies on my own. Without fail, I end up chatting to the waitresses for much of the time, and then slope off before the dancing starts in the evening. This one couldn't be avoided, though, it was the marriage of an old friend and she begged me to go, even though I didn't know anyone else. I didn't have the heart to refuse.

There were a few awkward moments when other guests realised that I was in fact a singleton, and not waiting for a partner who'd nipped to the loo, or the bar; they smiled at me kindly. There are always advantages in every situation, though, if you look for them. There was no one to say 'are you going to eat all those?' when standing in a corner and getting stuck into the canapés – or amuse bouches as they are so whimsically named, these days.

The usual half a quail's egg sandwiched between a halved cherry tomato; a sliver of smoked salmon on half (true, I swear!) a small circular cracker, or a microscopic bacon and goat's cheese tartlet weren't particularly amoozing, though. I reckon I could have got a dozen in my mouth at once and still had room for a fun-sized Mars bar. I'd starved myself for a couple of days in an unsuccessful attempt to force my growing body into a rare frock, so I was ravenous until the main meal was served a good hour later. It was a lovely wedding, though, as these things go.

The following day, I decided to re-jig the goat's cheese tart into a slightly larger version and substitute pigeon meat for the bacon. They are scrumptious and would make a classy addition to any picnic, or 'micnic' as my youngest grandson insisted on calling the practice of eating sarnies in the park, until he learned to talk – sounds like an Irish arrest. Or, if you've eaten a surfeit of amuse bouches the evening before, followed by a hefty, and delicious four-course wedding breakfast, one of these pigeon tarts is just enough for a tasty but light lunch for a single lady – and they're so easy to make.

INGREDIENTS:

Shortcrust pastry
1 pigeon breast, cut into strips
1 red onion, sliced
A little sugar
A couple of drips of balsamic vinegar
Goat's cheese sliced thinly
Sliced tomato
Sage or basil leaves to garnish

METHOD:

Roll out the pastry and line a couple of small quiche tins – or one large one if you're doubling up on ingredients.
Slice the onions and fry very gently in a little oil for about 20 minutes, with the sugar and balsamic, so that they caramelise.
Allow to cool and then spread in the base of the pastry-lined tins.
Slice the pigeon breast thinly and place on top of the onions.
Put sliced goat's cheese slices on top of the meat, drizzle with a little olive oil and then pop 'em back into a moderate (180 degrees) oven for about 20 minutes.
Serve with a leafy salad.

You will need ...

Fry onions, sugar and vinegar ...

... gently until caramelised.

Onions into pastry cases.

Add sliced pigeon.

Add the topping.

PIGEON

P-uffins

I have a seven-year-old grandson, Thomas, who has a dairy allergy and reacts very badly when anything triggers it. He doesn't go without much, there are substitutes for practically everything these days, but he knows how poorly he can be if he eats, drinks, or touches anything containing a dairy product, and it's so serious that I can't kiss his cheek after I've had a cup of milky coffee, unless I wash my mouth first. There's a silver lining, as ever, because if it were not for my attempts to create something delicious for Thomas to eat, that will not cause him harm, many of my experimental recipes would not have seen the light of day.

A few months ago, while playing in the kitchen, I made the usual basic muffin batter - I substitute soya milk and vegetable oil for the cow's milk and butter - and then added some blueberries and a couple of packets of dairy-free, white chocolate buttons. I'd sourced some brown muffin cases similar to the ones used in the coffee houses, and my grandsons were so impressed that I began to experiment further.

Having exhausted many combinations of dried/fresh fruit, nuts and preserves, I branched out into the savoury muffin category, beginning with a Mediterranean-style that eventually morphed into these pigeon and bacon beauties – add the cheese if you're not allergic. They can be served warm and dipped into soup for a light lunch in the winter; or eaten cold, in the middle of a field in summer, accompanied by tomatoes that have been left for 30 minutes to warm through in the sun, and washed down with red wine - or fruit juice if you're seven years old.

INGREDIENTS:

One or two pigeon breasts, diced finely
A couple of rashers of bacon, diced
A finely chopped red onion
10oz plain flour sieved with a level tablespoon of baking powder
Pinch of salt, squashed garlic, black pepper, tspn of dried basil
6 tablespoons sunflower (vegetable) oil
9 fluid oz soya milk whisked with a stock cube and two eggs
A few sun-dried tomatoes, and one fresh tomato, all small dice
*2oz grated strong cheese, and a handful for topping (leave this out if you're going for the dairy-free option)

METHOD:

Preheat oven to 180°C and place muffin cases in a baking tin.
Fry pigeon, bacon and onion for a few minutes in a little oil.
Place all dry ingredients into a large bowl: flour, salt, baking powder, *cheese, herbs, pepper.
In another bowl: oil, milk, stock pod, eggs, tomatoes, onion, garlic, pigeon, and bacon.
Work quickly now. Upend the mixture in the 'wet' bowl into the dry ingredients and stir a few times until roughly combined. Don't overdo it. The baking powder will react with the liquid immediately and you need to get it all into the oven as soon as possible.
Place spoonfuls into the muffin cases and sprinkle with grated cheese. I know it looks a mess but you must complete this last stage in about 90 seconds. Bake for about 20 minutes at 180°C.

You will need ...

Fry ingredients for a few minutes.

Separate bowls – wet and dry.

Mix for ten seconds, tops!

Into cases, top with cheese.

Bake until golden.

Pigeon Eggs

I had this idea when I was attempting to eat a Scotch egg at a summer picnic. It wasn't very inspiring, just an egg covered in bland sausage meat and 'orange' breadcrumbs, and I knew I could do better than that. I vowed to source some pigeon eggs, substitute minced pigeon for some of the sausage meat, add a few spices, and make baby Scotch eggs. I got quite excited about it.

Ever tried to source pigeon eggs? I couldn't understand why I can't get them anywhere. We eat quail eggs … hen, duck, goose … why not pigeon? Was there some kind of law against it? I could understand why pheasant or grouse eggs are not readily available; they're probably too valuable because they are hatched for shoots, but pigeons?

I asked the question on a forum and no one seems to know why pigeons are shot for meat, but their eggs have been spurned so completely. One reply was that 'pigeons are dusty'. There is, so I was told, dust on the feathers so 'it stands to reason' that there will be dust in the eggs. Erm … would that not apply to the breast meat, as well? Eventually, I asked a shooting friend if he knew the answer to this mystery and he laughed at me.

"Who do you think is going to harvest them, Rosie?" he asked. "They don't live in nice cosy coops, or pens, you know. They nest in trees. It wouldn't be worthwhile, even if you could find them."

I hadn't thought of that, it's obvious, really. Standard hens' eggs it is, then.

Any road up, back to this recipe: I tarted up some plain sausage meat by crumbling half a dried chilli into it, adding a finely chopped onion, a teaspoon each of mace and ground black pepper, and then mixed in the minced pigeon meat, and an egg to bind it all together. It's a good idea to chill this mixture for at least half an hour because then it's easier to mould and doesn't stick to your hands so much.

This version of the Scotch egg turned out as a flavour bomb, and you can serve it as a light lunch with a salad and some homemade, spiced tomato chutney. (see page 208)

INGREDIENTS:

Two eggs
250g sausage meat, tarted up with:
Chilli, fresh or dried, to taste.
A small, finely chopped onion
One teaspoonful each of mace and ground black pepper
One more egg, beaten, for coating
A little flour
Breadcrumbs
Oil for frying

METHOD:

Boil the eggs for ten minutes, only. Don't overcook them or they'll be like rubber.
Mix sausage meat, minced pigeon, chilli, onion and seasoning. Make sure all ingredients are combined.
Roll a peeled egg in the flour.
Mould a handful of pigeon meat mixture around the egg.
Coat with the flour, then beaten egg, and finally into the breadcrumbs.
If you want a very crisp covering, repeat the last step.
Fry in medium hot oil for about 15 minutes – turning often, until golden brown.
Drain on kitchen paper.

You will need …

Combine all ingredients.

Roll eggs in flour.

Place egg in the centre.

Mould mixture around egg.

Fry for 15 minutes, turning often.

PIGEON

Pigeon for Picnics

I often wonder who spends their time in the kitchen cooking the recipes that I churn out month after month in the mags, especially the ones involving pastry. They're directed mostly toward men – hunters, shooters, fishermen ... and the majority of the men I know – including my sons - are frightened of the 'p' word. Even in these enlightened times when you can buy any kind of pastry ready-made, they still shy away from making pies, flans or sausage rolls and leave that side of things to me. I'd love to find out how many men have a go, themselves, and how many say to their other halves, 'this looks like a good'un. Why don't you have a go?'

This dish is ideal for a picnic and I've made it before with beef and lamb, but pigeon meat is just as good, if not better, because it allows the cooking time to be reduced, and remains tender while allowing the mushroom mixture to stay moist. Make sure everything is cut in fairly thick slices, otherwise it ends up as unrecognisable mush with lumps of pigeon in it.

I sprinkled a bit of smoked paprika on top of mine because I made an apple and gooseberry version with the other block of pastry and that looked the same. Knowing me, I'm likely to serve up the pigeon slices covered in custard if I can't tell the difference.

INGREDIENTS:

A couple of pigeon breasts.
Half a dozen shallots and two cloves of garlic.
Big field mushrooms, stalks removed and thickly sliced.
A mixture of buttons, chestnuts or shiitake, sliced – or just small mushrooms if you can't get other varieties. The shiitake have a gamey flavour all of their own, which complements the flavour of the pigeon, so include them if you can.
Splash of white wine.
Enough crème fraîche to make the mushroom mixture spreadable.
Pastry from a packet – you can use shortcrust as I have or, if you want it all fluffy and risen, use the puff option. That's not so convenient for a picnic, though.

METHOD:

Cut one block of pastry in half, and roll out into a rectangle wide enough to accommodate the width of the field mushrooms.
Add a teaspoonful of butter, for flavour, and a glug of oil to a shallow pan and fry the field mushroom slices gently for a couple of minutes. They should be as dry as possible. Remove from the pan with a slotted spoon, set aside, and allow to cool while you fry the shallots and garlic in the same pan as the mushroom juices with a little more oil.
When the shallots are tender, add the rest of the mushrooms and continue to fry gently for a couple of minutes until softened.
Finally, stir in the white wine and cook off the alcohol for a minute or two, then remove from the heat and add the crème fraîche.
Assemble like this:
Place the cooled field mushrooms along the length of the rectangle of pastry, as a kind of base, then arrange the pigeon breasts on top.
Spread the mushroom/shallot mixture over the top of the pigeon breasts.
Roll out the other half of the pastry to fit, egg-wash the edges to seal, bung it on top and crimp round the edges.
Egg-wash, make a couple of small slashes to let out steam and place in a moderate oven for 30 minutes.
Serve on a hot, summer day, beside a river – washed down with ice-cold cider.

You will need ...

Place pastry on baking sheet.

Pigeon strips on pastry.

Fry mushroom mixture ...

Add to pigeon pieces.

Pastry on top, and egg-wash.

Victorian Woodie Wellington

Sometimes, it's tricky to think of new recipes. There are only so many combinations of ingredients, so I came up with a plan. I riffle through my vast collection of cookery books and then stand in front of open kitchen cupboards, gazing at the shelves stocked with ingredients, waiting for inspiration.

Just as I was about to give up and go for a walk along the beach, a packet popped through my letterbox. It was a book written by Rob Collins, 'Recipes from the Hedgerow'. Well, I can tell you that I was impressed and couldn't wait to try out some of the recipes within it. I found one that Rob calls 'Victorian Pigeon Pie' that I have adapted with substituted ingredients, partly because I couldn't be bothered to go shopping and decided to use what I had in the house, and more importantly because I didn't want to crib it completely – that's hardly fair after Rob's gone to all the trouble of writing it down!

I didn't agree with Rob's statement at the beginning of this pigeon recipe, 'pigeons are rarely seen on restaurant menus today', though. That may be true in Rob's neck of the woods, but here in the south-east, they are becoming more and more popular – and very expensive if you go to the West End of London for a meal.

I've had friends ask me more for pigeon recipes than rabbit, and I'm always surprised when the feedback is, 'that was fantastic; have you got any more?' This pigeon pie is portable; Rob's tells us that it was a favourite snack at Victorian race meetings, but it is equally tasty and convenient for a picnic on the beach or in a park, a hike through the woods, or any outside space, really.

Knock up a couple of apple turnovers, made with the leftover pastry, add a handful of Babybels, a cold drink or two, and you've got a complete picnic lunch menu that is easy to eat, and carry to your chosen venue.

INGREDIENTS:

About half a pound of rump steak, or 'quick-fry' steak, sliced thinly.
1 pigeon, halved
2 hard-boiled eggs, yolks only
Half a pound of pork sausage meat
1 garlic clove
Thyme
Sage
2 slices bacon
1 slab frozen puff pastry

METHOD:

Preheat the oven to 180°C or equivalent.
Line a deep pie dish with pastry.
Place the steak on top.
Pigeon halves go on top of the steak.
Take the yolks out of the eggs and place (whole) between the pigeon pieces.
Mix the garlic, thyme and sage into the sausage meat and add chunks of it randomly on top of the pigeon.
Lay bacon slices over.
Top with the rest of the puff pastry, brush with beaten egg and bake for about an hour.
Serve by the side of a river, on a beach, or under a huge oak tree in the middle of nowhere.

You will need …

Line a deep pie dish.

Steak and pigeon on top.

Mix sausage meat with herbs.

Top with bacon.

Pastry top, and egg wash.

Pigeon Pie – Or Not

Three pigeons narrowly escaped being disposed of at the local rubbish tip. I'd been having the annual 'clear the garden up' session which, in our household, seemed to be an inevitable advent to warmer weather. Where did it all come from? That's what I wanted to know. Every winter I made sure that the garden was sorted before the frost and snow arrived, and yet, come the few days of sunshine in early spring when everyone goes mad, and there it all was again.

I had filled several black sacks with junk from the shed, where my family had a habit of throwing things what might come in handy but rarely did, and packed a number of cardboard boxes with brambles and garden rubbish collected from next-door; our elderly neighbour was very frail and couldn't do it any more. I'd broken up a wind-damaged fence panel, tied up the big bits with garden twine and left everything in a heap while I went out to open the boot of the car preparatory to loading it all up and departing tip-wards. It was going to take at least three trips. I'm sure my family used to get vibes when I was about to go into tip mode – they went out; usually in different directions, and I was always on my own when these jobs needed doing.

At around lunchtime, while I was away for the second tip trip, my eldest, who had gone with a friend on an early morning hunting jaunt, returned home. I was to find out later that he'd placed a cardboard box among my 'waiting to be shifted' pile of garbage, before sauntering down to the local pub for a well-earned pint. I wondered, sometimes, how he ever made it through grammar school. Surely, he didn't think that I had put all those boxes there for decoration. It should have been obvious that they were awaiting disposal.

Fortunately, I ran out of steam after the second tip visit and decided that a cup of coffee was necessary to keep up my strength. By this time, I had also lost interest in the whole operation so the last few cardboard boxes were still there when the hunters came home expecting a three-course meal. My sons used to call me Super Crone because I could usually manage to be in two places at once and their meals were always on tap when required. Not today; I was knackered.

"Help me to take this last lot down to the tip," I bribed. "Then, I'll cook you some lunch."
Suddenly, they had to visit the loo, wash hands, change clothes before they could join in. Strangely, it took the exact amount of time required for me to load up the car again.

By the time we arrived at the tip it was packed, with a queue of cars stretching several hundred yards and dozens of people milling about, clutching black sacks and waiting for a chance, amid the melee, to hurl them into a bin. I had the 'pigeon' box poised over the tip crusher, ready to drop it in, when there was a yell of despair from the eldest.
"Don't do it!" he cried, as all the other tip users stared at me, open-mouthed, no doubt under the impression that

I was considering suicide. "Don't put my pigeons in the crusher, Ma!" This last plea cried out in plaintive and heart-rending tones.

Great! Now they think I'm either a pigeon-hater or a cruel parent. The RSPB/NSPCC will get a few phone calls this afternoon reporting my car registration number and I'll get a visit from someone in uniform. Thank goodness I had disposed of all the rubbish; a number of heads were shaking in disapproval and I dared not go down to the tip again, not in the near future, anyway.

Having saved the pigeons from a fate worse than death – an odd choice of phrase, considering they were already dead – I had no alternative but to cook the little devils. I'd usually put that off as long as possible, mainly because the family refused to eat them unless they were heavily disguised as something else - usually burgers - and scoffed after the pubs had turned out. Often, they had been thrown away during the six-monthly clearout of the freezer, the most popular excuses to myself being 'freezer burn', 'been in there six months, not worth the risk of food poisoning' and so on. This time, however, there was no escape.

As I hadn't prepared anything for lunch, it seemed poetically justified that I should make them eat the cause of my embarrassment, so while the boys were in the garden preparing the birds for cooking, I searched Mrs Beeton, for a recipe. Pigeon pie sounded okay, they'd usually eat stuff covered in flaky pastry.

'Take three pigeons - I was on a winner, already! - a pound and a half of rump steak, three slices of ham, four eggs, puff pastry ... sufficient for six persons, average cost 5s 3d' - yeah, maybe in 1861 and, besides how was this a 'pigeon' pie?

I fried the breasts in butter and black pepper for about five minutes, threw a handful of chopped, fresh herbs over them and served them to the lads with garlic bread to provide bulk. The completed dish was extremely tasty and, to my surprise, eaten with gusto.

Needless to say, I had to cook another meal later on. Apart from the fact that the other members of the family had to be fed, pigeon sandwiches are not enough to stave off the hunger pangs of growing boys – not for more than an hour or two.

PIGEON
- Autumn -

PIGEON

Easy Peasy Pigeon Pie

Pies don't come any simpler than this! I defy anyone to tell me that they can't cook when there are only a few ingredients required and when someone else has already done most of the work. The tinned soup has been slaved over by dedicated chefs – all right, an assembly line in Kings Lynn, but you get my drift – and the pastry (puff, which would take you ages to knock up) comes straight out of the freezer at a supermarket. All you have to do is a bit of chopping and rolling. It'll take you half an hour, tops, from start to finish and it's probably quicker than waiting for a curry to be delivered, not to mention far better for your cholesterol levels.

You can add any vegetables that you happen to have handy, too, if you need to bulk out the meat. Mushrooms would work a treat, cougettes, pre-cooked carrots ....

Here we go, then. On your marks, get ready … go!

INGREDIENTS:

One pack of already defrosted puff pastry, or you can even buy already prepared pie dishes now, I'm told, complete with a lid, for goodness sake! The puff pastry is better, though.

Four pigeon breasts sliced into evenly sized pieces.

One large onion

Herbs - mixed if dried from a jar or, if you're really giving it your all, chopped fresh thyme and parsley.

A tin of condensed soup I used chicken and white wine, but you can use plain chicken, or mushroom if you prefer.

Ground black pepper - and plenty of it. You won't need salt; there is enough in the soup.

METHOD:

Preheat the oven to 180°C

Peel and chop the onion, fairly coarsely, you want to know it's there in the finished article and it's not just for seasoning but also for texture. So many folk I know always mince or finely chop onions so that they become invisible, but sometimes it's good to use them as a vegetable and not only as a background flavour.

In a large pan, brown the meat with the onions over a medium heat for two or three minutes. Throw in a teaspoonful (or a handful, if fresh) of your chosen herbs and add the black pepper.

Remove the pan from the heat and bung in the soup. Stir it around a bit and then portion the mixture into your pie dishes.

Roll out the pastry so that it fits the top of the dish. Tuck it in round the edges, egg wash it – or you can use milk – and shove it in the oven on 180 degrees for about 20 minutes, or until the top is golden brown.

While you're waiting for the pies to cook you could be knocking up the mashed spuds and opening a packet of frozen peas to go with.

You really should give this a go. It looks quite impressive, too. Whoever you are cooking for will think you've been in the kitchen for hours. Think of the brownie points you can rack up for hardly any effort at all!

You will need ...

Brown the meat and onions.

Add a tin of soup.

Bung it into a couple of pie dishes.

Roll out pastry.

Bake until golden.

Fajitas

In my neck of the woods, there have been some weird and wonderful things on offer at barbecue parties. Some of my friends are excellent cooks and love to experiment with the exotic so we've eaten alligator, shark, ostrich, wild boar – oh, yes, and rabbit and pigeon. You'd be surprised at the number of people who consider the last two meats to be 'exotic.'

I witnessed a middle-aged man being chased around a half-acre field by another middle-aged man armed with a rabbit kebab.

"Go on Dan, just taste it and I'll leave you alone!"

"No, I can't. It's rabbit. Poppy (13-year-old daughter) has got a rabbit."

"It's not Thumper, you doughnut. Shot it myself last night."

"No, no! Aren't there any sausages left?" … and more of the same for a good half an hour. It was pathetic; funny, though.

So, if we're cooking 'exotic' we might as well go for it with fajitas, which are not too uncommon these days, but made with pigeon breasts you just might get a reputation of being more adventurous than the cook who serves up wild boar, which is only undomesticated pork when you think about it.

I'm not usually a fan of Mexican food, it's a bit too 'in yer face' for me, but these fajitas were received with enthusiasm when I tried them out on some friends, so I'm passing the recipe on. Recently, I discovered 'Discovery' products – tortillas, salsa and fajita spice mix: all neatly arranged in packs and jars, ready and waiting to be tarted up by the chef. As a rule, pride will not allow me to use fast food, ready-meals, or pre-cooked ingredients. So, on the rare occasions that I open a packet, I have to tweak and add spices or fresh veg. It's probably a psychiatric problem and I need therapy, but it's too late now, even if I were willing to change my viewpoint on what constitutes a healthy diet.

INGREDIENTS:

A couple of pigeon breasts, sliced.
Two rashers of smoked streaky bacon, diced.
One onion, mushrooms, half each of a red,
a green and a yellow pepper, sliced.
Fajita spice mix – Discovery is a good one.
To make your own, see page 206

METHOD:

Slice the pigeon breasts as thinly as you can, then place the meat into a plastic bag with the spice mix and squidge it until the meat is coated. Leave to fester while you slice the rest of the veg.
Fry pigeon, bacon and onions for a few minutes, medium heat, until the onions are tender., then add sliced peppers and mushrooms and cook for another two minutes. Turn it into a dish and keep warm while you make a salsa – or a finely diced salad as it used to be called before the advent of TV chefs – and warm up the tortillas in a large frying pan. No oil!
Salsa: Cut spring onions, cucumber and tomatoes into small dice, add salt and black pepper. You can also make a dip by adding the zest and juice of a lime to a carton of natural yoghurt, to cool things down a tad if you've overdone the spice mix.

You will need ...

Slice onions, pigeon, bacon.

Fry for five minutes.

Add peppers, mushrooms.

Filling and salsa.

Roll up, roll up!

Kentucky-fried Pigeon

Quite a few of my male friends are interested in cooking and/or food, and it's not unusual for quite in-depth telephone conversations to take place regarding the preparation of ingredients. Cooking is one of my passions and I'm finding that female friends don't share my interest any more, sadly. There are exceptions, but mostly they open packets or jars, throw the contents over meat and 'stir-fry'. They cook, they tell me, because they have to, not for enjoyment.

On the other hand, the boys are consumed with curiosity and enjoy experimenting. There is a certain amount of science involved, I suppose; some ingredients chemically react together; some flavourings complement each other, and some very definitely do not. Men tend to understand the Heston Blumenthal philosophy toward food, whereas most of the women I know just find his efforts amusing.

Anyway, one such telephone conversation that took place with a young man who has a sense of humour and considerable culinary prowess, resulted in a suggestion when I complained about being unable to think of a pigeon recipe for the magazine column. 'You could always do a KFP?' said Elton, literally taking the p.

What a brilliant idea! I wouldn't have thought of that in a million years; it's not very PC these days, to advocate deep-frying and I'd get hate-mail, or at least gentle chastisement mail. I went for a walk along the beach for a think about how to do it and came up with this.

INGREDIENTS:

4 pigeon breasts
Sunflower oil
1 lemon
2 cloves garlic, squashed
2 bay leaves, crumpled
A couple of sage leaves and a few springs of thyme
The herbs can be the dried variety if you can't get fresh
2 heaped tablespoons plain flour
1 egg
A pinch each of salt and cayenne pepper, a level teaspoon each of dried oregano or basil, paprika, black pepper, dried onion, and ginger.
Milk, to mix

METHOD:

Cut the pigeon breasts into thin strips and marinade in the lemon juice, garlic and herbs for at least an hour - or longer if you have the time.
When ready to cook, dry the pigeon strips on kitchen paper.
Put the oil into a wok, or deep pan, to heat while you prepare the batter mix.
Put the flour into a large basin, make a well in the centre and then add the egg and all the spices. I always get the spices ready round the edge of a plate before I start, that way I don't forget what I've put in.
Mix it all together, and then gradually add milk until the batter is the consistency of thick cream.
Dip the pigeon strips into the batter and fry in batches, half a dozen at a time, until golden – this should take about two minutes, per batch. Drain on kitchen paper and serve with fries and baked beans, or just eat them as a snack as they come out of the pan.
It turned out to be really tasty, and I wouldn't mind betting they'd be just as good using squirrel – KFS.

You will need ...

Marinate the pigeon.

Whisk batter ingredients.

Looks like single cream.

Fry in batches.

Kids love it!

Pigeon Pick-me-up

I'm a great believer in giving into comfort food when the need arises. We all have days when spirits are low for no apparent reason; sometimes it's just the same old daily grind that gets to us and then we need something to give us a bit of a lift. Most of us go for the foods that our mothers gave us when we were kids. Fruit crumble and custard, stews with dumplings, sausage and mash, egg and chips and so on. Trouble is, too much feel-good food shows around the waist and in the doctor's notes when you complain of aching joints and high blood pressure symptoms, so in this recipe I've tried to combine cosiness with healthy eating. Any kind of game is the leanest meat you can get so a little indulgence with accompaniments balances it out.

I don't get the blues very often but when I do, I usually go for something sweet. There is only so much chocolate and ice cream that the palate can tolerate, though, and even these rescue remedies can fail to do the job. When that happens, a more robust solution must be found. Mashed potato is a good'un and rich, brown gravy always reminds me of my mother's cooking, so I combined the two, added a couple of tweaks of my own and came up with this comforting and slightly rustic dish. Even if you don't need comforting, you can still give it a go and impress your mates by calling it pigeon avec melange de pommes de terre, et jus. It's delicious whatever you call it and whatever mood you're in, and because it's so low calorie, guilt-free and easy to cook, you can follow it up with a plate of profiteroles, a pavlova, or a knickerbocker glory. What? It's just a suggestion! If you need comfort, you've got to go for it.

INGREDIENTS:

Two pigeon breasts per person
Potatoes, crème fraiche (or milk and butter, or cream, or all three – depending how fed up you are)
Something green
For the sauce:
Olive oil
Mushrooms, quartered
Two garlic cloves, squashed
Beef stock cube or one of those stock gel capsule thingys
Half a pint of water
Pepper – no salt, the stock cube/capsule contains enough already
Couple of drops of Tabasco or any hot sauce
Knob of butter

METHOD:

Sear the pigeon breasts for a few minutes on both sides, and then reduce the heat to moderate and cook until they take on colour and juices run clear when poked with a sharp knife.
Remove to a plate to rest. Keep warm.

Make your sauce:
Glug of olive oil into a pan, add squashed garlic and mushrooms. Fry gently for two minutes.
Add stock cube and water, pepper and Tabasco. Stir well and boil rapidly until the liquid has reduced by half and the sauce thickens. At the last minute, add a knob of butter. This gives you the rich flavour and makes the sauce all shiny.

Serve with a green vegetable and make sure you slosh the gravy all over the mashed potato. Eat it all, place hands on full belly, smile and breathe sigh of satisfaction. I guarantee you'll feel better for it.

You will need …

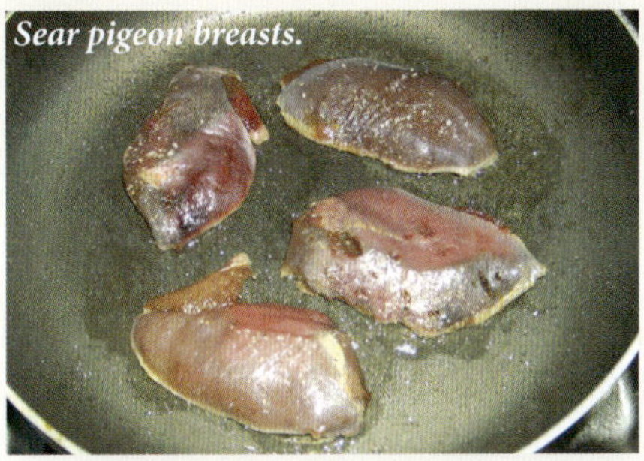
Sear pigeon breasts.

Cook through, gently.

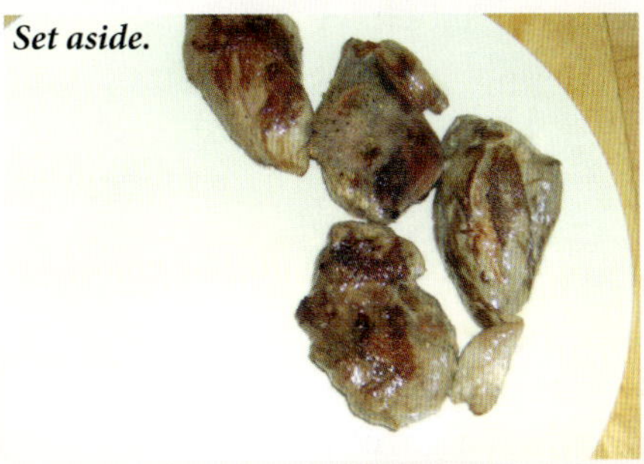
Set aside.

Fry mushrooms.

Add sauce ingredients.

Pigeon Pasta

I eat a great deal of pasta, because I'm always so busy. I live alone so sometimes I forget to eat at all and wonder why I feel light-headed at the end of a stint in front of the computer. When it dawns on my ancient brain that the cause this time for the not completely unaccustomed wobbliness is probably lack of nourishment, I go for the quickest option. Pasta cooks in ten minutes, three if it's fresh, and there are so many ways to serve it that I never get fed up.

I do tend to use the same old sauces, though, especially those that I can produce in bulk and freeze. A frozen portion of Bolognese topping takes two minutes to reheat in a microwave, or if I've had the forethought to remove it for defrosting before the start of my day, I throw it into a pan of hot, drained pasta, swish it around a bit and then decant into a bowl - easy, mega-fast and tasty.

I was fortunate enough to be taught how to cook authentic Italian food by my ex-husband's grandmother, who hailed from Genzano di Roma. She showed me how a basic tomato sauce could be made, preserved in jars, or frozen, and used as a foundation for many other things. It could be reduced by half and spread on pizze; with the addition of a few chopped olives and fresh basil leaves it makes a delicious sauce for steak; and tomato-based pasta sauces include Milanese, puttenesca, vongole alla Romana, with the addition of mushrooms and ham, chilli and clams, respectively. This list goes on ....

I had one pigeon breast in the 'fridge and that wouldn't make a meal on its own so I went into pasta mode and knocked it into a kind of bolognese-style sauce. It was lush – which is my grandson's version of luscious, I presume – and different! You should try it.

INGREDIENTS:

A finely chopped onion; I've used a red one for sweetness.
A clove of garlic, squashed.
One small carrot, diced.
Two rashers of bacon cut into small dice so that it almost disappears into the sauce.
One level tablespoonful of dried basil – or a couple of handfuls of fresh basil.
One large tin of tomatoes, chopped.
A couple of squirts or a small tin of tomato puree.
No salt. Half a teaspoonful of sugar, ground black pepper.
Half a pint of vegetable stock – use a cube!
This makes enough sauce for four people so you can freeze three-quarters of it for another day.
One pigeon breast per person, sliced thinly.

METHOD:

Place onion, garlic, carrot and half the bacon, into a saucepan and fry gently until the vegetables are tender. Do not let them brown.
Add the basil, tomatoes and purée, seasoning and stock.
Bring to the boil and simmer for at least 20 minutes, with the lid off, until the sauce is thick and gloopy. Fry pigeon and the rest of the bacon for a few minutes. Place a tablespoonful or two of sauce into a shallow pan. Add the meat. Cook for five minutes only, add your cooked pasta, swish around and serve. It's almost like magic!

You will need ...

Fry vegetables and bacon.

Add tomatoes and stock.

Fry pigeon and bacon.

Add sauce to pan ...

... and then the pasta.

Pigeon and Chicken Loaf

I spent half an hour thinking about a snappy title for this recipe, to include the words 'pigeon, chicken and loaf'. While the title I came up with doesn't sparkle with originality, it provoked memories of a childhood spent in a small community of a dozen prefabs built on a bombsite after the war. I could almost smell the dog daisies, groundsel and chickens' bread. See? I've got chicken and loaf into it already.

Mrs Fidgeon was an old lady who lived in the first 'proper' house in the street, and we kids called her Mrs Pigeon, because that's really funny when you're six. She kept chickens, and we were impressed. She must have been fed up with us peering over her back fence to catch a glimpse of these wondrous feathered creatures, but she never told us to 'clear orf' like some of the neighbours did.

On Mrs F's baking days, all her stale bread would be placed in the bottom of her oven, and left there on a low heat until it became crisp; then she'd feed it to her hens – if there was any left. We developed a taste for this delicacy and a call over the fence to beg, "Mrs Pidgin, you got any chicken's bread?" would always result in a tray of toasty crusts that we could break our teeth on. It had a distinctive taste and I've tried to reproduce it several times since, but never succeeded. I still bake stale bread, though, and whiz it into breadcrumbs to include in recipes like this. So, there's the 'pigeon' train of thought and I have to tell you that these tenuous links with the title have nothing whatsoever to do with the content of this dish, apart from breadcrumbs.

Recently, I had one of my 'clearing out the freezer' days and found a few pigeon breasts which would have been insufficient on their own, but combined with a redundant chicken breast and a few other ingredients they made a meal to feed a family. So, this is what I turned out and it was very tasty when served with some rice that I knocked up to include some dodgy-looking vegetables that were trying to escape from the bottom of the 'fridge. I reckon the whole meal cost me a couple of quid and I call that a 1950s result!

INGREDIENTS:

Three or four pigeon breasts, and one chicken breast
A cupful of breadcrumbs
One onion, a clove of garlic, a pinch of dried thyme, black pepper
One chicken stock cube dissolved in two tablespoons of water
Two rashers of bacon
Three hard-boiled eggs and an egg for binding

METHOD:

Mince pigeon and chicken pieces and place into a large bowl.
Chop the onion finely, squash garlic and add to the meat.
Add the breadcrumbs, thyme, pepper, beaten egg and chicken stock - mix well.
Line a loaf tin with greaseproof paper and lay the bacon on top.
Put half the meat mixture on the bacon and then add the whole hard-boiled eggs.
Cover the eggs with the other half of the meat mixture and smooth down with a palette knife. Make sure that the eggs are covered.
Place into a medium hot oven (175°C) for about 40 minutes.
Leave to rest for ten minutes while you cook the rice. (See page 208)
Serve piping hot with toast for a light lunch, or as a main meal with creamed potatoes and something green.

You will need ...

Bacon into lined tin.

Minced meat in a bowl.

Half meat mixture in, then eggs.

Top with rest of meat.

Turn loaf upside down.

PIGEON

Positive Pigeon

I've given up watching the news. All we hear about is the recession, unemployment, whole countries murdering each other in the name of religion or greed, or both … there's rarely anything uplifting. I watched a news item recently featuring a young woman with a couple of kids who was bemoaning the fact that she couldn't afford to feed them on the amount of benefit she received, the inevitable fag (£8-odd a packet) held expensively, in one hand. I'd love to have been able to speak to her and offer this recipe. It costs peanuts - especially if you leave out the saffron - it's filling, delicious and nourishing, and kids love it because it's so colourful.

It's just a case of knowing how-to. At school, I was fascinated by the fact that half a dozen ordinary substances could be fashioned into something extraordinary, just by using a little imagination combined with the chemical reactions that occur when mixtures are heated. My father encouraged me by taking my early attempts to work, for his lunch. He swore that he ate everything I cooked, although I suspect that a convenient waste bin was more likely to have been the recipient. If nothing else, today's students will learn how to feed their kids a balanced diet on a pittance, as I had to; you never know what life is going to throw at you – it's good to be prepared.

The saffron in this recipe is expensive, but if you do use it, just put the strands into a cup, add boiling water and leave to steep for two minutes. It's then ready to use – and you must put in the whole lot, strands, water and all – or you can use the cheaper turmeric.

There is very little fat in this recipe. Just a teaspoon of olive oil to get the chorizo going is all you'll need. The fat released from the chorizo as it fries gently will be sufficient to brown the pigeon meat, before you add the rest of the ingredients. This positive plateful is guaranteed to cheer up the most dejected, and disillusioned diner – and it's ready to eat in minutes.

INGREDIENTS:

Two pigeon breasts, sliced thinly – yes, really, that's all you'll need to feed two people.
Chorizo – diced quite small
One red onion, half of a yellow and an orange pepper, cherry tomatoes, frozen peas
Two small handfuls of bomba rice, if you can get it - or supermarket own-brand paella rice. Please don't use long grain; it doesn't absorb the liquid and flavours so well.
A pinch of saffron (optional), and a teaspoonful of hot paprika
One chicken stock cube dissolved in about half a pint of water

METHOD:

Fry the chorizo gently in a teaspoon of olive oil until the fat is released - two minutes.
Add the sliced pigeon breast meat and fry gently until brown.
Add the onion, peppers, tomatoes, peas and rice.
Stir for a few seconds, so that the rice and vegetables are coated with oil.
Add the saffron and its liquid, the paprika and the stock, and season to taste.
Bring to the boil, simmer for ten minutes, lid off, and then stir.
Simmer for a further five minutes, lid on. If it looks dry, add a little boiling water.
Serve with a green salad, and chutney.

You will need ...

Steep the saffron.

Fry the chorizo.

Add the pigeon ...

... and vegetables ...

...then the rice.

Remember Remember

Way back when, there was no such thing as an organised firework display. Households held their own modest, family celebration in the garden, with a small bonfire, a guy of sorts, a few quids-worth of fireworks and 'traditional' food. There was always at least one Catherine wheel that wouldn't whizz round on a fence post, ditto a rocket that refused to launch from its milk bottle pad, and sparklers.

With the advent of Health and Safety laws, and awareness of what we were doing to our environment, most of the family bonfire dos ceased and the heart and soul was ripped out of the season. Instead, we have massive, impersonal displays where an average-sized family has to pay a king's ransom to gain access, and even more for a 'barbecued' burger or hot-dog.

Our small November the 5th parties were fun. They lasted for about an hour and my boys loved it. Nan and Granddad were always there and we ate Bonfire Night food; cheap and cheerful, but special because it was eaten in a smoke-filled garden, while Granddad rushed about like a mad person in an attempt to sustain some kind of pyrotechnic continuity. Heinz tomato soup (oxtail for the youngest because he wouldn't entertain a tomato in any guise), and homemade burgers in baps was the menu for about 15 years, and it was the same when they grew up – eaten indoors, before the pub.

Nowadays, my grandchildren go to organised events where they view fireworks from some distance away, and are bought glowsticks in place of sparklers, and flat burgers washed down with a carton of something. Their parents have the hassle of trying to find somewhere to park before fighting their way out at the end of the show – and it's supposed to be fun! I say, bring it all back. Once a year, get some common sense on the go, so that you can ignore all the health and safety nonsense, light a small bonfire to dance around, buy some sparklers and make some homemade burgers. Two hours, tops – that's all I'm asking. Give your kids something to 'remember, remember the 5th of November' for – apart from the capture and execution of Mr Fawkes.

INGREDIENTS:

Baps or ciabatta
Pigeon meat, chopped, 4oz of sausage meat, and an egg to bind
White onions, chopped
Seasoning: garlic or onion salt, pepper, pinch of cayenne.
Matzo meal or breadcrumbs for coating
Red onions, sliced
Cheese slices
Tomato, sliced thickly
Relish, or ketchup, and dill pickle (optional)

METHOD:

Slice the baps in half, reassemble and place in a warm oven to heat through while you make the patties.
Place the meats in a bowl with the white onion, egg and seasoning.
Form into patties, roll in the Matzo meal or breadcrumbs and set aside.
Heat the oil and cook the patties in small batches until golden brown.
Drain on kitchen paper, then assemble the burgers and accompany with Heinz tomato soup, chips and a sparkler.

You will need ...

Mince the pigeon.

Mix the meats.

Roll in breadcrumbs.

Fry until golden.

Self-assembly job.

Stone Age Hunter

We're all a bit Jekyll and Hyde-ish. We all have a number of facets to our personalities, but the transformation that can occur when your child prepares to realise his killing instinct can be quite awe-inspiring. Your junior airgunner may be gentle and kind, he may be considerate, compassionate, buy Christmas gifts for the family pets, be altogether angelic, but ask a teenaged cherub to help out by culling the pigeon population in a farmer's fields and you can watch a transformation occur within minutes.

Before your very eyes, he will transmogrify into a stone-age hunter, a precision machine. All he needs is a Davy Crockett hat or a Terminator 3 outfit to complete the image. He is on a mission to wage war against hostile invaders of the cornfields. He has been given the instructions of his assignment by his commander, Farmer Giles, and he marches off into the sunrise, head held high, adrenalin flowing, rifle gleaming, raring to go against all odds.

'It's disgusting,' I hear plaintive cries from the animal rights brigade, 'killing all those innocent creatures for no reason,' and I agree, up to a point. I don't particularly relish blood sports, but let's get it into perspective. The pigeons destroy crops and have to be controlled. There is a reason, and mostly, the meat is eaten – even if it's only by the local ferret population.

You will notice a theme running through this book, more than one actually; I feel very strongly about the opening of packets in order to feed your family, I don't waste anything edible, if I can help it, and I can't stand hypocrites! I stood behind an earth mother in the supermarket queue the other day, at least I think it was a mother, it could quite easily have been a father, it can be quite hard to tell sometimes. There were badges all over her coat: Save the Whales; Ban Fox Hunting; Leave the Dolphins alone etc., and in her trolley she had vegetarian sausages and cheese, soya mince substitute, lentils, and the like, together with several tins of cat food containing rabbit, chicken and liver. She was praising the merits of 'natural' food to the check-out girly, declaring that eating meat was totally unnecessary, while gazing sideways disapprovingly at my pork chops and leg of lamb.

I felt like asking her why it was okay for her cats to eat animals, while we meat eaters are frowned upon if we purchase a pound of mince. What did she mean by 'natural' anyway? There was no sign of a tin containing a hint of mouse, starling or essence of dustbin sack, and I've never seen a cat creep up on a fully grown hen or catch a cow and rip out its liver. She should have had a badge saying, 'Save a Chicken Today – and Feed it to Your Cat.' I'm not having a go at true vegetarians. I admire anyone who has the courage to carry their convictions into their diet, but it seems a mite hypocritical to bend the rules to suit one's convenience. I mentioned this to a friend recently, who doesn't eat meat because of 'cruelty to the animals'. She explained that cats and dogs HAVE to eat meat because they're carnivores - and we don't; we're not, so we shouldn't. She's never had a steak cooked by Pierre Marco White, though.
Anyway, back to the huntsman. Hunting can be good for your teenager; it teaches self-discipline and patience. It's no

good charging across the fields, firing at will. A certain amount of control has to be exercised while the quarry is stalked and observed. One shot, all the pigeons disappear and a great deal of patience has to be summoned by your offspring as he waits for them to lull themselves into a false sense of security. For a pigeon to indulge in a good lull takes at least 20 minutes, so in a couple of hours he could bag about six birds, if he's very lucky. That's hardly enough to decimate the species, but while the escapees are busy lulling, they are not munching the farmer's profits, and that is the object of the exercise.

Rats are also the target, on occasions. Funnily enough, no one seems to mind if the rat population is wiped out, but they're animals too, aren't they? The rat-hunting expeditions are, by necessity, nocturnal events and can be a team effort. Three rifle-boys have been known to sit for hours in a remote barn, in almost complete darkness except for a Mag-lite mounted on the scope of their rifles, while they wait for the rodents to emerge into the 'killing zone', the small area where they have smeared the last of the family's peanut butter and the cat's evening meals for the next week. You will hear about these ratting episodes - which is the nearest you want to get, judging by the relish with which the stories are related - usually at mealtimes.

Apparently, the hunters listen to the squeaking and keep perfectly still, the latter a feat in itself for an active 17-year old, until they are certain of success. I had always assumed that rats were reasonably intelligent. They can find their way out of mazes and negotiate the most complicated of assault courses in an attempt to feed under laboratory conditions, and yet, even before the removal of the corpses of their brethren, they return confidently. You'd think that they would realise that something in that barn wasn't quite right!

The juniors are not allowed to touch the rats under any circumstances, which is a relief, otherwise they may be tempted to bring them home. The farmer burns the animals because of the risk of Weil's disease which can be fatal to humans. However, the danger adds a fillip to the rat-hunting trips and your youngsters will talk about it for weeks unless you shut them up.

If your teenager is fortunate enough - if that's the right phrase - to be allowed to indulge his baser instincts by shooting rats, do not think that you are overreacting if you insist that he disinfects everything, including himself, with carbolic before he sets foot in the house. For about a week you will find yourself twitching every time he goes near the larder or fridge, but don't worry, it's a perfectly normal response. It is also normal to erect a tent in the garden and refuse him admittance to the house at all until you are satisfied that all traces of rat have vanished. You will never use the expression 'squeaky clean' again.

PIGEON

- Winter -

PIGEON

Camberwell Hotpot

The smell of a Lancashire hotpot simmering away in the oven always evokes childhood memories of my grandmother's kitchen, although her version of it should have been Camberwell hotpot, since she was a South London gal and never went within sniffing distance of Lancashire. I thought I might give it a go, substituting pigeon for the more usually favoured scrag end of lamb and, sure enough, as it began to bubble the memories crowded in.

I'd often have to walk through a pea-souper fog for my after-school visits to my maternal grandparents in winter. There was a 100-yard dash along a back alley, up the garden path past the coal hole where I thought the demons lived, and the outside toilet where they probably really did, until I could burst through the back door and into a scullery. A huge butler sink sported a spotless, wooden draining board, and a pine table that had been scrubbed to within an inch of its life stood beside shelves holding kitchen equipment. There was a walk-in larder where the milk bottle was kept in a saucepan of cold water on the concrete floor, winter and summer. Refrigerators were a luxury and only for the quite well off.

The scullery door opened into a large kitchen and Granddad sat at the table, a plate piled high with 'doorstep' slices of bread and butter in front of him. I still have the bread knife that he used, still as good as new. My grandmother, on hearing my noisy and panic-stricken approach, transferred the hotpot to the table from the smallest of three ovens in a black-leaded range. This cooking stove was a magnificent piece of Victorian engineering and took up the whole of one wall, not like the pseudo, cosmetically-enhanced, compact 'ranges' available today. It was a beast; a fire-eating dragon powered by coal and coke and capable of producing the most delectable food you can imagine. Bread, apple pies, slow-cooked meats, and rice/sago puddings covered in nutmeg that, try as I might, I have been unable to reproduce to quite the same creaminess.

I wallowed in nostalgia for a good couple of hours, drinking tea and remembering my childhood, until my pigeon hotpot was ready to eat. You could also make individual hotpots to offer to elderly relatives, but this may invoke memories of their childhoods and you'll have to listen and nod along. Make sure you have plenty of time.

INGREDIENTS:

Pigeon breasts, cut into pieces
A large onion, two carrots, two sticks of celery and a leek, all finely sliced
Four large potatoes cut into quarter-inch thick slices
Chicken stock
Salt, pepper, and a handful of fresh thyme, or just a pinch if dried

METHOD:

First, roll the pigeon pieces in flour, then fry them for one minute each side in a little hot oil, just to seal the juices, then place all the prepared vegetables, except the spuds, into a large mixing bowl and stir them around with the salt, pepper and thyme.
You will need a fairly deep dish for this. Start with a layer of potato to cover the bottom of the dish, then continue to layer, alternately, the meat and the mixed vegetables. Finish with a layer of potato - that's potato top and bottom, meat and veg between - and add stock until it just reaches the top layer of potato.
Cover with tin foil or a lid and place into a medium hot oven, 180° C, for about an hour, or until the potatoes are tender.
Remove the lid/foil, brush the potatoes with a little melted butter/oil and bake for a further 20 minutes, until the top is golden and crunchy.

You will need ...

Fry the pigeon.

Chop the vegetables.

Into a pot; top with potato.

Bake until browned on top.

A childhood favourite.

Currying Favour

I get quite a few invitations to dinner parties, birthday bashes and work-related gatherings at this time of the year, and I'm always asked to take along a batch of sausage rolls. Sometimes, I wonder if that's the only reason I'm asked to attend, but I don't mind, it's quite flattering really. There is the bog-standard version of this recipe elsewhere within these pages, but so many people have asked me how to make them that I'm repeating it here, with a twist.

You can make these 'sausage' rolls with any kind of meat that you happen to have handy, apart from chicken or turkey. With a little imagination, though, you can combine most ingredients and come out with something original and tasty. (See page 46)

The method is the same every time; just roll out the pastry into a long strip, place the filling along it, fold it over, egg wash the top and cut into bite-sized pieces. Maybe that's where I go wrong, they're a bit too handy to pick up three at a time. I might not have to make so many if they were bigger … or not.

Anyway, this time I've used the base of sausage meat and onion, as before, but added some curry spices, a hit of chilli and some pigeon meat. They are yummy, I promise you, and that's not just my opinion. Recently, I took some to a tradeshow and they went down a storm. I've been told to keep a ready supply in the freezer for when my presence – and the sausage rolls – might be required at another function.

I might even branch out and use up all the odd bits of meat lurking at the back of my freezer. One of my favourite occupations is playing in the kitchen, making something really delicious out of the most unlikely ingredients … and winter's here, so it's an excuse to be all warm and toasty indoors with the oven on, experimenting to my heart's content. Make sure that you don't have the oven too hot or the meat will not cook through.

INGREDIENTS:

Sausage meat
Pigeon meat, chopped finely
A small cupful of matzos meal, or breadcrumbs
Chopped onion
Dollop of curry paste, or 2 teaspoons of garam masala
Half a teaspoon of dried chilli flakes, or one chopped, fresh chilli
Two eggs
Half a teaspoon of salt and plenty of black pepper
Ready to roll pastry – shortcrust, or puff
Beaten egg to with which to brush the tops

METHOD:

Combine sausage meat and finely chopped pigeon meat in a bowl with the matzos meal or breadcrumbs, add the chopped onion, seasoning and the eggs. I go hands-in, but you can use a fork, and mix well.

Do the 'one long sausage roll' trick as described, cut into whatever-sized pieces takes your fancy and bake in a medium-hot oven – about 170° C or equivalent – for about 25 minutes, or until they are golden brown and irresistible. You might have to taste one, or two, just to make sure they're suitable to serve to others.

You will need …

Combine all ingredients.

Add seasoning, mix well.

Make one long sausage roll.

Egg-wash the top.

Cut into bite-sized pieces.

PIGEON

Peaceful Pigeon Pancakes

A few days before my dear old mum died, we spent one hospital visiting time talking about food, almost to the exclusion of everything else. Cookery was always our common interest and we enjoyed a couple of hours discussing recipes and how things used to be, when we could buy mutton easily and scallops were a cheap Sunday teatime treat. "Eggs and bacon seem to be going out of fashion," she said - they were feeding her slop and she loved her egg and bacon breakfasts - and then, sternly, "Never waste food, my girl!" I told her that I wouldn't dare, in case she found out and put me on the naughty step. We spoke about the wonderful meals she made when I was a small child in the '50s, when rationing was still in place. Convenience food was largely unavailable back then, but Mum wouldn't have considered using it anyway. It was a matter of pride; her idea of convenience food was shoving an Oxo cube into her gravy.

Mum taught me to respect food and to prepare it with love; apart from bread when I should beat the living daylights out of it, she said. To offer a carefully prepared meal to a child or a partner is to give a part of yourself to them, and should reflect the love behind it. The opening of a ready-meal and reheating it in a microwave just doesn't hack it.

A reorganisation of the freezer unearthed a pigeon. I found chillies, tomatoes and bacon in the fridge. I had honey, white wine vinegar and garlic in the store cupboard, and the makings for a couple of pancakes so eventually, I was all set to play in the kitchen. The finished product ticked several boxes; I didn't have to think too much in the preparation stage, it was comforting to eat, and I made a delicious and nourishing meal for myself with very little effort and a few ingredients. Mum would have approved.

INGREDIENTS:

One pigeon per person.
Two rashers of bacon.
Honey, white wine vinegar, squashed garlic mixture for basting.
For the pancakes: 2oz plain flour, one egg, a pinch of salt and pepper, and half a pint of milk.
Salsa: Thinly sliced red onion, sliced tomato, half a finely-chopped chilli, a glug of balsamic vinegar.

METHOD:

Mix the basting ingredients together and paint the pigeon, then wrap it in bacon and roast in a moderate oven - about 180°C - for half an hour. Knock up the pancake batter and let it stand for 15 minutes. Set aside and make the salsa; Place the red onion, tomato and chilli into a bowl and add a little balsamic vinegar. Swish it round a bit and leave to marinate until you're ready to use it.
Remove the meat from the pigeon and keep warm with the bacon – which will be crunchy.
Fry a couple of tablespoons of the pancake batter in very little oil, for a minute or two each side.
Place the pancake on a warm plate, add a portion of pigeon meat and top with salsa. Fold the bottom up, sides in, like swaddling a baby; add a dollop of crème fraîche, if you fancy it, curl up in front of the telly and eat. This is even more comforting if accompanied by a glass or two of something alcoholic.

You will need ...

Paint the pigeon.

Whisk the batter ...

...until it looks like cream.

Salsa ingredients.

Self-assembly.

PIGEON

Imagination Pie

I can't be the only one who has opened the 'fridge door, midweek, and seen nothing but leftovers. I'm talking about those cold, boiled potatoes that you cooked too many of and decided to save for 'tomorrow', but you know they'll end up in the bin. Or the two rashers of bacon/three sausages left in the packet from Sunday's breakfast that will most likely accompany the spuds; maybe a couple of pigeon breasts that are nowhere near enough to feed four hungry people, vegetables that are on the verge of a 'best by' date ...

I hate wasting food and always manage to come up with something reasonably tasty by using the lonely ingredients in my 'fridge. This dubious talent stems from watching my grandmother 'create' in the kitchen. She was notoriously mean, never wasted a crumb and despite being a very wealthy woman because of frugality in all aspects of her life, died almost penniless and in anguish as she watched her fortune (and my inheritance) dwindle and disappear in nursing home fees. However, she did leave me a gift, in a manner of speaking, which came in really handy in the many times of need/penury that have occurred during my life; the ability to take a handful of ingredients and turn them into something tasty – providing I have access to herbs and spices.

This Imagination Pie was inspired by an egg and bacon pie that Grandma used to make and is so-called because imagination is one of the necessary components. You can add anything you happen to find lurking in the cold: sliced cooked spuds, a slice of ham, frozen peas, grated cheese … really, anything. You can serve this hot as a main course with mashed potatoes and peas, warm with chutney as a lunchtime snack, or cold if you want something substantial when you're on the move. I really like this pie, not only because it's tasty, but also because I didn't have to go shopping for ingredients - it feels as if it's free!

INGREDIENTS:

Puff pastry – found in the freezer, left over from last Christmas and still edible.

Four sausages, filling removed and mixed with a chopped onion, a squashed clove of garlic, a pinch of dried thyme, and some black pepper.

A couple of pigeon breasts, sliced and three rashers of bacon.

A couple of onions, thinly sliced, two tomatoes, sliced thickly, alf a dozen mushrooms, quartered, and four eggs – and one to egg-wash the pastry.

METHOD:

Roll two-thirds of the pastry fairly thinly and big enough to overlap a two-inch deep baking tin, and then layer your ingredients:

Spread the prepared sausage meat evenly across the bottom of the tin. Place the pigeon breasts in next and the bacon rashers on top. Make a layer of sliced onions, then tomatoes, and finally the mushrooms. The important bit is to make little 'nests', one in each corner, before breaking the eggs very carefully into them. The eggs must remain whole! Fold the excess pastry over the top of the pie, egg wash, and then roll out the rest of the pastry to make a lid. Place this on the top and bake in a medium hot oven – 180° – for about 40 minutes. I dusted mine with a little smoked paprika to make it look pretty.

A jumble of leftovers.

Layer meat mixture, pigeon and bacon.

Then layers of veg.

Add eggs – gently, don't break them!

Tuck them in and add the lid.

Serve warm with chutney

PIGEON

Pigeon Crumble

You can make savoury crumbles as well as the more popular fruit variety, but not many people do, probably because of the childhood association with custard. If you can control the impulse to hurl vanilla sauce all over it, though, a savoury crumble ticks all the boxes for a tasty and satisfying winter supper. I came up with this one when trying to create something new for an impromptu dinner party. The weather was dire and I really didn't want to go shopping and I had a couple of pigeon breasts, but there would be three of us, so I had to pad it out somehow. Chicken's always a good bet to accompany flying game and I've always got a few lurking in the freezer for emergencies, so it was just a case of defrosting one of them.

The crumble went down a treat, despite one comedian asking 'where's the custard' as I placed it on the table – there's always one! I threw a few roasties in the oven with it while it was baking, too, so there was hardly any effort involved, apart from slicing the vegetables. That's my kind of cookery!

It is so easy; you can prepare it in advance and put into the oven 30 minutes before your guests are due to arrive, so that they say 'ooh, something smells good' as they walk through the door, and by the time you've had your first glass of wine, it'll be ready to serve. Or, if you're not having guests, just get on with it, cook and eat. It's delicious, either way.

INGREDIENTS:

Two pigeon and two chicken breasts, sliced and rolled in seasoned flour.
Two red onions and two carrots, sliced.
Mushrooms, quartered and half a green and a yellow pepper, sliced.
A couple of large, fresh tomatoes, sliced, or a tin of chopped ones.
Half a pint of chicken stock and salt and pepper to taste.
For the crumble:
4oz plain flour.
2oz butter – or margarine.
Pinch of salt, ground black pepper, mixed herbs, pinch of cayenne.
2oz extra-strong cheddar, grated

METHOD:

Fry floured meat in a little olive oil for three minutes until it begins to take on colour.
Add all the vegetables, stock and seasoning.
Bring to the boil and then simmer for about 15 minutes, lid off.

Place mixture into an ovenproof dish and then make the crumble by rubbing in the flour and margarine with your fingertips – it takes seconds - until it resembles breadcrumbs. Add the cheese and seasoning, then sprinkle over the meat and vegetable mixture. Pat it down a bit and place into a moderate oven – about 170° – for about 40 minutes or until the top is golden brown. Serve with the roasties that you bunged in the oven with it – you did, didn't you? Enjoy!

You will need ...

Fry the meat.

Add vegetables and stock.

Decant into a dish.

Add topping and cheese.

Bake for 40 minutes.

Pigeon au Vin

One bright but very frosty Sunday morning, I went along with my friend, Mark, to one of his local 'shooting for pest control' venues. It was blowing an easterly hooli and perishing cold but he still insisted that I strip off in the middle of an open field to replace my warm and sensible but colourful clothing ('You didn't think that one, through, Rosie. How the hell do you think I'm going to get anything with you dressed like that?') with the camo gear that he had thoughtfully brought along for me.

It might be an idea, he'd said when I'd begged him for pigeons, if I got into the spirit of the thing and witnessed the necessary skill required – not to mention the trouble he had to go to - in order to provide me with my vital ingredients. This, he assumed, would justify his demand for food from my kitchen once a month. It didn't work because there was no hardship involved at all. I loved it.

We walked for about five miles, keeping to the lee of the hedgerows, and while Mark was pigeon watching, I kept quiet and still, as instructed, but took careful note of my surroundings, mentally filing away other stuff that I could possibly use in the kitchen at a later date. When in season, I could gather hazelnuts. Elder trees would give me fruit for wine or flowers for cordial. Blackthorn for sloes and brambles which would yield blackberries for crumbles or jelly. I'd almost lost interest in the pigeons, but Mark managed to bag four and I was quite happy to wander homeward with my gifts.

INGREDIENTS:

To feed 4 people:
Eight pigeon breasts
Three shallots – I'm using the Egyptian ones, but the best are round and grown in Brittany or the UK. If you can get hold of these you'll need, half a dozen, roughly chopped.
One squashed clove of garlic.
Button mushrooms – a punnet
Salt, pepper, thyme
Half a bottle of good red wine – if you use the cheap stuff it'll taste of acid. Your meal will only ever be as good as the ingredients you use.

METHOD:

I found some baby carrots to accompany the finished dish – beautifully sweet and I have to confess that there were not so many when I had finished cooking as when I started – but you can serve with creamed potatoes and any vegetable that you fancy.

Begin with a slug of olive oil in a wok/pan. Once hot, throw in the shallots, garlic, thyme, salt and pepper and pigeon breasts. I slice mine into strips so that they cook quicker and more evenly but you can put them in whole. Fry on medium heat, stirring all the time, for about four minutes. Then add the mushrooms and continue to cook for two minutes. Turn the heat up, add the red wine, let it bubble at high heat for about a minute, then turn down to simmer gently for about ten minutes. This will reduce the liquid and you'll end up with the most amazing red wine sauce.
I love sweet potato mash, but you can serve with any vegetables that you prefer.

Roast Pigeon

As I was raking through the freezer for something different, buried among the large number of individual pots containing Bolognese sauce that I make and portion-freeze, I came across a solitary pigeon. I'd forgotten about it because I usually cook game when I have company, so one lonely pigeon isn't enough. It had been left until I had time to visit a farmer's market and purchase some mates for it.

I rely on fast, home-cooked, but frozen-in-advance, food when I come home from wherever I've been, and game needs a bit of nurturing to do it justice, and therefore time – and sometimes thyme.

Any road up, getting back to this pigeon that I found, as I said, it did look a tad forlorn so I had a rummage round the fridge as well, to see what I could find to go with it. I found a few vegetables and some streaky bacon; sufficient ingredients to make a lonely pigeon feel that it had friends.

This dish cheered me up no end on a cold and frosty Sunday evening and my renewed brightness had nothing whatsoever to do with the two Cadbury's Flakes and hot, strong caffeine that I had for pudding.

INGREDIENTS:

One pigeon per person
Four rashers of streaky bacon
A few spuds, cut into chunks and par-boiled for ten minutes
One large onion cut into quarters/eighths or half a dozen pickling onions
Carrots, cut in half.
Three sticks of celery

METHOD:

Place a roasting tin containing a glug of oil into a hot oven for five minutes. The oven should be on the highest setting. Chop the carrots and celery into large-ish chunks and wrap the pigeon in the streaky bacon.

Spread carrots, onions, celery and par-boiled potatoes evenly in the hot oil. Place the pigeon on top of the vegetables, black pepper over the whole lot – no salt, there's already enough in the bacon - and put the tin back into the oven.

Immediately, turn the oven down to a medium heat and roast for about an hour. After about 40 minutes into the cooking time, if you think that the bacon is getting a bit too crispy, place a piece of tinfoil over the pigeon breast. This sounds like a long time to cook a small pigeon but you will find that, because it is covered completely in bacon, the result will be a moist, perfectly cooked bird and vegetables just right, soft and slightly caramelised.

At the end of the cooking time, remove everything from the tin and keep it warm. Deglaze the roasting tin by placing over medium heat on the hob and adding half a pint of chicken stock (or water and a stock cube). You can add half a glass of white wine if you really want to push the boat out. Reduce the liquid by half, stir in a knob of butter for richness, and you're ready to go!

You can serve it with a green vegetable if you wish, but I just settle for the root veg and a glass of Merlot – your call!

Pigeon and Pork Terrine

This terrine is so versatile that you can make it at any time of the year. It can be served hot with roast root vegetables and gravy for a hearty, warming supper in the middle of winter, but it's equally good eaten cold, out-of-doors on a summer afternoon, with a crisp, green salad, and a glass of chilled Chablis. You can take it anywhere. If you slice into a baguette with tomatoes, lettuce and a touch of mayo, it becomes a portable, balanced meal – vegetables, protein and carbs all in one handy package. I've made this particular meatloaf and served it at a dinner party, as a starter, or taken it to the beach in the summer. The kids absolutely love it - and you can freeze it, whole or in slices; like I said, versatile.

Today, though, since summer seems a million years away, I'm cooking pigeon and pork loaf – terrine is just a posh word for it – in the bleak midwinter. It's freezing outside, literally, and the aroma of this dish as it cooks seems to make the whole house seem cosy. As a rule, I use pork and veal, or chicken and ham, but it's good sometimes to experiment with flavours and, more often than not, you can discover something special that is unique to you.

Give this a go. It looks complicated, I know, but I can assure you that it isn't and it's well worth the small effort involved.

INGREDIENTS:

About a dozen rashers of streaky bacon
1 chopped onion
Couple of shallots
1 clove garlic, squashed
4 pigeon breasts, very thinly sliced or minced
12 oz minced pork - you can buy belly pork for this. It's cheap and has a wonderful flavour
1 cup of fresh white breadcrumbs
1 egg
About 4 tablespoons brandy
Chopped parsley
Vegetable, or chicken, stock cube

METHOD:

Line a loaf tin, or a deep cake tin, with bacon so that it overhangs the sides.
Grab a mixing bowl, put everything else into it, mix it about a bit and then dump it into the prepared tin. Spread it around and pat it down so that it's level and packed tightly with no air bubbles.
Fold the overhanging bacon on to the top of the terrine. Cover with foil and put the whole caboodle into a larger, roasting tin that you have half-filled with boiling water.
Put it in the pre-heated oven for an hour and a quarter.
Remove the terrine, take of the foil, and run a skewer into it. If the skewer comes out clean, it's done. If it doesn't, then bung it back into the oven for another ten minutes, or so.
When it's cooked, pour off the excess juices, double wrap it with foil, put a tea towel over it, foil and all, and place a couple of weights on the top – large tins of baked beans (still in the tin, obviously) will do, and leave it for half an hour to compress. It will still be warm by the time you plate up. Alternatively, if you want to serve it cold, put it in the fridge, complete with weights, overnight before cutting into slices.

You will need ...

Union Jack bacon.

Mix everything together.

Press it down firmly.

Fold over the bacon.

Slice to serve or freeze.

Thereby Hangs a Tail

You can meet the most interesting people in pubs. A mature gent came into my local one day, where I sat nursing a Diet Coke while waiting for my boys to return from a hunting trip. I knew him by sight already and we began to talk about the weather and progressed to his stories of the 'good old days'. I'd already explained why I was sitting alone in a pub, and where my boys were.
"Just after the war when I was a lad," he said. "I had an air pistol. It was my dad's really, but I used to borrow it while he was on a late shift, and put it back cleaned before he came home."
I could sense a story coming on. "Tell me," I urged.
"It was a Webley Mark 1," he said. "Cost about thirty bob in those days. A .22, it was, great little shooter."

He went on to tell me a story that I found hard to believe, but didn't like to say so, particularly as he'd just bought me a gin and tonic. Our local rubbish tip is an efficient and cleanly run haven of respectability now, but way back in 1946, he told me, it was a different story. The town's household and factory waste was piled up in putrid heaps and allowed to decay before being bulldozed into surrounding marshland. Hundreds of gulls picked at the best bits, the stench was awful, and there were rats galore.

My new friend told me that he and a pal or two used to take their air pistols and torches and cycle over to the tip at dusk to shoot as many rats as they had pellets for. There were no pest control agencies in those days; landowners were responsible for keeping vermin numbers in check, and the young lads were actively encouraged by the local authority to indulge their hunting instincts. In fact, he assured me, they were paid a couple of shillings (10p) for every dozen rats' tails handed in at the police station. That bit I found hard to take. I couldn't imagine our eternally under-funded police department paying out, and as for actually handling rats' tails … Mind you, I suppose times have changed since then and people are more aware of the health risks.

Half an hour later the boys breezed in after locking their rifles in the boot of the car, and I introduced them to my companion, They were intrigued when they heard of the 'rats' tails for bounty' story.
"Are you quite sure it was the police station?" I asked him, and he assured me that it was, but now he came to think of it, although he remembered shooting the rats, collecting the tails and taking them to the police station, he couldn't remember what he did with the money. He looked quite worried as we left, in case he was owed several shillings from way back when.

First thing on Monday morning, I rang the local police station and spoke to a young PC who thought I was winding him up.
"No, really," I assured him. "It's a genuine enquiry. I need to know if it could be true."
"I dunno," he said. "Sounds a bit strange to me. Hold on a minute. I'll go and ask my sergeant."

After a while he returned somewhat apologetically, because he'd sniggered during most of our conversation, and referred me to the Essex County Police Archives. "Ask for Fred Feather," he advised. "He's a good bloke."

Fred turned out to be a very good bloke. He assured me that my story seemed feasible, because he knew for a fact that the forestry commission used to pay a bob per squirrel tail, but he wasn't so sure about the rats' tale. He told me that he'd look through the land registry archives for documentary evidence, but suggested flying a kite in the local paper to ask for information from readers. This seemed like a good idea, and as I wrote for the local rag at the time, twice weekly, I mentioned it in my column, but there was no response.

I was determined to get to the bottom of it somehow. I couldn't let it go so I spoke to one of the local reporters who was in charge of local history features and he told me of a piece he'd read that covered a 'Rat 'n' Sparrow' club. There were many such clubs in the late '40s, he told me, and they met at their local pub where a few shillings were presented each week to the member with the largest tally. It didn't verify my story though, and I was still puzzled by the police involvement.

Another call from 'Archive Fred', told me that our neighbourhood police station could well have been the reception point for rats' tails. The airgunner would have had to be authorised by the police before any money was paid out – and our particular station was the only one in Essex not owned by the police department. It was owned by the council and until 1960 the same building housed the council offices, which could have explained why the tails were handed in there, but I still couldn't prove who had actually paid up – council or police department.

Did this kind of primitive vermin control actually take place years ago? Were airgunners paid for producing the evidence of their rat-hunting adventures? The mystery continues.

RABBIT

- Spring -

RABBIT

Bunny Milla-aze

The whole family call spag-bol 'pasketti Bolla-aze' now, since that's what my granddaughter, Mia, used to call all her pasta suppers, regardless of recipe, when she couldn't pronounce Italian words. I don't know why we still do it. We certainly didn't help the child to learn, but she did that against the odds and now corrects us and asks why we can't speak properly. Anyway, I've only told you that to explain the name of the recipe, which is nothing like a spag bol. It's a variation of spaghetti Milanese, which my late, ex-mum-in-law used to make, and I could eat it every day, it's so yummy.

Tera was from Rome, but she taught me to cook authentic Italian dishes from all over her country. I had no idea that there was such a divide until she told me, for example, that there was a difference between a lasagne cooked in Naples, to one baked in Florence. Tera would recoil in horror if I put cheese anywhere near my lasagne until after it was cooked, and yet many recipes, from further south, require cheese to be added to the white sauce. It's a matter of preference, I suppose, but lasagne still doesn't taste right to me if it's got cheese in it, rather than on it.

I was wrong to generalise. Of course there are regional variations; we have them here in the UK, and in my family, from street to street. My Somerset-born and bred grandmother made a rice pudding with fresh cream and sultanas, whereas South-London Nan reckoned that to be 'posh', and knocked one up with evaporated milk and nutmeg, both equally delicious puds, but different.

In Italian households, pasta dishes are usually eaten as a starter, rather than a main course, and the popular assumption that Italian food is boring because 'it's all pasta and pizza' couldn't be further from the truth. This recipe is intended to be eaten before the main event, but can easily be served as a snack for lunch, or a late supper, if you make the sauce in bulk and freeze in portions. Dried pasta only takes about 12 minutes to cook, and the sauce a couple of minutes to reheat in a microwave.

INGREDIENTS:

The meat from two rabbit legs, minced or chopped
Four rashers of streaky bacon, diced
Two cloves of garlic
One large onion, and a carrot finely chopped
A handful of button mushrooms, sliced
One tin of tomatoes, chopped
Half a pint of hot chicken stock (made with a stock-pod or cube)
Pinch of sugar, and of salt; black pepper to taste
Dried oregano and fresh basil to garnish

METHOD:

In a large pan, fry the bacon, garlic, onion and carrot and rabbit meat gently in a little olive oil until the onion is softened. This takes a few minutes.
Add the mushrooms and oregano and cook for a further two minutes, stirring all the time.
Add the tin of tomatoes, stock, sugar, salt and pepper. Not too much salt, it's already in the bacon.
Bring to the boil, then simmer for at least half an hour, or until the sauce has reduced by half.
Cook your pasta for ten minutes and serve topped with the sauce and garnished with fresh basil.

You will need ...

All prepped and ready.

Fry vegetables gently.

Add tomatoes, stock and seasoning.

Boil pasta.

Sauce reduced by half.

Chinese Slow-cooked Rabbit

I knew it was a long shot, but nothing ventured, nothing gained, so I called in at my local Asda on the way home from work to see if I could buy a rabbit. They've recently upped their game (pardon the pun) and added venison and wild boar sausages to their repertoire, so I thought I might be in with a chance.

"No, sorry," said the very polite and friendly meat-counter assistant. "We don't stock it fresh. You could try the frozen food aisle, though, they might have some."

"Ooh no!" gasped the frozen food attendant, as if I'd asked her for babies' fingers, or curried puppy. "We don't do that, although they do have it in tins, you know - in the pet food aisle."

I didn't tell her that I don't have any pets and the rabbit was for my own consumption, she'd seemed shocked enough when she'd thought it was for my cat.

After phoning around and being told by several establishments that there was no demand for rabbit, these days, I managed to get one from a butcher who specialises in 'ethnic' meats – although he just stared at me blankly when I asked him how rabbit fits under that particular umbrella. He did have a good selection of produce, though, and I ended up spending far more than I'd intended: rib eye steaks and ox tail, along with two fine bunnies.

Anyway, this is what I came up with. It's extremely tasty and if you've got access to a rabbit and a slow cooker, very simple to knock up. Even simmered gently on the hob, it's a doddle and it can either be a satisfying but light Saturday evening meal, or with the addition of a few dumplings, a hefty plateful of comfort food. I always cook my rabbit on the bone because I think the meat is sweeter and the bones give more flavour to the dish, but that's just a personal opinion. If you want to take all the meat from the bones, it's probably easier to eat. You can't get much simpler than this. I call it 'a bloke in a hurry' recipe.

INGREDIENTS:

A rabbit
A pack of frozen Chinese vegetables
Olive oil for frying
A pack of Knorr Golden Vegetable soup mix
Enough water to cover.
Seasoning – black pepper, salt, dash of chilli oil, soy sauce
A little crème fraîche to garnish

METHOD:

Pre-heat the slow cooker.
Place olive oil into a large pan and fry the rabbit pieces until they take on a bit of colour.
Put the frozen vegetables into the base of the slow cooker, and the rabbit on top.
Make up the soup mix – instructions on the packet.
Throw in the seasoning.
Run away.
Six to eight hours later, you'll have the most wonderful, fragrant, braised rabbit.
Stir in a little crème fraîche and serve with mashed potatoes, rice or pasta.
If you want dumplings, add them about 20 minutes before serving. (See page **)

You will need ...

Brown rabbit pieces.

Place in slow cooker.

Add soup mix.

Thick and scrumptious.

Dumplings optional.

RABBIT

Hungarian Rabbit Goulash

First, shoot a Hungarian rabbit … not really, that's just me being stupid. I know that among the readership, there will be some hungry'uns but I'm a bit worried in case there are any Hungarians because I could be in big trouble since there is only a tenuous link between their homeland and this recipe. I did use genuine, Hungarian, smoked paprika and the goulash was served in a beautiful dish bought for me by a friend who went on a business trip to Budapest, but apart from that, Hungarian it ain't. It's delicious, though, and I couldn't think of anything else to call it so I beg poetic licence.

This dish was cooked on a miserable, grey day when it was cold, raining, and blowing a hooli. I was busy writing, with a deadline fast approaching, and slightly fed up because I wanted to walk along the beach as I often do in extreme weather, but had to work instead. The aroma of onions, paprika and herbs wafting into my home office offered instant comfort and I became more cheerful by the minute as I anticipated a tasty dinner. It doesn't take much to keep me happy. Low maintenance, that's me. I've always been a long walks and peanuts woman. A decent meal, the heating turned up a notch on a cold, spring day and I'm more or less content.

You can serve this goulash with a green vegetable which is miles better for you, but I was in need of as much comfort food as I could get so I knocked up a batch of seedy rolls to go with mine; lovely for dipping in the sauce. The rolls take just 45 minutes, including proving time, but supermarket tiger bread works just as well if you can't be bothered to bake. I haven't included the recipe for the rolls because you should be eating broccoli, anyway, and I'm very good at not practising what I preach. This dish can be cooked a day or two before you intend to eat it and left in a refrigerator to allow flavours to infuse. I'll bet you don't do that, though. I couldn't wait!

INGREDIENTS:

Rabbit pieces
Two onions, sliced fairly thickly
One tablespoonful paprika, a pinch of salt and pepper
A couple of sprigs of fresh thyme, or half a teaspoonful of the dried stuff
Large tin of tomatoes, chopped, and a small tin of tomato purée
Stock cube – chicken or vegetable
About a pint of water

Four large potatoes cut into small chunks
A good handful of mushrooms, quartered

METHOD:

Fry the rabbit pieces in oil with the onions over a gentle heat, until the meat shows some colour.
Stir in the paprika, a little salt and pepper, chopped tomatoes, purée and thyme.
Add the stock cube and about a pint of water. Bring to the boil and then turn down to simmer.
Cover and cook for 30 minutes.
After 30 minutes, add the potatoes, turn up the heat slightly to a fast simmer and cook for a further 45 minutes. Ten minutes before the end of cooking time, add the mushrooms, and adjust seasoning.

You will need ...

Fry rabbit and onions.

Add 'dry' ingredients.

Add tomatoes and stock.

Simmer gently.

Add mushrooms.

RABBIT

Rabbit Cacciatore

This is so easy you can knock it up in a trice, go to the pub for an hour and come back to a hearty, tasty meal, and very little effort is required for an outstanding result. That's what I call convenience food!

I used to make this dish with chicken to a recipe perfected by my Italian ex-mother-in-law. She was an amazing woman and fascinating to watch in the kitchen. She made everything look so easy and although I managed to emulate her prowess with savoury dishes, I could never match her expertise in the cake-making department. She was a superb patissiere. I make a mean carrot cake, but that's about it.

Anyway, all that has nothing to do with this recipe, but I'm going to pass on a tip that mum-in-law gave to me many years ago: Always assemble your ingredients before you begin - that way, you won't leave anything out. She suggested that I do this after I'd left the sugar out of a very impressive-looking and eagerly anticipated lemon meringue pie. It was horrible; even when offered a sugar shaker and sweetened cream my boys still wouldn't eat it. Trust me; gathering ingredients in readiness is a good idea.

INGREDIENTS:

One whole rabbit, jointed and coated in seasoned flour.
One medium-sized leek, finely chopped.
A punnet of small mushrooms, or half a dozen flats, sliced.
One large tin of chopped tomatoes.
A small tin of tomato puree.
One bay leaf.
Two cloves of garlic, squashed, or a good squirt of the stuff from a tube.
A couple of chicken stock cubes and a pint of water – you can add a glass of white wine, but that's not essential.

Salt and pepper,

METHOD:

Put a glug of olive oil into a large pan, place rabbit pieces into it and cook, over medium heat, until they start to show a golden colour. I always coat my rabbit with flour, but it isn't vital if you can't be bothered. It does make the gravy thicker and gives the rabbit a savoury coating, though.
Add the chopped leek and cook for a minute or two before adding everything else.
Now you've thrown all the ingredients into the pot, just bring it to the boil, then reduce the heat, bung a lid on and simmer gently until you're hungry – at least 45 minutes. You can continue cooking for a couple of hours, providing it's over a very low heat and you give it a stir occasionally, but that's all the attention it's going to need.
If you think the gravy isn't thick enough, remove the lid and simmer until the liquid reduces. One of the secrets of being a half-decent cook is to keep on tasting your dish and to adjust the seasoning as you go. You could, if you like your food with a kick, add a little cayenne pepper or a teaspoonful of chopped chilli when you add the tomatoes. You could finish it off with a dollop of crème fraîche and a sprinkle of smoked paprika, or you could just be a bloke and eat it straight out of the pot, in front of the telly, with chunks of crusty bread to mop up the gravy.

You will need ...

Fry rabbit pieces.

Add chopped leeks.

Add everything else.

Lid off and simmer.

Any pasta shape.

Rabbit Nuggets

When my boys were teenagers, I discovered that they would eat anything if it was flat, patty-shaped, shoved in a homemade bap and topped with tomato ketchup. I tried to point out once, when told 'I don't like cottage pie' that exactly the same ingredients were used to make burger and chips; the cottage pie was just a different shape and not dripping with grease. You can imagine the response I received, but I gave in and made cottage pie for the 'grown ups' and assembled the rest of the meat and spuds into burger and chips for the rebels. It was a healthier version than the local McD's, but the boys didn't know that, and I didn't stop there. All manner of concoctions were flattened, made into sandwiches or subs and eaten with considerable smacking of lips and praise for the cook. Strangely, the Sunday roast was never refused.

I have grandchildren now and sometimes my daughters-in-law complain that mealtimes are a battleground because the infants have discovered the phrase, 'I don't like …' I know all about that. Their fathers were exactly the same. I've passed on the burger/cottage pie secret, along with several others like blitzing some of the broccoli into the gravy – it was ages before they sussed that one – and mincing onions so that they almost dissolve into a stew.

Anyway, I was recounting all this to a friend and she came up with an idea. "What about rabbit nuggets and chips?" she said. "I bet you haven't tried that! You don't even have to tell them what it is. They'll think it's chicken." A wise move, considering that the baby girls had a pet rabbit called Rosie. Holly was only just two and tried repeatedly to get into the hutch so it wouldn't have been a good plan to suggest that she eat a relation of her best friend, with chips or not. So, I made 'nuggets and chips' (See what I did there? No mention of the source) and they went down a storm. Even if you don't have small children, you should have a go at this. It is seriously good. Using low-fat oven chips and baking the nuggets instead of frying makes this a very healthy dish. If you do go for the baking method, though, be prepared for a certain amount of criticism. It won't 'look right' to youthful eyes!

INGREDIENTS:

Small chunks of rabbit meat
One egg
Breadcrumbs
Oil for frying
Seasoning:
A squashed clove of garlic, or an inch of garlic puree
Paprika
Dried thyme
Black pepper and a pinch of salt

METHOD:

First, put the chips in a hot oven. They will take longer to cook than the meat.
Heat the oil in a large frying pan, or use a deep-fat fryer. Don't have the oil too hot, you want to cook the rabbit and that should take about five minutes.
Line up your ingredients next to the hot oil so you can operate 'conveyor-belt-style'.
Mix all the seasoning ingredients in a shallow bowl.
Whisk the egg into another bowl, and breadcrumbs go in another.
Turn the rabbit chunks in the seasoning, making sure that they're covered.
Roll them in the egg, then in breadcrumbs. If you want a crunchier, thicker coating, egg and breadcrumb again.
Place the nuggets gently into the hot oil and turn until they are golden brown.
Remove from the oil and drain on kitchen paper.
Serve with chips - and peas if you can get away with it, or more likely baked beans.

You will need ...

Seasoning and egg; breadcrumbs.

Roll nuggets in egg, breadcrumbs.

Fry gently ...

... in batches.

Place on kitchen paper.

Rockin' Rabbit Rogon

This is one of my favourite rabbit recipes because it's so simple that anyone can do it. There are few opportunities in life to achieve spectacular results for very little effort but this is one of them. A minimum of preparation will allow you to walk away and leave a pot of ingredients to simmer magically for 45 minutes, and by the time you return to the kitchen, the meat will be succulent, the sauce spicy and delicious. All you had to do, was to chop up a rabbit and throw four things into a pan. How bad is that?

I really like Patak's curry pastes. 'Cook in' sauces contain too many preservatives and chemicals for me, but by using the pastes I am in control of the amount of kick in the finished dish. I have tried the already prepared jars of sauce but they have been formulated to someone else's palate, and I haven't found one that agrees with my idea of how things should taste. I recommend that you give the curry pastes a go. One jar, kept in the fridge will last you for months and there are several recipes in which you can use it. You could add half a teaspoonful of it to mayonnaise for a summer Rabbit Elizabeth (see page 128) or mix it with a little lemon juice and olive oil and use it as a barbecue marinade for meat or shellfish.

If you're health-conscious, or on a diet, you can be reassured that this rabbit recipe is virtually cholesterol free and contains so few calories that it can safely be followed by a small portion of rich, chocolate torte, with minimal damage to the waistline.

INGREDIENTS:

A rabbit, jointed
A couple of red onions – or white if that's all you've got
Large tin of chopped tomatoes
One generous tablespoonful of Patak's Rogon Josh Curry Paste

METHOD:

Joint the rabbit – four limbs and cut the saddle in half so that you have a total of six pieces. I prefer meat on the bone because it offers a better flavour.
Fry the rabbit pieces in hot oil for two minutes, with the chopped onions, in a large pan. I cook mine in a wok but you can use a large-ish saucepan. Keep stirring it about so that the onions don't burn.
Add tinned tomatoes. Fill the tomato tin with hot water from a kettle and add to the pot.
Stir in the curry paste.
Bring to the boil and simmer for about 40 minutes or until the sauce has reduced by at least half. It should be gloopy. Do not season until the end of the cooking time. The flavour will become more intense as the sauce thickens.
You can serve your Rockin' Rabbit Rogon with crusty bread, or boiled rice. I add a tablespoonful of crème fraîche or Greek yoghurt to mine at the last minute and garnish with chopped coriander or flat-leaf parsley, especially if I have kids to feed and the sauce is a bit too exuberant for them. You don't have to bother with all that, though. Just eat and enjoy!

You will need …

Fry rabbit and onions.

Add tomatoes and paste.

Simmer until gloopy.

Serve with crusty bread …

… or corn bread and boiled rice.

RABBIT

Spicy Rabbit and Rice

When either of my sons comes to visit, I often receive a prior phone call asking what I'm intending to cook for their dinner and if it's not what they fancy, they'll offer 'a suggestion.' The boys do most of the cooking for their families and I don't know why my sons have this possessive attitude toward cookery. Maybe it's because I always let them join in when they were children and I was constantly in the kitchen creating something or other out of very little. I don't know, but their partners seem quite happy with the arrangement, so it's worked out all right.

One of the most frequent requests is for spicy chicken and rice, a dish that I first developed over 30 years ago. I had an Italian friend who had left home when she was 16, was used to not having enough to eat, and could create a substantial and tasty meal from very few ingredients. She taught me how to cook with herbs and spices and this rice dish was one of her inventions when all I had in the house was leftover chicken, two rashers of bacon, a small cabbage and some garlic – and the rice, obviously. It has become more elaborate over the years and this is my take on Yuli's 'spicy meat and rice.'

INGREDIENTS:

Rabbit meat from the saddle, and portions left on the bone. This recipe will feed four people but if you're only feeding two you can freeze the boned portions and save them for another dish; the saddle meat will be enough.

Streaky bacon, diced – or cheat and buy lardons.
Chorizo sausage, sliced.
Two cloves of garlic, squashed.
Sliced vegetables. I've used red and spring onions, mushrooms and tomatoes. You can add a handful of peas near the end of the cooking time, if you wish.
A teaspoonful each of turmeric and smoked paprika, salt and pepper to taste.
A chicken stock cube and about a pint of water.

Rice. Do not use the long-grain or risotto varieties! You need to buy paella rice, Bomba if you can get it, but most supermarkets do their own brand. The other stuff will not absorb enough liquid and just doesn't work as well. I never weigh anything but add a mugful of rice.

METHOD:

You will need a large frying pan or a wok. Fry the bacon and chorizo for a few minutes until the oil/fat is released. Then add the chopped saddle meat and brown it; keep turning, it will take a couple of minutes. Add the vegetables, including the garlic, and stir until well mixed with the meat mixture.
Now stir in the spices and then sprinkle the rice over the top. Stir it in and add three-quarters of the stock, bring it to the boil and turn down the heat so it's just bubbling gently. No lid.

It will take about 15 to 20 minutes to cook. After ten minutes, have a look at it and if it seems a bit dry, gently stir in a bit more stock.

That's it. It's so easy to do, once you've assembled the ingredients, just a case of 'sling it all in a pan and run away.'

You will need ...

Fry meats and veg.

Add spices and stir.

Sprinkle rice.

Add stock.

Fry rabbit pieces.

RABBIT

Rabbit Saltimbocca

I watched the late Clarissa Dickson-Wright make rabbit saltimbocca on a TV programme and it took me back to when I was newly married and my Italian mum-in-law made saltimbocca with veal, prosciutto and sage leaves. She fried it in butter, topped it off with a slug of Marsala and it was amazing. I'd never tasted anything like it and decided there and then that she would teach me everything she knew about Italian cuisine. We ate veal scallopini, osso buco, veal Milanese … in fact we enjoyed veal on a regular basis until it became politically incorrect to eat baby cows and it was all but removed from butchers' counters.

These days, locally at least, veal is still difficult to find and various friends have suggested that I make saltimbocca with pork instead – 'You'll never know the difference.' I tried it once but the texture is wrong so I put the recipe aside. The rabbit idea seemed to be a way back, though, so I thought I'd give it a go, not holding out too much hope, if I'm honest.

My mum, who spoke in clichés for several of her latter years always used to say, 'Don't spoil the ship for a ha'porth of tar' so bearing those words of wisdom in mind, I attempted to buy a bottle of Marsala. I got it from

Tesco eventually, after assistants in two off-licences and one other supermarket said they'd never heard of it. It cost a bit more than a ha'porth, but it'll last me a year or more, and it's fantastic in zabaglione or tiramisu, so I consider it to be an investment.

The result was surprisingly delicious. The sage leaves melded with the ham and brought out the flavour of the rabbit. Clarissa D-W used beer, but trust me, if you can stretch to a bottle of Marsala, it is well worth the money.

INGREDIENTS:

One loin/saddle of rabbit
Four sage leaves
Two rashers of streaky bacon
Butter for frying
Two tablespoons of Marsala

METHOD:

Cut the meat from the loin, in two pieces.
Place a length of Clingfilm on a work surface, one piece of loin on top and then cover with some more Clingfilm. Do this with the other piece of loin.
Start in the middle, working your way outward, and bash gently with a rolling pin until the meat is flat, thin, and twice its original size. Be gentle. Don't beat the living daylights out of it - it's done you no harm.
Assemble the saltimbocca: Make a kind of rabbit sandwich with sage leaves and bacon in the middle. Squash down gently.
Heat the butter in a pan and fry the rabbit on a low heat for a few minutes each side, until the meat is opaque. Add a glug of Marsala halfway through the cooking time and pour the sauce over the rabbit when you serve it. It's too good to waste.
Serve with crusty bread and a side salad, or with chips if you're a bloke.

You will need ...

Cut meat from saddle.

Beat until flat.

Place sage on top ...

... then bacon.

Fry like a sandwich.

Rabbit-tin On

Some of my friends treat me to restaurant meals regularly and will never allow me to pay my way, so I cook for them instead. These particular friends were less than enthusiastic when I suggested rabbit for dinner, having been force-fed it as children after WW2 when it was one of the few meats readily available. I live within walking distance of a chippy so I suggested that they could always grab cod and chips if they really couldn't face the rabbit. My friends eat in all the best places, at home and abroad, and although I knew they wouldn't want me to get stressed about it, or go to an enormous amount of trouble, I didn't want to go down my normal 'rustic' route; rabbit pie, with roasties and parsnips, or rabbit stew with dumplings. I can do 'fine dining' when I have to!

I went for a walk and a power-think along the beach and came up with this offering. My inspiration was a TV programme that showed Jamie Oliver cooking a picnic lunch for himself and his nieces, to eat at the end of Southend pier. He'd used the 'poor man's tagine' method – a tin foil pyramid – so that the meat and veg effectively steam themselves into submission, and all the flavours are infused. Mr Oliver and his companions ate his creation cold, for obvious reasons, but I could dish up, straight from oven to plate. My friends would be impressed, and there'd be hardly any washing up.

Well, I surpassed myself. They ate every scrap and the chip shop wasn't even mentioned. This is such a simple way of cooking anything that you could class it as convenience food. If you have family members who arrive home at different times, you can make these individual parcels and reheat as required, and the dish doesn't suffer from being cooked twice, in fact, the flavours will intensify. You can use any combination of vegetables, too. I used root veg for this one, but it would be equally delicious Mediterranean style; tomatoes, mushrooms, courgette, red pepper, and you could add half a finely sliced chilli for a bit of a kick. There is no need to add water with the wine, the vegetables will cook down and provide moisture.

Give this a go. My best meals seem to be created when I'm in experimental mode, and this is one of them. Just one little tip – leave the parcels to cool for five minutes before allowing your diners to open their own parcels, or they could end up with no eyebrows. Give them the health and safety lecture while they're waiting.

INGREDIENTS:

1 rabbit, jointed.
Finely sliced vegetables – try to keep them the same size.
Onion, celeriac, carrot, swede, turnip, parsnip.
Squashed garlic
White wine
Stock cube – chicken or vegetable
Bay leaf, parsley
Salt and pepper

METHOD:

Brown the rabbit in a little olive oil.
Place individual meat portions on large pieces of tinfoil.
Add the sliced vegetables and seasoning, garlic, bay leaf and parsley.
Crumble the stock cube into the wine.
Squish up the sides of the foil, and carefully add wine.
Pull up the sides of the foil to make a 'pillow' and seal, making sure that there is plenty of air inside the parcel.
Place on a baking tray and bake for an hour and a half on 170°
Serve with an assortment of vegetables or cous cous (see page **).

You will need ...

Brown the rabbit.

Slice your veg.

Meat and veg in tinfoil.

Add wine mixture.

Make your parcels.

Morning Coffee

It's amazing how news get around. I had a phone call from a stranger who had heard through the grapevine that I was something of an expert regarding young airgunners. That was never true; I was only knowledgeable regarding the behaviour of my own sons, but this poor woman was desperate for someone to talk to about how to cope. Her 14-year-old was so desperate to own a rifle that he'd taken on two paper rounds in order to accumulate enough cash to finance his heart's desire, and he was saving every penny.

It was only a matter of time, she told me, and she didn't like the idea one bit so I invited her round for a coffee and a chat. Naturally enough, her main reservation leaned toward the safety angle. She was terrified that her son would cause himself an injury and mildly apprehensive that he would have the means to inflict damage on others. I told her that she must expect a certain amount of destruction while her youngster was a novice, but to get it all into perspective. A strict safety lesson from his parents would make the boy only too aware of the dangers of irresponsible behaviour and so it was very unlikely that he would hurt anyone.

We could even enlist the help of my eldest, I told her. He'd been through it all twice, by learning from his own experience and that of his younger brother. Besides, if her youngster was determined enough to earn the price of a rifle himself, rather than resorting to the pressurised nagging that most kids employ until they get their own way, then that was to his credit and he should be encouraged to continue.

Surely, it would be worth losing a flowerpot or two in the name of enterprise, there were bound to be accidents, and airgunning is a great sport for young and old alike; they're out in the fresh air instead of sitting glued to a TV or a game console. They're meeting all kinds of people of all ages, learning self-discipline, concentration, about conservation, the environment ... she gave in.

The eldest was only too pleased to offer his services. His limited expertise was gradually imparted to the new boy who began to be a regular visitor – very regular – every weekend for a couple of months. He was using number two son's Webley Eclipse until he had saved enough to buy his own rifle, and was he eager to learn, or what! He had been told that as soon as he had proved himself capable, my boys would ask the farmer if they could take him along for the day to the farmland where they go hunting. It would be okay and perfectly legal since the eldest had just reached his 21st birthday.

First, our new friend must apply himself to plenty of practice, vital if he was considering a venture out into the fields, and if he was going to shoot live quarry his aim must be as accurate as possible, so it became necessary to create more challenging targets in the garden.

Luckily for the riflemen, I had cleared out the attic a couple of months previously and carted the whole lot to a car boot sale. Never again! It was so cold that a punter offered me a couple of quid for an old blanket that I'd wrapped myself in, and I wouldn't part with it. I made about £10 profit and brought half the stuff home again, which once more lay festering in the attic, with no purpose in life. It would be a good idea to allow the boys to shoot at the breakable bits and then dump the shattered remains at the tip. They sorted out all the old crockery, made a range similar to the ones you see in fairgrounds, cardboard boxes made into shelves at varying heights in front of a large and secure backdrop, with cups and plates arranged in neat rows ready for pot-shots.

We stood well back and invited our novice's mum to watch as her son tried to convince her that he'd be all right in the fields. The afternoon took on the ambience of a country fair as I served tea and homemade cakes to assorted, interested friends and neighbours in the garden.

By the end of the afternoon, everyone was happy and at ease with airguns and as they were leaving, our young friend turned to my eldest.
"Erm … Dave," he said hesitatingly. "I've got a mate. He's in my class at school and he wants to get an airgun, too. I don't suppose you would …"
Maybe we should have opened an airgun school.

(Webley) Eclipse of the son.

RABBIT
- Summer -

Kerabs and Risi Pisi

It's that time of year again, when men can be seen sweating in front of hot charcoal while poking bits of meat around until the food, and often the chef, becomes overcooked and unidentifiable. Admittedly, the cremated offerings can be served with charm and a chivalrous flourish, but some of them are surprisingly pink inside, given the cinder-like crunchiness of the outer coating, and you'll be hard-pushed to name the animal of origin. It's all nuked beyond recognition but if you don't eat it with relish and appreciation – the more relish the better, in my experience – sensitive male feelings, fuelled by an excess of lager, can be damaged and it could be minutes until the lure of hot coal gets the better of him and he just has to have another go.

I attended an al fresco party recently and was offered some decent grub because 'barbecue man' had partly cooked most of it in the oven before slinging it over the charcoal for flavour. His attempt at barbecued salmon, however, was a total disaster. Barbecued leather would have been more like it, but he's a lovely bloke so we all resolutely chewed each mouthful 100 times and washed it down with plenty of liquid. His mushroom and white wine sauce was delicious, although he wouldn't give us the recipe – he'd probably thrown away the tin.

If you are one of the few who tries very hard but doesn't get it right every time, or lives in a flat, as I do, with no facility to barbecue anything, here's a foolproof way of serving a delicious, barbecue-flavoured dish, with minimum effort. You'll still get the same adulation and praise, but this time it'll be genuine.

INGREDIENTS:

Chunks of rabbit meat cut from the legs and saddle
Marinade: balsamic vinegar, garlic granules, salt pepper.
Mushrooms, cherry tomatoes, baby onions/shallots, chunks of green/yellow pepper … Please don't use pineapple; that goes with salty or fatty meats like gammon, or pork - used with chicken, only if you're in Hawaii – never rabbit. Better yet, pair it with ice cream. It's up to you, obviously, there aren't any hard and fast rules really, but I'd think twice!
Vegetable oil.
Barbecue spice.

-METHOD:

Thread rabbit cubes, mushrooms, tomatoes, onions, and peppers on to skewers; baste with the oil and pat barbecue spice into the meat and vegetables.
Fry briskly, turning until the rabbit has taken on some colour, then turn down the heat and cook gently until the onions are tender and slightly caramelised. When the onions are cooked, so is everything else.
While the kerabs are cooking, place a cup of basmati rice and two cups of water into a saucepan. Add a teaspoonful of salt, bring to the boil, cook away surface water, cover, turn it down to simmer and cook for 12 minutes. Then, lightly whisk two eggs, and cook in a large frying pan, scrambled egg-style, but try to separate the cooked egg into small chunks. When the eggs have nearly set, add the cooked rice and a handful of frozen peas. Stir it about a bit for two minutes; the peas will still be a bit crunchy.
Place the skewers on top of the rice, pour a glass of white wine to go with it, and even if it's raining outside, you can kid yourself you're at a barbecue!

You will need …

Thread on to skewers.

Brush with seasoning.

Fry gently.

Rice, eggs and peas …

… in a pan and cook through.

RABBIT

Quesadillas

I seem to have become one of those 'ladies who lunch'. My friends and I don't have a great deal of money so it's never exactly luncheon at the Ritz, but it's nice to spend an hour or so, gossiping over a cuppa and a snack. During the summer we meet up at the local ice-cream parlour and indulge ourselves with take-away coffee and a tub of rum 'n' raisin while sitting on a bench on the foreshore, but in the cooler weather lunchtime get-togethers are usually held at someone's house – mine, more often than not. It's no fun sitting outside when it's blowing a hooli or seriously raining.

I don't mind being the one who entertains, but trying to think up new, cheap and easy snacks can become a bit of a headache. I discovered soft tortillas and found out that you can make the equivalent of a hot toastie with these little gems. Although you use more or less the same ingredients, it looks different and seems to taste better than when the same stuff is shoved between two slices of cotton-wool bread and heated through in a Breville.

This recipe can be served as a lunchtime snack or for a supper dish if you team it with a baked potato. Try it! Quesadillas are delicious, quick to prepare, and cheap.

INGREDIENTS:

Saddle meat from one rabbit
Juice from one lemon, one clove of garlic, squashed, and chilli (fresh, sliced, or a few dried chilli flakes) for marinade.
Any vegetables that you happen to have hanging about.
I've used a red onion, a couple of mushrooms, and a yellow pepper, all thinly sliced, but you could include sliced tomatoes, courgette, sweetcorn – whatever you fancy.
Grated cheddar cheese
Soft tortillas

METHOD:

Slice the saddle meat into thin, flat strips and marinate in lemon juice, garlic, and chilli for about 20 minutes.
Stir-fry in very little oil for about two minutes, until the rabbit starts to take on some colour. Remove from the heat.
Put a squirt of oil into a pan and wipe it around with kitchen paper so that there is just a light covering.
Place a soft tortilla into the pan, over medium heat.
Arrange the cooked rabbit strips on top of it, add the thinly sliced vegetables, and then a layer of grated cheese.
Cook gently for a couple of minutes, than gently lift up one edge of the tortilla and have a look. When the underside has turned golden, slap on another tortilla, squash down with the palm of your hand and flip the whole thing over. Use a fish slice, it isn't Shrove Tuesday..
After two minutes, check that the underside is toasted, slide on to a cutting board and cut into four. I use a pizza-slicing wheel; it's more efficient and neater than a knife.
Serve with a salad and a bowl of mayo topped with smoked paprika. Delish!

Slice rabbit into strips.

Marinade for 20 minutes.

Fry until golden.

Get ready.

Assemble ingredients.

Fry for a few minutes.

Rabbit Elizabeth

I went to a friend's house on a sunny summer day for an early al fresco dinner and she served me with Chicken Elizabeth accompanied by various delicious homemade side dishes. The vegetables were from her garden and the chicken dish was absolutely superb, so I asked her for her recipe so that I could reproduce it for you, but with rabbit.

It's not a complicated dish to cook, but it's time-consuming – not for you, for the rabbit – because the meat has to be cooked first and allowed to cool before the rest of the procedure can be carried out. Plus, it has to be assembled the day before you want to eat it so that the flavours can combine.

You can clean a rifle, or play with your pellets, while the rabbit braises gently in an oven for a couple of hours or until you can pull it from the bones with a fork, and then go out to play while it goes completely cold.

The Elizabeth sauce takes about 15 minutes to knock up but, trust me, it is very much worth the hassle. For the health conscious, I've suggested that you replace half of the fresh cream with crème fraîche, but quite honestly, I can't see the point. I go to a Harvester restaurant once a month with some friends, eat steak, chips and all the trimmings followed by Eton mess or knickerbocker glory – and drink Diet Coke. Where's the sense in that! Use all cream … and full fat mayonnaise. Life's too short to deny yourself anything, really.

INGREDIENTS:

One rabbit, a couple of carrots and onions, bay leaves and about a pint of chicken or vegetable stock.
One medium onion, finely chopped
Olive oil for frying
A good tablespoonful of curry paste, or a very good quality curry powder
One teaspoon tomato puree
Salt and pepper to taste
Half a jar of redcurrant jelly
Four heaped tablespoons of mayonnaise
Quarter pint of fresh double cream, or make up a quarter pint half cream and half crème fraîche.

METHOD:

Braise the rabbit and vegetables in the stock for a couple of hours in a moderate oven, or until you can pull the meat off with a fork. Make sure you cover it tightly; you don't want to roast it.
Shred the meat and then allow to cool completely.
Fry the chopped onion gently in olive oil for a few minutes until it's translucent. Do not allow it to colour. Then add the curry paste/powder, tomato puree, redcurrant jelly and seasoning.
Bring to the boil and then simmer very gently, stirring occasionally. As it cooks the mixture will thicken and you don't want it to stick to the pan.
After about 15 minutes it will be reduced by half and have the consistency of jam.
Allow the sauce to become completely cold.
Place the shredded rabbit meat into a large bowl, then add the cold sauce, and 4 heaped tablespoons of mayonnaise and the cream/crème fraîche.
Mix well, cover with Clingfilm and refrigerate overnight.
Serve with a huge salad and baby new potatoes, or just crusty bread and a chilled white wine. Wonderful summer grub.

Braise rabbit.

Ingredients for sauce.

Cook onion and seasoning.

Shred rabbit into a bowl.

Add cold sauce …

… and mayonnaise.

Rabbit in Oatmeal

Every now and then, I go through my kitchen cupboards ready to throw out anything that's well past its sell-by date. I do this on a fairly regular basis so there is rarely anything that's completely rank, but I sometimes find stuff that's on the verge. I hate waste and never throw anything away so whatever I discover lurking at the back of shelves has to be incorporated into something else, even if it's only added to soup. This harks back to the days when I was so hard up that there was little money for food, and I even made soup from vegetable parings. Once it had been cooked, seasoned and whizzed in a food processor, the kids had no idea that Mum's 'magic' soup was not made from whole vegetables. Old habits die hard – I don't waste anything if I can help it.

I found some porridge oats buried at the back of the 'packets' cupboard, bought last winter while on an economy drive, and abandoned in favour of 'ready oats', because that's quicker than standing in front of the stove and stirring for ten minutes on a cold and frosty morning.

Rabbit in oatmeal, I decided, was the way to go. I used to make a similar dish with chicken, years ago, when my youngest son wouldn't eat anything unless it was coated in breadcrumbs and/or stuffed in a bun. One evening while rapidly running out of patience, I'd also run out of breadcrumbs, couldn't be bothered to whizz fresh ones and settled for oats because the packet was handy. The result was surprisingly tasty and became such a popular family meal that I began to mass produce it and freeze individual portions. You can do the same with the rabbit version, if you can get it as far as the freezer. It really is delicious.

INGREDIENTS:

Rabbit pieces
A couple of tablespoons of flour
Beaten egg
Porridge oats
Oil for frying – about an inch deep
Seasoning: salt, pepper, thyme, cayenne pepper or Tabasco

METHOD:

Mix the seasoning ingredients together and rub well into the rabbit pieces. Leave to marinate for at least four hours; overnight in the 'fridge would be even better.
When you're ready to eat, place the flour, beaten egg and porridge oats into three separate shallow bowls, and heat the oil in a frying pan.
Turn a piece of rabbit in the flour, shake off the excess, swish it through the egg mix, then coat it with oats ready to chuck into the frying pan. This conveyor belt procedure is repeated until all the rabbit pieces have been dealt with.
Fry in small batches, no more than three pieces at a time, over a medium heat for a few minutes, each side, until the oats take on a bit of colour.
Remove from the pan and set aside while you cook the rest of the rabbit pieces, then place on a baking tray and cook them in a hot oven for about 20 minutes, or until the rabbit is tender.
Meanwhile, you can mash some spuds and cook some frozen peas to go with it, and a homemade chutney makes a good accompaniment. Serve and enjoy.

You will need ...

Conveyor belt system.

Flour and egg wash.

Oats - cover well.

Fry in batches.

Golden and gorgeous.

Rabbit Satay

I didn't have to leave the house for this rabbit. It was delivered by some compassionate hunting friends whose only request for payment was a share in the spoils, once cooked. I'd had that flu virus that's been going about so the lads felt sorry for me and dropped it off – with a bonus. The hunter had made a pig's ear of jointing the bunny, felt guilty and so bunged some extra meat into the bag as recompense for his bungling. I ended up with a five-legged bunny. How bad is that!

Once recovered from the lurgy – or the 'algae', as my grandson when aged three used to call it – I had some friends round for dinner. They always ask me for a preview of the menu so I suggested a rabbit pie this time; something easy because I was still feeling a tad fragile. They were, mostly, quite gentle in their rejection of this idea for a main course, but grudgingly agreed to give the rabbit a go if was served as a starter, disguised as something else, and closely followed by roast leg of lamb with several veg and copious amounts of home-made treacle pud for afters. They turned up bearing gifts, ate everything, accused me of trying to pass off chicken breast as rabbit, and demanded that next time I intend to serve it I sort out my priorities and make sure there's enough to go round.

You will be impressed with this starter. It's tasty and a bit different – and, in case you're wondering what I did with the rest of the rabbit, that's been transformed into an Italian feast and is sitting in my freezer waiting for another day.

INGREDIENTS:

To feed four people:
Kebab skewers:
One saddle section of rabbit – dice the meat into inch-square chunks
Cherry tomatoes
Button mushrooms – or large mushrooms cut into quarters

For the marinade:
Half a cup of cider vinegar
Same amount of olive oil
Fresh thyme, chopped
One squashed clove of garlic
Salt, pepper

METHOD:

Combine all ingredients - make sure that the marinade mixture is rubbed well into the meat – and leave in the fridge to soak up the flavours for as long as you can. Couple of hours minimum and overnight if possible. Thread on to skewers in any order you like. You can also use rolled up streaky bacon rashers for added flavour, red or green pepper slices – anything that takes your fancy.

The longer you leave it, the more tender the meat will be. It really does taste like chicken, too, and the acid in the vinegar sort of cooks it so it will only take a few minutes to brown on a griddle or barbecue. Brush the veg with some of the marinade mixture and don't forget to turn it now and again. Serve it with a Satay sauce. (see page 208)

Marinade - you will need ...

Marinate overnight.

Satay sauce – you will need ...

Combine ingredients.

Thread onto skewers.

Griddle until browned.

Stuffed Rabbit

I was whingeing at work. It doesn't happen often because it's a negative occupation, takes up far too much of my time and energy, and doesn't get me anywhere. Mostly, I look for the positive and get on with it, so when I do whimper a bit, people take notice. Our local farmer's market takes place on the second and fourth Saturday of every month, so my brain tells me that it's every two weeks. Sometimes, though, there are five weekends in a month and quite often, I forget that and turn up when there's no one there. This had been one of those times and I was fed up because I'd run out of rabbits. I felt better after I'd complained to anyone who would listen about the calendar's lack of consideration toward elderly brain cells, even when no one sympathised or offered me chocolate/a cuddle/strong coffee. Maybe there's something to be said for the occasional grumble, after all.

The following morning, one of the lads in the design office presented me with a roasting tin containing three fresh, plump rabbits that he'd shot, skinned and paunched for me, and they were much bigger than the ones I usually get from the farmers' market. I was told that they were woodland rabbits, so they'd have a slightly different diet to those shot in the fields and there was a possibility that there could be a difference in flavour. Google is my friend when I need to find out facts in a hurry, but when I typed in 'rabbits', I got 'where to buy pet rabbits, how to care for them, how to litter-train, how to read your pet rabbit's body language ...' and a couple of dubious sites that seemed to be devoted to some kind of plastic variety. I tried 'wild rabbit+habitat+food', and received a similar list of results. No one, it seemed, could tell me how the diet, and therefore flavour, of wooded rabbits was different to the rest of their kin. There was only one way to find out.

I settled on baking the rabbit because I didn't want the meat submerged in gravy, and it was fantastic. I ate far more than I should have, but was comforted by a Google assurance that rabbit meat is lower in fat and cholesterol than chicken. One of the advantages of getting older, I've found, is a selective memory. You can conveniently forget about the sausage meat, gravy, and mashed potato and kid yourself that you've over-eaten an almost calorie-free meal. There's always a positive, if you look for it!

INGREDIENTS:

One whole rabbit
Breadcrumbs, thyme (fresh or dried), and a chopped onion (or a small pack of sage and onion stuffing mix)
A few mushrooms, one Bramley cooking apple, peeled and diced
One pack sausage meat
One egg
Salt and pepper and half a pint of chicken stock

METHOD:

Mix the stuffing ingredients: breadcrumbs, thyme, and chopped onion, mushrooms, and apple.
Add the sausage meat and combine - hands in! – then stir in the egg, season with salt and pepper, and mix well. Stuff the rabbit with the sausage meat mixture.
Place the rabbit into a shallow, ovenproof dish and arrange the leftover stuffing around it.
Add the stock, ensuring that it leaves most of the meat above the liquid, and cook for two hours at 160°C, or until the rabbit is fork-tender. If you think it is browning too much, cover it with tinfoil.
Remove the foil 10 minutes before serving, pour the stock into a jug and add a little of the stuffing, then whiz with a hand blender to make a delicious thick gravy.

You will need ...

Chop the vegetables.

Mix the stuffing ingredients.

Stuff the rabbit.

Bake until tender.

Whizz the stock and meat juices.

RABBIT

Rabbit Roulade

I was asked recently how I manage to dream up these recipes on a regular basis and it's about time I let everyone into my 'secret'. I take my rabbit, pigeon, or squirrel (occasionally), and then stand in front of my open store cupboards/fridge to see which ingredients I can combine to make something worth eating.

There are a few recipes on the Internet, or in cookery books that can be adapted to rabbit or pigeon, but mostly, I gain inspiration from my own imagination, or that of my friends and family, and there are always the ancient cookery books that you can pick up from boot fairs, or charity shops. Some of them hold a mine of information. I bought one for 50p that told of a time when rabbits were bred specifically for food and, by necessity, became a staple in the UK.

A friend of mine, Joe Walker, just 14 years old at the time, helped his father to breed Ermine Rex rabbits. Originally, they were bred for shows, but during World War II the government insisted that half of all domestic rabbits were bred for food. They offered a small monetary allowance as an incentive so that breeders were able to fatten up their bunnies until they were huge by comparison with the wildies, and excellent for roasting, stewing … and display, apparently.

Anyway, for my ordinary-sized rabbit, I used odd items that I found in my cupboards, none of which were in sufficient quantity to combine in another particular dish, bunged them all into a pastry cocoon and hoped for the best. I'm telling you, you should try this. It is absolutely and accidentally delicious.

INGREDIENTS:

Rabbit meat, diced
Onions, mushrooms, sliced
Garlic clove, squashed
Crumbled stock cube – chicken or vegetable – dissolved in 200ml water
A glug of white wine
Crème fraîche
A couple of asparagus spears – or you could use spinach
Bacon rashers
Filo pastry and melted butter for painting

METHOD:

Fry the sliced onion and diced rabbit meat gently for about five minutes, until the onions are softened but still translucent. Add the sliced mushrooms, garlic, the stock cube, and white wine and simmer for ten minutes. Allow to cool and then add the crème fraîche. Chill in the fridge for at least half an hour so that the mixture thickens. Preheat the oven to 190°C. Assemble the roulade on a baking sheet, so that you don't have to transfer it when filled. It will break and leave you with a terrible mess, and don't ask me how I know. Use four sheets of filo pastry and brush each one with melted butter as you use them. Lay them on top of each other, and don't forget to butter the top one. Place bacon rashers on top of the pastry; spread the meat mixture over the top to within half-an-inch of the sides. Lay asparagus spears across the top and then begin to roll it up, being careful to keep all the filling inside the pastry. Brush the top with melted butter and place into the hot oven for about 20 minutes.

You will need ...

Fry rabbit and onions.

Add mushrooms, stock and wine.

Place bacon onto pastry.

Top with meat and asparagus.

Brush with melted butter.

Mrs Upwardly-Thrusting

Between writing and looking after the family, I taught theory of music and piano to kids of all ages – I still do. Occasionally, a new pupil arrived on the scene and I knew instinctively that this one wasn't going to work out well. In my music room there were remnants of the past; certificates and diplomas together with a large collection of every kind of recorded music. I give the impression of being quite a responsible adult, qualified and trusted to educate youngsters in the finer points of musicianship, so imagine the culture shock to the mother of a prospective new pupil when she noticed Airgun World, hot from the press and mid-read on my dining room table.

"I do, hope, Mrs Barham, that you are not personally involved with these dreadful things," she declared loftily, waving her hand in the general direction of the magazine.
"Of course not, how stupid of me," she continued, dismissively. "One of your sons, obviously - yet another phase to be endured, I suppose - how dreadful for you."
"Erm I write for the magazine, actually," I admitted.
She gazed at me in disbelief. "You do what?" she asked ungrammatically, while bristling into the epitome of outraged upper-middle class.
I'd had enough.

"I write for Airgun World, and have done for several years." I told her firmly. "Both my sons are crazy about shooting. They're out now, as a matter of fact, shooting rabbits."
"Rabbits!" she exclaimed.
"Yes. You know what rabbits are - furry creatures with long ears and buck teeth."
Sarcasm was beginning to set in, brought about by mild irritation at her attitude.
"Disgusting," she shuddered, pulling her genuine coney coat closer around her shoulders for comfort. "I don't agree with blood sports."
I tried to make her feel better.
"The rabbits have to be culled," I told her. "The boys are doing the farmer a favour, really, and they shoot targets as well … belong to a rifle club or two, and they're insured with the BASC."

"One should not encourage teenage violence," she stated firmly. "I've read reports in newspapers about the misuse of air rifles. Why, only last week there was an article in the Daily Grunge about young boys taking pot-shots at passers-by. Air rifles can be dangers in the wrong hands. I'm surprised you allow it.'

I argued that a bread knife or a claw hammer could be dangerous in the wrong hands. "Give a teenager of either sex a length of elastic and a bag of marbles, stand well clear, and watch developments," I told her, "and in any case, it's down to the parent to make sure that junior airgunners have a responsible attitude toward their sport. It's no good shouting a casual 'be careful' as a teenager departs on a hunting trip or to target practice," I said, gazing thoughtfully at her daughter who was listening avidly, and thoroughly enjoying this difference of opinion.

"Parents should take full responsibility," I continued, well into my stride by this time, soapbox firmly in position. "Clearly the parents in the reported incident were lacking in the responsibility department."
"You can't blame the parents," she said. "Best prohibit the activity altogether. One cannot be behind one's children all the time."
"Yes, that's true," I agreed, "but that particular newspaper item stated that the rifle used actually belonged to the father, and for the same reason that one does not leave a packet of razor blades or a box of matches within easy reach of a three-year-old, the airgun should have been kept in a locked cupboard, for the child's safety, apart from anything else - and to leave ammunition readily accessible is asking for trouble."
"You've just told me that your sons are out on their own; that doesn't seem very responsible to me."
"My sons are now old enough, by law, to be in possession of an air rifle." I was becoming really fed up and resenting the fact that I had to justify myself to this woman. They are very well aware of the dangers of irresponsibility with an air rifle and of the damage they could cause if they're not sensible, 'cos I've made damned sure of it, and so should other parents."

Mrs UT was surprised at my vehemence in defence of airgunners.
"I'm sorry," she said, shepherding her daughter out of my house, "but I don't think you'll be a suitable teacher for my Elaine."
That was a relief because I didn't think so either. Elaine was a little madam, with no sense of humour, even less musical talent, and sporting an ego beyond her years, given to her and nurtured by her parents. It wasn't her fault she was obnoxious, I know, but I didn't fancy having to cope with her for half an hour a week followed by running the gauntlet with her mother every time Airgun World popped through the letterbox.

RABBIT

- Autumn -

RABBIT

Bunny Biriani

I hate it when the weather is hot, mainly because it limits my cooking sessions. Meals are assembled with as little time spent in the kitchen as possible, and as I cook when I'm fed up, bored or feeling lonely, I get irritable when I can't get my therapy. As someone, quite cruelly told me once – it's a good thing I live on my own!

Anyway, once the really hot days are over, and I've simmered down a bit, this oven-baked curry dish is one of my favourites for an early autumn evening. It looks complicated but isn't really because although several things are cooked separately at the same time, they are then just mixed together. Sometimes, I do mix fresh ginger, garlic, and home-ground spices together, but as I've mentioned elsewhere in this book, it's so much easier to use Patak's pastes and they're authentic Indian mixes so there's only a slight difference in taste from fresh. Do not use any make of curry sauce from a jar, though, or you'll ruin your biriani. I'm all for saving myself prep time, but only if my 'cheat' ingredients aren't refined foods.

It can be eaten cold if there's an Indian summer – it is a curry, after all – and if you fancy something a bit different for a picnic, but it's great for a dinner party, too.

INGREDIENTS:

For the marinade:
A large tub of natural yoghurt
1 tbsp curry paste – use Patak's from the jar, or make your own (see page 207)
1 tsp salt

Rabbit meat
Half a dozen strands of saffron
A large onion, sliced, and a few chilli flakes
8oz (about 225g) basmati rice and 5 fl oz (50ml) chicken stock.
A handful of frozen peas, and a few sultanas (optional)

METHOD:

Marinate the meat, and soak the rice in salted water, for three hours. This is the secret of a good biriani; soaking the rice makes it grain-separate. At the same time, soak the saffron in a little hot water for about 20 minutes to infuse. Your finished dish will be a beautiful, golden yellow, but if you choose to replace the saffron with a tsp of turmeric, just add it to the stock. Put the rice into a pan of water, bring to the boil, and cook for five minutes. It is now half-cooked. Remove from the heat and drain.

While the rice is cooking, fry the onions and chilli flakes in a little vegetable oil and a knob of butter until they start to take on colour. Place the marinated rabbit pieces – and the marinade – into a large ovenproof dish. Place half of the fried onions evenly over the surface, and then the peas and sultanas. Gently spoon the rice over the top and then place the peas/sultanas and the rest of the onions on top of it. Finally, add the saffron and water, sprinkling evenly over the surface so that some rice grains will be yellow and some will remain white. Add the stock carefully. Don't disturb the topping. Wrap tightly in tinfoil and cook in a low oven - about 160° - for at least an hour. Check that the meat is cooked. If it isn't, give it another 15 minutes.

Once cooked, gently fork it through so that the ingredients are mixed together and then serve with some naan bread, chutney, lime pickle, or whatever takes your fancy.

You will need …

Rabbit and marinade in a large dish.

Fry onions and chilli flakes.

Add half the onions, the peas and sultanas in an even layer.

Drizzle saffron and water

Fork through and serve.

RABBIT

Cannelloni Coniglio

Translated, cannelloni coniglio is rabbit stuffed into pasta tubes, covered in a sauce and baked in the oven. I haven't made it for years, and in fact made it with chicken originally. My ex-husband's Italian grandmother used to live alternate years in England and Italy, spending twelve months with each of her two daughters. When Nonna stayed with my mum-in-law, she spent much of her time in the kitchen, cooking wonderful Italian meals for the family and I was her shadow. Unfortunately, Nonna spoke not a word of English and I didn't know any Italian, apart from spaghetti Bolognese and I was pronouncing that wrongly, I found out later.

So, because I wanted to learn properly how to cook all things Italian, and not just pasta, I took Italian lessons and did okay, enough to converse with Nonna in the kitchen, anyway, and to teach English to Italian students which earned me enough money to buy ingredients.

Nonna made her own pasta and the authentic way to make this dish is to spread the meat mixture on a square of fresh pasta, as if you were putting butter on toast, only thicker, and then roll up each one, Swiss roll style. I don't have the time, or inclination, to make pasta, though, so I use the dried stuff and, although it has a different texture, it still works. It looks a bit complicated but it really isn't. It takes longer to write about than it does to make. Give it a go. You'll love it!

INGREDIENTS:

Dried cannelloni tubes
Minced rabbit
Breadcrumbs
Half a teaspoon of nutmeg
Two teaspoons of dried oregano, or a big handful of chopped fresh if you can get it
About a tablespoonful of parmesan cheese
A finely chopped onion
2 squashed garlic cloves
A tin of tomatoes
A small tin of tomato puree
Half a pint of chicken stock – stock pod in half a pint of water, if you like
Handful of fresh, chopped basil, or two teaspoonsful of the dried stuff
Pinch of salt, one of sugar and loads of black pepper

METHOD:

Prep the cannelloni:
Mix all the filling ingredients together well and, using a teaspoon, poke it into the cannelloni tubes.
Line them up in an oven-proof dish and set aside.

Make the sauce:
Fry chopped onion and garlic in a little olive oil over a medium heat, so that the garlic doesn't burn, and then throw in the tomatoes, puree, stock, basil and seasoning.
Bring to the boil and then simmer for about 20 minutes – lid off, so it thickens.
I added a layer of mushrooms, but they're optional.
Pour the sauce over the cannelloni so that the pasta is covered and bake in a moderate oven, 180° C, for about half and hour.

Serve with a green salad, if you like and/or crusty bread. I like to sprinkle Cheddar over mine. Red wine to go with it, of course.

You will need

Mix filling ingredients ...

... and poke it into the tubes.

Fry onion and garlic.

I added mushrooms.

Cover with the sauce.

RABBIT

Lou-easy-ana Rabbit

I love the autumn. The warm days and cool evenings suit most of us and it's just how our temperate climate should be. Unaccustomed heat in this country feels unnatural to the British. Anything over 80 degrees for more than a few days in August and the headlines scream, 'heatwave!' and there are warnings about taking extra care of small children and the elderly in case they dehydrate. It's okay if we're abroad, heat is expected then and holidays booked on the strength of it, but we're always surprised by it at home, and not always pleasantly. It makes me smile when our weathermen tell us that we'll be 'enjoying' tropical temperatures for a week, when I know that most of my friends and family will just moan about how hot it is.

I often cook meals in advance, and there are still shades of when my dear old mum was alive and I cooked a week's dinners for her to freeze, so I often make far too much for me to eat in one sitting. The dishes I cook in May can be frozen and then defrosted and eaten on a cool autumn evening, and this one tastes even better after the freezing process. I don't understand the science behind why the flavour of spicy food seems to improve after having been frozen, but it certainly appears to work.

I adapted this from a recipe found in a very small, home-printed cookery book that was bought for me by a friend when he went to New Orleans for a holiday a few years back. The marinating process incorporates all the flavours and it is well worth taking the time to do it. You'll notice that there are no suggested quantities, it's all a matter of taste and doesn't really matter too much, but be careful not to use too much white wine vinegar in the marinade or the finished dish will be acidic and you'll have to add a dollop of crème fraîche to counteract it.

INGREDIENTS:

One jointed rabbit
Onion,garlic
Spring onions
Mushrooms
Green pepper
Salt black pepper, parsley, white wine vinegar
Cayenne
Chicken stock cube
White wine

METHOD:

Wash and dry the rabbit pieces and place in a large bowl.
Combine the salt, black pepper, cayenne pepper, onion, garlic, parsley, and vinegar. Pour over the rabbit and turn the pieces, making sure that they are covered with the marinade. Cover the bowl with cling film and marinate overnight in a refrigerator.
Preheat the oven to as hot as it will go.
Transfer the rabbit and the marinade to a baking dish. Cover tightly with tinfoil, place in the oven, and then turn the heat down to 180°C and bake for about an hour.
Add remaining ingredients: mushrooms, green pepper, spring onions, then combine the white wine and stock cube/pod and pour over the rabbit. Cover with foil and bake for another hour, until the rabbit is fork-tender. Serve with creamed potatoes and curly kale, or whatever you happen to have handy.

You will need ...

Combine marinade ingredients ...

... and marinade the rabbit.

Rabbit and marinade in a dish.

Chop the veg.

Bake for an hour.

RABBIT

Rabbit Cassoulet

Quite often, in a quest for something different to eat, I rake through the freezer and store cupboards searching for items that I can put together to make something tasty. This time around I came across a couple of Toulouse sausages bought on impulse when the French market was in town, six months before, and frozen for later use. I don't like to eat these on their own because of the fairly high fat content, but combined with a lean meat, they do add flavour to a dish.

Rabbit is about the leanest meat you can get so it seemed a good idea to use that with the sausages, along with some other stuff that I already had in the larder. It's quite exciting when you're not quite sure how it's going to turn out, but taste the mixture as you add ingredients, and remember that the intensity of flavour will increase as some of the liquid evaporates, so allow for that.

It turned out all right. In fact, it was delicious, and even my elderly mum put in an order for a repeat performance. She had reached the stage in her life where food was of little interest and for her to wax even slightly lyrical meant that this dish was something special. Maybe it's a good excuse to nip across the Channel for a pound of sausages, although you can replace the Toulouse ones with the Cumberland variety; they both contain sufficient fat to enhance the flavours of this cassoulet.

Many people assume that fat is bad and we are in danger of getting sucked into the 'eat hardly any fat and you'll live longer' philosophy embraced by many, these days. This may be true for those who constantly consume vast amounts of the stuff, but as we have to eat to live, we should enjoy what we're eating, and a certain amount of fat is necessary to give flavour and depth to our food. There is no need to survive on green salad and grilled chicken breast, skin removed, in order to eat healthily. Everything in moderation is the key.

INGREDIENTS:

Diced rabbit
Toulouse or Cumberland sausages
Shallots
Carrots
Garlic
Parsley, bay leaves, thyme
A tin each of tomatoes and haricot beans
A couple of glugs of red wine and a chicken stock cube dissolved in half a pint of water.

METHOD:

Use a fairly large pan and brown the sausages in a little oil, just for a few minutes until they take on colour. Remove and set aside to cool.
Add chopped shallots, garlic and rabbit meat to pan and fry gently for five minutes or until the shallots are tender but translucent. You don't want them to brown.
Slice the sausages into chunks and add to the pan.
Add tomatoes, beans, diced carrots and herbs, stock and wine and simmer for about 45 minutes.
Transfer into an ovenproof dish and bake in a moderate oven for another 45 minutes.
Serve with chips, or a baked potato.

You will need ...

Fry shallots, garlic, rabbit.

Add sausages and veg.

Simmer for 45 minutes.

Transfer to oven-proof dish.

Transfer to oven-proof dish.

RABBIT

Yin Yang Rabbit

Life is a balancing act, we all know that. There has to be light and dark, bitter and sweet, joy and pain, and so on; it's the natural order of things. The Chinese philosophy of yin and yang became the thread for this recipe after watching a TV consumer programme about the fallacy of 'low fat' foodstuffs being better for you than those that taste like real food. The amount of sugar added to compensate for the removal of the fat, is staggering, largely unadvertised, and just as harmful – if not more. Yes, it's a tenuous link to spiced rabbit, but that's the way my brain works, I'm afraid. For me, one of the attractions of eating wild meat is the lack of additives and the fact that it is as lean as you can get. There's only one downside, from a cook's point of view, and that is the necessity to add fat if you want the meat to remain moist when you dry-cook it; fat means flavour, of course, but I have a way around it.

Last Christmas, I prepared half a dozen duck legs, a small joint of pork, a spiced gammon ham, and a small chicken for the children, all under seven, in case they didn't fancy the more 'exotic' meats. The chicken remained completely untouched, the ample remains of the pork and ham were taken home to various points north and south, and there wasn't a scrap of leftover duck to be found. The little ones loved it, much to the chagrin of some of the grown-ups who were forced to share – because I was in charge of the forcing department. I've since tried the same deal with rabbit and it's not the same texture because there is no fat to make it crispy, as there is on a duck, but the flavour is the same, the meat is as tender as you like, and I'm betting that when I produce it for the next family gathering, there won't be any of that left either.

You will need to marinade the meat overnight in a 'fridge, and make sure that it's covered tightly while cooking, but I guarantee it's worth the effort for a guilt-free, flavoursome meal with all of the yumminess and none of the fat. A perfect balance between naughty and nice – a yin-yang result!

INGREDIENTS:

For the 'twos' marinade:
Two teaspoons ground ginger
Two teaspoons cinnamon
Two star anise, or a teaspoon of five-spice powder
Two tablespoons of Marsala, or dry sherry
Two tablespoons of soy sauce
Two squashed garlic cloves
Two tablespoons of honey

METHOD:

Place all ingredients into a large bowl, coat the rabbit pieces in this mixture - it will stick - cover with Clingfilm and leave in a 'fridge overnight.

Just before you're ready to cook, remove the rabbit pieces and wipe off the excess marinade with kitchen paper.
Place into an ovenproof dish with a cupful of water, cover tightly with tinfoil and bake in a moderate oven for at least an hour and a half. Give the meat a poke and if it isn't tender, put it back into the oven for another 30 minutes.

You will need ...

Mix marinade ingredients.

Coat rabbit pieces.

Into an ovenproof dish.

Test after an hour.

Cook for another 30 minutes.

Rabbit Enchiladas

This recipe was inspired – or not – by a meal I had in a local restaurant. I'd been looking forward to it for weeks and the meal, when it was eventually served, was well below standard. I don't mind paying for something that I can't do better myself - Chinese food, for example. I've tried and tried, but it always turns out like a dodgy attempt at Far Eastern cuisine by an Englishwoman - which it is, of course. When I'm faced with food that doesn't come up to scratch and I know I could have made it ten times better, though, I resent having to pay for it. Obviously, I did so on this occasion, I'm not writing this from the local nick, but I didn't leave a tip.

I ordered enchiladas – forgot to mention it was a Mexican place – and it sounded great on the menu: Succulent chunks of suntanned hen and freshly-picked-half-an-hour-ago vegetables, wrapped in a light wheaten pancake and covered with cheese grated on the thighs of a Latin American virgin. All right, I might be exaggerating, but you know how they dress up the menus these days, and it was something like that. It sounded fantastic, anyway, and by the time I'd had a few tequilas, which I shall blame on the abysmal service, I was more than ready to eat.

It was presented with a flourish by a pretty waiter, with very little English, or so he pretended; he was more than likely born in Cambridge. Mind you, I'd have feigned ignorance of the language, too, if I'd had to serve up crap to paying customers.

Really, I'm not exaggerating. It was bland, considering that we'd been expecting Mexican heat, the vegetables were soggy and the sauce had separated. I was determined to have a go at it when I got home, and I did, substituting the chicken in favour of rabbit, but you could do it with pigeon, too. I felt like taking a sample of it back to the restaurant, just to prove a point, but that might have been a step too far. I just enjoyed the fact that mine was better than theirs.

INGREDIENTS:

Finely chopped rabbit meat
Chopped onion
One clove of garlic and a roasted red pepper
120 grams grated cheese – strong Cheddar, or Monterey Jack if you can get it.
Mozzarella, thinly sliced
1 pack of mini wraps, or tortillas
For the salsa:
Onion, garlic, tinned tomatoes, tomato puree, chilli, balsamic, seasoning.

METHOD:

Make the salsa: Fry chopped onion for a few minutes, then add the rest of the ingredients. Bring to the boil, simmer, lid off, until the liquid has reduced by two-thirds. The salsa should be thick.
Cook the filling: Add all ingredients to a pan - apart from the cheese - with a little olive oil, and fry gently for ten minutes until the onions are soft and the meat is tender. Add two tablespoons of the salsa mix and a handful of the grated Cheddar. Stir until well mixed.
Place a tablespoonful of the filling into the centre of each tortilla, roll up and place into an ovenproof dish. Continue until the dish is full - one layer only. Pour over the rest of the salsa, place the sliced mozzeralla and the rest of the Cheddar on top.
Bake in a hot oven for 15 minutes until the cheese has melted and turned golden brown. Serve with salad and a glass of something.

Fry onions.

Add all other ingredients.

Add salsa and cheese.

Dollop onto tortilla.

Roll up, and into dish.

Top with mozzarella.

Wartime Rabbit

'During the war ..., and for a decade after it, we had to eat what we could get. There were no convenience foods. No one had ever heard of fresh chillies, coriander, or butternut squash. Olive oil was bought in small bottles from the chemist and used as a skin treatment. The population ate whale meat and the National loaf. We had chicken once a year, at Christmas if we were lucky, and we were fitter than the youngsters of today'. All of this and more, uttered by the older relatives and usually triggered by one of my boys saying something like 'I don't like mushrooms' at a family get-together meal. On and on they'd go, like Uncle Albert.

The truth is that the average diet in the 1940s, by necessity, was restricted, bland and lacking in variety. Saturated fat was used for frying, roasting, cake-making, and there was very little sugar available. Homegrown vegetables and fruit supplemented the rations of those who had space to cultivate them, but mealtimes represented a challenge to the cook on every level. Maybe people were fitter then, but that's because they didn't eat so much and very few families had cars. They didn't live any longer than people today – it just seemed like it.

Eventually, the members of the older generation in my family died off, the lectures on fussy eaters stopped, and I inherited all manner of ancient bits and pieces, including a paperback cookery book, published in 1946 by the Daily Mirror and titled 'Patsy's Christmas Reflections.' I found within its pages a recipe for baked rabbit, right next to one for stewed whale meat, and decided to give it a go. For the best part of 40 years, I'd been bombarded with how tasty and good for you these wartime recipes were. It was time to try one out and it was surprisingly delicious. It's very simple and I have to admit now that my late grandparents weren't wrong all of the time. Sorry I took the mickey, Grandma!

INGREDIENTS:

A jointed rabbit
A cupful of fresh, white breadcrumbs
1 large onion
Three carrots
A couple of sticks of celery
Dried sage, salt and pepper.
Olive oil and half a pint of chicken stock.

METHOD1:

Patsy's 1940s version: 'Boil and chop up 3 or 4 nice onions – have ready a good heaped breakfast cupful of breadcrumbs…and mix them together to a paste with the onions, salt and pepper, a little dried sage and about 1 ounce of melted dripping.
'Melt another bit of dripping in a baking tin and spread half of the mixture on it. Arrange the pieces of rabbit on this. 'Cover with the rest of the mixture and bake in a moderate oven for about an hour.' Mmmn … yummy! Probably.

METHOD2:

Chop the potherbs (vegetables for those of you not still living in the 1940s) into equal-sized pieces and fry gently in a glug of olive oil for a few minutes.
Transfer to a baking tin. Fry the rabbit pieces until browned on both sides, then sling it on top of the vegetables. Add the stock, salt, pepper and sage and cover the whole lot with the breadcrumbs. Dot with butter and bake in a medium oven - 180°C - for about an hour. If the breadcrumbs look as if they are browning too quickly, stick a piece of tinfoil over the top and turn the oven down to 170°.

You will need…

Chop potherbs.

'Patsy's Reflections' in glorious 1946 colour!

Rabbit pieces on top of potherbs…

… top with breadcrumbs.

Bake until it looks like this.

Rabbit Rissoles

I was always taught that the less popular and therefore cheaper cuts of meat or poultry have more flavour than the overpriced 'upmarket' displays of fillet steak or pork tenderloin. Whether this is a fact, or if it seems to be so because we tend to spend more time tarting up the cheaper cuts, is open to debate. It was a family legend, anyway, first told to me by my maternal grandmother. She had seven surviving children and couldn't afford to buy 'fancy' food, as she called it, but made the most delicious stews, pies and puddings out of 'six-pennorth of pieces and a few pot-herbs'.

Translated, this meant sixpence spent at the butcher's on scraps of beef or mutton that were the trimmings from joints of meat, and a handful of carrots, onions, turnips and celery sticks. The butcher used the off-cuts from the pork joints for sausages, I imagine; the family ate plenty of those, and always with a different gravy, for variety.

The philosophy was carried down through the years to my mother, and then to me, and I still prefer forerib of beef, a slow-cooked piece of brisket, or neck of lamb stew/curry to the more expensive delicacies on offer at my local farm shop. So, even though I can now afford to buy whatever I fancy, the old habit of concocting dishes from very little continues and I get a real buzz out of creating something tasty.

I found some minced rabbit meat at the back of the freezer, left over from a previous dish and given the 'waste not, want not' treatment – ie, prepared and then frozen for later. Tarted up with a few ingredients gleaned from the kitchen cupboards this made an excellent lunch for me and a couple of friends. I served it with purple sprouting broccoli and steamed new potatoes, but in hindsight, salad might have been a better idea. They said it was too filling, that was after eating every scrap, though!

INGREDIENTS:

Minced rabbit meat
Two rashers of bacon, cut into small dice
A couple of handfuls of white breadcrumbs
A small onion and one carrot, finely diced
Chopped fresh thyme, or a pinch of the dried stuff
Seasoning: pepper, a crumbled chicken stock cube, or a
One egg to bind
One egg and a handful of semolina to coat
Oil for shallow frying.

METHOD:

In a large mixing bowl, place rabbit, bacon and breadcrumbs.
Never waste leftover bread, by the way. It takes minutes to zap in a food processor, and you'll have a constant supply of breadcrumbs that you can use straight from the freezer for all kinds of dishes, sweet and savoury.
Fry the onion and carrot gently for a few minutes, until they soften.
Add the vegetables to the meat and breadcrumb mixture, add thyme and seasoning and mix together thoroughly with the beaten egg.
Lightly whisk the other egg into a shallow bowl, and place semolina in another bowl so you have a kind of assembly line.
Shape the meat mixture into rissole shapes, coat with beaten egg, then semolina and fry gently for two minutes on each side, or until golden brown.
Serve with salad for a light lunch, or with broccoli and spuds for a hearty dinner, apparently.

You will need …

Make your own breadcrumbs.

Fry carrot and onion.

All ingredients in a bowl.

Egg and breadcrumb.

Fry until golden.

Attila the Gun

Way back in the '80s our first-born pair, the Webley and Tasco twins, were fostered out to a close friend. It wasn't a permanent thing, you understand, and that fact was made abundantly clear before the deal was struck, just until some newly-purchased land could be brought into some kind of order. Close friend was not the proud owner of an air rifle, and his family had just bought a couple of acres of England, way out in the wilds of Lincolnshire – and I mean wild.

The area was reminiscent of the scene in Sleeping Beauty when the handsome prince has to hack his way through thorn bushes and the like in order to offer the kiss of life to his princess, and the only way the other lads could wheedle their way into this paradise for junior airgunners was to lend a rifle to the son of the landowner.

The small acreage had been untouched by human hand or foot for over ten years, so the accompanying cottage situated in the middle of this wilderness was practically derelict with no amenities of any kind, although there was running cold water indoors, but only when it rained. They could do no damage; the windows of the cottage were already shattered and there were no neighbours to annoy, which was just as well since close friend had little sense of direction in the aiming towards a target department. He was, so I was told when Sunday outings to the cottage began, a danger to himself and those around him. That didn't do much for my peace of mind, I can tell you.

If I tell you that the boys dubbed their friend Attila the Gun, due to his uncoordinated and erratic attempts with an air rifle, you may understand what I'm getting at. Living proof that even the short-term wearing of baseball caps, regardless of the legend emblazoned across the peak, can cause brain damage.

Fortunately, his way-off target shots took place on his own land, and only involved the destruction of several small bushes and the occasional already dead branch of a tree. There was no wildlife within spitting distance of the boys because they made enough noise to wake the dead – and certainly enough to frighten off anything within a five-mile radius.

By the time they got around to paper targets and tin cans, Attila had had a bit of practice and the involuntary ducking of heads and nervous tics of his fellows began to subside. They had decided that it would be brilliant if they could spend a whole weekend at the cottage with a view to organising their own FT competition for the Sunday morning, following a Saturday of ground clearance, and general back-breaking toil to the placate the parents of the close friend.

I suggested that they take a tent - at least it had a roof - but they dismissed this idea as a negative thought pointing toward no sense of adventure, and besides, they had an old tarpaulin that could easily be battened down over the bits of missing roof. They would pack all the equipment that they had taken on previous camping trips, of course; heat, light, food, water ... but this time there would be no need to pitch a tent, not a strong point at the best of times. They organised everything quite well, to my surprise, even to the extent of photo-copying a hundred or so paper animal targets as well as the usual concentric circles with a pin-head in the middle.

It's a shame that their culinary preparations didn't reach the same standard as the shooting groundwork. I found out afterwards that they'd only taken one small saucepan with them. They had therefore found it necessary to half-fry the sausages in it first, before adding tinned tomatoes, baked beans and grated cheese. They brought the whole thing to a rolling boil and then consumed it with bread and butter, while exclaiming how fantastic it was. The recipe was repeated on numerous fishing trips, too, and became a staple. I was told that it tasted a bit like chewing gum with lumps in, but they ate it anyway. They had a serious competition the next day and had to keep their collective strength up.

The FT event was a great success, and even Attila managed to hit quite a few of the paper crows, he wasn't quite so hot on the paper circles, but that says quite a bit about his mentality. They set up a pyramid of empty tin cans, the bulk of which I suspected had originally contained lager – just imagine how many tins of baked beans and/or tomatoes they would need to open to make a pyramid! The effect on their digestive systems doesn't bear thinking about – but they wouldn't confirm the fact. They know the rules concerning the combination of guns and alcohol, and although they never drink when they are shooting, they could still have the alcohol in their blood the following morning, if they drink enough of it the night before. Accidents can happen no matter how responsible they think they are, so there was no mention of lager in my presence.

The paper targets were pinned up in the most inaccessible places, but to compensate, a row of Extra Strong mints was carefully arranged at a range of about 15 yards for Atilla to practise on first, before the rest of his friends left the area while he had a shot at a tree target.

All too soon it seemed, Atilla's parents decided that enough was enough. They had the cottage refurbished and began to spend their weekends in it, so that put a stop to the boys' weekly visits. Nothing lasts forever; Webley and Tasco came home.

RABBIT
- Winter -

Classic Rabbit Pie

As I write, the weather has taken a turn toward winter. Days are sunny, but with sufficient nip in the air to ensure that my walks along the beach are brisk and over with as quickly as possible so that I can get home for hot chocolate and biscuits. This time of the year, I don't stop to wonder at the flora and fauna along the shoreline. By nightfall, it is so cold that my thoughts turn to comfort food. Although I'm fairly keen to ward off the inevitable winter layer of fat that most of us start to acquire around this time of year, I'm not so desperate that I'll forgo the delight of puddings, pies and hearty soups and stews. There's nothing cosier than a plateful of home-cooked deliciousness when rain is battering at the windows and there's a north-easterly howling over the roof. This classic rabbit pie will give you the half-remembered reassurance of a childhood security blanket, although I'm not suggesting that you carry it around with you all day.

You can cheat, and shove the filling into the bottom of a pie dish and just drape the pastry over the top. Not quite the same, in my opinion, but it means that you can have a thicker crust and you don't have to faff about making a circle of pastry fit into the bottom of the dish. It's a fantastic winter day special and comforting as all get out, I promise you, especially if you accompany it with a few glasses of a seriously good red wine, followed by something from the Simple Puds section.

INGREDIENTS:

A pack of Jus-Rol shortcrust pastry
One rabbit, jointed
An onion, a couple of carrots, half a head of celery – all chopped
Some shallots and a handful of frozen peas
One pint of chicken stock
Seasoned flour

METHOD:

Place the meat in a plastic bag with the seasoned flour and shake it about a bit.
Fry the rabbit gently in olive oil, for about five minutes, until slightly browned.
In a large pot fry onions, carrot, celery, shallots for a couple of minutes, then add the rabbit, peas, and chicken stock. Bring to the boil and simmer for about an hour, or until the rabbit is tender. Remove from the heat.
Let it get cold. An hour before you're hungry, roll out the pastry and line a pie dish ready to receive your rabbit and veg mixture; I take all the meat off the bones. Use a slotted spoon to transfer the meat and vegetables into the prepared pie dish, leaving most of the gravy in the pot. Add a pastry lid, glaze with egg and bake in a moderate oven (180°C) for about an hour, or until golden brown.
Make a sauce by reducing the saved gravy by a third, and serve with mashed spuds and a green vegetable.

You will need ...

Brown rabbit pieces.

Add vegetables and stock.

Stew until tender.

Into a lined pie dish.

Egg wash and bake.

Bunny Burgers

This one's for cold winter nights when it's dark and misty and you want comfort food. It's easy, takes five minutes to prepare and ten minutes to cook. There's a bit of chilling time in the middle but you can be having a beer in front of the fire while you're waiting – or you can prepare the burger mix earlier in the day and bung it in the fridge until you're ready to create. The beer idea sounds a better idea to me, though.

You really cannot beat fresh meat, from whichever source, and it doesn't come much fresher than when you shoot it yourself. I had a strange conversation with a friend recently who told me that she wouldn't dream of eating anything shot by her son or partner. She never visits her local butcher, either, but buys all her meat from an 'up-market' supermarket – are there such places?

"I like to know exactly what I'm buying, where it comes from and be confident that it's fresh," she said, and became quite agitated when I tried to promote the benefits of buying locally-reared meat – and not just to the consumer.

"You can't get much fresher than meat killed in the morning of the day on which you cook it," I pointed out, but she refused to listen and flipped her hand at me dismissively when I dared to suggest that rabbit and pigeon are really nice to eat. I didn't dare to mention squirrel in case she had a fit of the vapours. She wasn't having any of it. Oh well, you can't convince everyone.

You can serve the bunny burgers as a main course with creamed spuds and a green veg or, for those of you who have teenagers who are going through a picky stage, you could go down the traditional route. In my experience, young teens – especially boys - will eat anything if it's squashed very flat, put in a bun with ketchup and accompanied by chips. You can even sneak in a lettuce leaf, or two, if they're hungry enough not to notice.

INGREDIENTS:

Rabbit meat, sliced from the saddle and legs, and then chopped, or minced. Two pork sausages with skins removed, or the equivalent in sausage meat.
A finely chopped onion
A handful of oatmeal (porridge oats will do)
A couple of boiled potatoes
One egg
One garlic clove, squashed
Salt and black pepper
Oil for frying
Seasoned flour or semolina for coating

METHOD:

I prefer to finely chop the rabbit meat because it adds a bit of texture, but if you don't fancy that you can use a food processor or mincer to reduce it to lumpy sludge.
Place all the ingredients in a large bowl and mix well. Get your hands in and squash it all together thoroughly and then cover and leave in a fridge for at least half an hour.
Remove from the fridge and form into burger-sized patties.
Put the semolina, or seasoned flour, on to a flat dish and coat the burgers on both sides.
Fry very gently over a low heat for five minutes on each side, until golden brown.

You will need ...

Rabbit, onion and oatmeal.

Add the egg ...

... and boiled potatoes.

Coat with semolina.

Fry until browned.

Credit Crunch Rabbit Stew

One of the positive aspects of an economic downturn, and there are several positives if you know where to look, is the discovery by many that it is possible to cook cheap meals from scratch. At last, consumers are learning that the price of one trolley-load of ready-meals will buy a family enough proper food for a fortnight, and if a credit crunch encourages those who open packets at meal times to spend half an hour in the kitchen each day, then I'm all for it. It's far better for your digestion; you know exactly what's in it, and it tastes of fresh ingredients. Food doesn't have to be fried to a crisp, or served hot from a cardboard box.

This recipe, which fed three hungry people and a small cat, cost me exactly £3.45 and about 20 minutes in preparation time. I suppose you could say that I cheated a bit because the rabbit was a donation, but it's still a very cheap, tasty and satisfying meal and I could have used cheap cuts of any other meat to achieve the same deal.

INGREDIENTS:

One rabbit

One 'stew-pack' – that's a couple of onions, half a dozen carrots, a parsnip, and a small swede, bagged up and sold in most supermarkets and some greengrocers.

Or, you can do as I did and just grab a couple of onions and a handful of carrots.

Fresh thyme if you can get it, dried if you can't.

A stock cube, or two.

Potatoes

Peas

METHOD:

Brown the rabbit pieces in a little olive oil; add the chopped onions, carrots and thyme.

Add about two pints of stock – chicken is good, or try the new Knorr Stock Pots. They are little plastic capsules of pure genius; as close to the real thing as you can get without boiling up a chicken carcass for an hour. You'll need two, though, in two pints of water, for flavour intensity.

Bring to the boil and then turn down to a simmer; do not put a lid on the pot. Continue to cook gently while you relax in front of the telly.

After about an hour, add some previously cooked, boiled potatoes and a small pack of frozen peas. Allow to come up to heat until the liquid is bubbling slightly once more.

Lid off, give it another ten minutes to reduce slightly and you're ready to serve.

If you want dumplings with it, and my friends and family always do, just sling equal proportions of flour and suet into a bowl with a pinch of salt. Gradually add cold water and mix until it's a dough.

Plop golf-ball-sized lumps into the stew, lid on for 12 minutes. Or cheat, as I did, and buy a packet. You don't have to measure anything, it's as cheap as chips, and the dumplings will taste just as good, especially if you add salt, pepper, and a few mixed herbs into the mix.

You will need …

Brown the rabbit.

Add the vegetables.

Simmer until tender.

Cheat or see page 206.

One pot meal!

RABBIT

Old-fashioned Slow-cooked Rabbit

In the south-east, we had cool-ish weather all the way through the summer and early autumn – apart from a couple of hot days in June which we'd have made more of, had we known. The forecast was for a cold winter, too, and as the weather begins to cool down significantly, my thoughts turn to winter food. Every year during late autumn, I start to plan dishes for the freezer in readiness for the days when I come in from work, cold, tired, fed up, and in need of a hot, comforting meal, near enough instantly. A proper, old-fashioned rabbit casserole works wonders on cold winter nights and freezes particularly well, and I'd have enough for four meals, or so I thought. I could save money on fuel by cooking in bulk and have delicious, welcoming meals in the bank, so to speak.

While having a rare clear out of my kitchen cupboards, I came across an ancient and over-sized slow-cooker, which I'd forgotten about. It must be at least 40 years old and it's been well used in the past but had remained hidden for over a decade in the 'corner' bit of cupboard that I can't see into, unless I lie on the kitchen floor - which is one of the reasons that clearing out my cupboards is not a regular activity. In these straitened times, it makes sense to save on fuel and the slow-cooker would certainly do that; the ingredients cost me about two quid – the rabbit was a gift -

so I began to feel quite smug, but pride comes before a fall, as my old, cliché-loving mum used to say.

Everything had been bubbling away nicely for six hours, when a surprise visitor turned up and waxed lyrical about the 'fantastic aromas' emanating from the kitchen. It reminded me of when my boys were young and their mates used to turn up at evening meal times - it was years before I cottoned on. We ended up eating the lot between us, every scrap, apart from a small bowl of broth, which I had the following day for lunch with a crusty roll. Oh, well, back to the drawing board.

INGREDIENTS:

Rabbit pieces, smoked bacon and chorizo
Chopped onion, celery, carrots
A pint of chicken stock (made with stock pods or cubes)
Half a bottle of white wine
Fresh thyme
Garlic
Salt and pepper

METHOD:

Fry rabbit pieces in the oil until they begin to brown, then remove from the pan and put aside.

In the same pan, fry bacon, chorizo, garlic and chopped onions for two minutes; add carrots, celery, and thyme and cook for one minute, then stir in the white wine. Season with salt and pepper.

Layer the meat and the vegetable mixture in the slow-cooker, starting with vegetables.

Replace the pan on the heat and de-glaze it with a few tablespoons of the stock. Make sure that all the sticky bits are incorporated – never waste the flavours from the frying pan - and then add the rest of the stock. Bring to the boil and pour the liquid over the layered meat and vegetables.

Leave it alone for as long as you like and then serve with spuds and a green vegetable, or vegetable rice, as I did.

You will need ...

Prep done.

Brown rabbit pieces.

Add the vegetables.

Layer veg, rabbit, veg, rabbit ...

It will fall off the bone.

RABBIT

Rabbit Cobbler

On cold, winter days, there's nothing like a rib-sticking stew and dumplings to warm you up. I've driven home in freezing fog, hungry, tired and more than a little pee'ed off, but a hot and hearty meal somehow makes everything all right again. If you have a slow cooker, you can bung all the ingredients for this recipe into it and let it bubble slowly all day, so that by the time you're ready to eat it, the rabbit meat will drop off the bones but the vegetables will be firm enough to be recognisable. You can bung a few spuds in as well, so that you don't have to do any cooking at all. I use my slow-cooker even when I'm working from home sometimes, because I don't have much time to prepare and cook a meal. Some of my friends think that because I work in my own house most of the time, I'm not really working and can't understand why I don't just drop everything and meet them for coffee! I've given up trying to explain.

Failing the slow cooker option, you can cook in the conventional way, freeze the meat and veg until required and then just reheat on the hob, place into a pre-heated oven and throw a few dumplings into the simmering pot for 15 minutes. I guarantee this dish will make you smile. The dumplings are crunchy on top and soft and juicy underneath so you have texture as well as taste. They're called 'boilie-bakes' in the Royal Navy, so I'm told by a reliable source. My mum used to call them 'cobbles' but she also said 'Cornish patsys' and once told me that she'd found 'weasels' in a bag of out-of-date flour, so it's anybody's guess. All I know is that they are delicious and finish off any stew/casserole to perfection.

INGREDIENTS:

One rabbit, portioned
A little flour, oil for frying
The holy trinity: 2 carrots, 2 medium onions, 2 sticks of celery
Chicken stock, about a pint, give or take.
Fresh thyme, or a teaspoon of the dried stuff
A handful of mushrooms, sliced

For the cobbles:
Flour, suet, salt and pepper and water to mix

METHOD:

Pre-heat the oven to 180°C. Coat the rabbit portions in a little plain flour, and then fry gently until golden brown. Remove the rabbit and set aside. Chop carrots, onions and celery and fry in the same pan for two minutes.
Place the vegetables into an oven-proof dish, place the rabbit on top, add the stock and thyme and cover tightly with foil. Bake for about two hours, or until the rabbit is tender, then remove foil and add mushrooms. Make sure they are immersed in the gravy.
Mix the flour, suet, salt and pepper together in a bowl, then add water and mix to a dough.
Divide into eight golf-ball-sized portions and place on top of the stew, pushing down gently until about a third of the dumpling is above the liquid. Replace the foil, and cook for another 20 minutes.

You will need …

Cut into chunks.

Brown the rabbit.

Vegetables into a dish.

Rabbit on top.

Add the cobbles.

Rabbit ‘n’ Pork

Too many people think they can’t cook, but most of them are wrong; anyone can do it, and with the right recipes they can do it very well indeed. According to my dear old mum’s nearly last words, wasting good food is a sin, a crime and a downright shame, and I had to promise never to do such a thing.

If you are a hunter and fortunate enough to have access to regular supplies of free-range meat, it follows that hunting and cooking should go hand-in-hand. Still not convinced? I promise that you will be if you try this recipe. A chance remark was overheard by a work colleague who revealed that he went hunting regularly and the following weekend, there he was on the doorstep with a couple of fine rabbits already skinned, paunched, and ready for my chopping board.

“How old d’you think they are?” I asked Mark.

“I dunno,” he said. “We didn’t exactly get into conversation … and, anyway, you gonna eat ‘em, or date ‘em?” ... but he didn’t say ‘date’. Honestly, the youth of today.

So, should I bake or braise? The bunnies looked quite plump and grown-up so I decided to play safe and stew them. One of my late father's favourite meals was rabbit and pork with dumplings so I'd make that and force-feed my friends with it. There's nothing like a cosy evening in convivial company, with a full, fragrant stock-pot and a bucket of Chateauneuf du somethingorother.

This stew is incredibly tasty, filling, easy to prepare and just the job for those who think they can't cook!

INGREDIENTS:

Two rabbits, jointed and floured
500gr lean pork belly, in one-inch pieces
Onion, celery, finely diced
One squashed clove of garlic
Six carrots, sliced and about 12 baby onions
Salt, pepper, thyme, bay leaves, flour
Two pints of chicken stock
2lbs potatoes, cut into chunks

METHOD:

Fry diced pork belly gently in a little oil for about ten minutes until golden brown, remove to a stock pot or large saucepan, and then add the rabbit pieces and fry for a further five minutes. Add the browned rabbit to the pork. Now add the sliced onion, celery, garlic, carrots and baby onions to the pan, keep it moving for a couple of minutes, add thyme, a bay leaf or two, salt and pepper, and transfer it all to the pot.

Pour the chicken stock into the pan in which you fried the meat. Scrape all the crunchy bits into the liquid and then add to the stock-pot. Bring the whole shebang to the boil, then simmer gently for about an hour or until the pork is tender.

Add potato chunks about half an hour into the cooking process, and dumplings (see page 206) 20 minutes before you intend to serve - lid on tight, no peeping and make sure that the liquid is on a fast simmer.

Fry the pork belly.

Then the rabbit pieces.

Transfer to stock pot.

Simmer for an hour.

Dumpling components.

Smells superb!

RABBIT

100-year-old Rabbit Pudding

Writer's block is something that I live with and mostly overcome but cook's block is another matter entirely and can last for days at a time while I live on pasta. I had responsibilities, though. I took on my mother's dietary requirements in 1985, when my father died and she lost the will to eat – or do anything much. This became the norm and she began putting in special requests. It got to the point where she couldn't even be bothered to do that so I had to come up with 'surprises' on a regular basis - hence, the 'cook's block' – and I still get it on occasion.

All it takes to get back on track, though, is a bit of inspiration. A snippet of overheard conversation, or a reference in a book or on TV, is usually enough to get me going again. Just before the birth of this recipe I watched the cook on BBC 2's 'Victorian Farm' making a rabbit pudding and mentioned it to Mum the following day. 'I haven't had a rabbit pudden for years,' she said. 'Your Nan used to make it with …' and she proceeded to give me the recipe.

So, here it is, reproduced in memory of my mother and grandmother. The white wine is my idea, though. Nan was a Guinness drinker. Wine was only for when you were poorly and always a claret, warmed up in a little glass with a handle. Come to think of it, she was quite often poorly!

It turned out to be nearly, as good as Nan's, according to my mother. Why not as good, or better? "Oh, she used to put chopped bacon in hers. I forgot to tell you!"

Put the chopped bacon in with the rabbit meat!

INGREDIENTS:

1 rabbit
1 onion, salt and black pepper
1 chicken stock cube, or pod
2 tablespoons white wine

For the suet crust:
250g self-raising flour
125g suet
Salt and black pepper
Cold water to mix

METHOD:

Remove the meat from the bones. Chop the onion into large chunks. Mix the rabbit and onion together and season well.

Place the flour, suet, salt and pepper in a large bowl. Add cold water, a little at a time, and mix until it forms a dough. Keep one third of it back for the lid, but roll out the rest of the suet pastry and cut into the centre – see pic – this will make it easier to line your pudding basin. Pack the basin in layers: start with onion, then rabbit, more onion etc until you reach the top. Plonk the stock pod on top, or crumble a stock cube, and add a couple of tablespoons of white wine and one of water.

Roll out the remaining third of the pastry for the lid, place on top and crimp round the edges, cover with tinfoil, leaving a pleat in the top to allow the pudding to rise.

Place the pudding in a steamer over simmering water for about four hours. You may need to top up the boiling water after two hours. Serve with new potatoes and carrots.

You will need …

Onion in chunks.

Take a slice out.

Stock pod on top.

Pastry lid on.

Steam for four hours.

Rabbit Scones

Sometimes, I just daydream about ingredients, and yes, I know what you're all thinking, and you're right – I do need to get out more. Friends often ask me to help out with the catering when they've got some kind of family do on, and I always comply; firstly, because I enjoy cooking anything at any time, and secondly because it's always nice when there's someone to eat my creations fresh, rather than me bunging it in the freezer for when the family descend on me en masse.

This recipe came about when I was making cheese scones for a mate's 50th birthday party. I like to play about with ingredients and try to combine those that aren't accepted as being a happy marriage, if you like, and the idea of a cheese scone mixture slathered over the top of a rabbit casserole seemed like a good idea.

Anyway, I ended up with enough of the cheese scone mix left over to use as a topping, but to cover it completely seemed a bit much so I carried on cutting the scone shapes and 'stepping-stoned' them across the casserole. It was one of my better brainwaves, because the scones spread slightly as they cooked, and divided themselves into portions.

The trick is to work as quickly as possible with the scone mixture once it has been combined. The baking powder will begin to work as soon as the wet ingredients are added and if you hang about, you'll end up with flat scones. Get everything ready to hand before you start.

You can make the same amount of scone mix that I did, knock out some proper scones for the freezer and then serve the finished rabbit dish all golden brown and crunchy on top, whilst soft and succulent underneath. It is remarkably easy and it makes a change from the usual winter dumpling deal.

INGREDIENTS:

Rabbit pieces
Chopped onions, celery, carrots
Chicken stock cube
Scones: 10oz self-raising flour
A large pinch of salt
Two heaped tsp of baking powder
Half a teaspoon of cayenne pepper
2oz parmesan and 2oz strong cheddar
Fresh thyme or a teaspoon of dried
A chicken stock cube, crumbled
One egg and 6fl oz milk
A tablespoon of oil – I used chilli, but you can use vegetable

METHOD:

Place all rabbit casserole ingredients into a large, oven-proof dish.
Cover with tinfoil and bake in a moderate oven (180°C) for about two hours, or until the rabbit meat is just tender.
Make up the scone mix as follows:
Place all the dry ingredients into a bowl and mix well.
All the liquid ingredients go into a jug, whisk until the egg is combined.
Add the contents of the jug to the flour mixture.
Shape gently into a firm dough
Roll out until about an inch thick, cut out into rounds and then place on top of the bubbling meat mixture. Cook for about 15 minutes, or until a skewer comes out clean from the scones. Serve with a green vegetable and creamed mashed potatoes.

You will need …

Dry ingredients.

Rabbit casserole.

Cut into rounds …

Place on top.

Bake for 15 minutes.

Up-market Rabbit Stew

I'm known for my cavalier approach to cooking. Rarely do I measure anything, unless it's for a soufflé or a sponge when these things matter, but prefer to just throw things into a pot and see what happens. Most of the time, I come up with tastiness, rarely there's a burst of avant-grade genius and I produce something fantastic, and occasionally there's a dismal failure. I have tried-and tested recipes that I cook all the time, but even then, they're not reproduced as faithful replicas because I can never remember what I put in them in the first place.

I fancied a bog-standard rabbit stew and dumplings. We'd had some foggy, damp and bone-chillingly cold evenings and a bunny stew is the ultimate comfort food. Then I had a conversation with a friend who told me that it was time I became a bit more refined. He suggested that I dispense with the thick gravy, chunky vegetables and huge fluffy dumplings, in favour of a more delicate, French-style concoction – with croutons. Croutons will never replace a suet-laden, herby-flavoured dumpling, in my opinion, but for the sake of this month's recipe and a love of experimentation in the kitchen, I agreed to go along with it and we mapped out a plan.

I'd already been 'up market' of the Farmer variety for my monthly supply of rabbit, pigeon, and 'fresh from the fields', local and in-season vegetables, so I had everything to hand, pretty much. The only extras were some celeriac, and a tin of butter beans. If you add the beans you won't need an extra carb - potatoes, rice, pasta – and it becomes a meal in one pot. How simple is that!

You can cook this in advance, it takes minutes to prepare and a couple of hours to cook, but it's a satisfying and comforting plateful of something to come home to on a cold winter night when you've been out all day – or you can bung it in a slow-cooker.

INGREDIENTS:

One rabbit, jointed and floured
Lardons, or diced streaky bacon.
One large onion
Two carrots
Celeriac – or celery if you can't find celeriac
Small tin of haricot beans
Glug of Marsala or medium sherry
Chicken stock
Thyme, black pepper
Olive oil for frying

METHOD:

Dredge rabbit pieces in seasoned flour, shake off the excess and fry until slightly brown. Remove and set aside.
Fry lardons and onions, carrots and celery gently in the olive oil until the onions are translucent but not coloured, then add carrots and celeriac.
Add the rabbit pieces to the vegetables and cook for a few minutes, then add the Marsala, stock and seasoning.
Bring to the boil, cover and simmer for about an hour, or until the rabbit is tender.
Add the tinned haricot beans about ten minutes before you want to serve it.
Sprinkle croutons generously over the top and enjoy. (See page 206 for croutons recipe).

You will need ...

Brown the rabbit.

Bacon and veg in a pot.

Rabbit on top.

Add stock.

Simmer until tender.

Blueing Compound

There are several phrases in the English language guaranteed to strike terror into the hearts and minds of airgunning motherhood; 'I've had a bit of an accident ... Can you lend me ... There's a comp on 50 miles away ... and 'I think I'd better re-blue my gun.'

Webley Tempest who lives in a fishing tackle box and is carted o'er hill and dale in all weathers, definitely looked a tad jaded. More than a bit, in fact, it was rusty around the edges due to being allowed to play in the rain without going through the usual, after-use grooming session regularly endured by its larger brothers. It could certainly benefit from a bit of TLC.

The eldest hadn't any spare cash, as usual, and was suddenly busy, so I was despatched along with my much ill-used purse to the nearest gun emporium to purchase a container of blueing compound. The proprietor showed me a shelf on which reposed tubes, plastic bottle, touch-up pens - I quite liked the sound of those until he explained their use - and so on, and I was invited to take my choice from a confusing array of products, designed for the purpose of refurbishment. I asked him to point me in the direction of the method that would cause me the least hassle and he sold me a tube of blueing gel.

It looked reasonably innocuous sitting there in its little tube. There was no government mental health warning upon its label; it did warn that it could be harmful if swallowed, but then so could number one son's cooking, and besides, who would be stupid enough to use acid as marmalade? Apart from that, there was nothing to suggest the possible onset of severe trauma. It really shouldn't be allowed.

The first step, according to the instructions, was to strip the gun down to the bare metal and the method was described in detail. Purse in hand, off I went to the hardware store to purchase various grades of wire wool. I knew that it would be my fault if the required abrasive wasn't available when the mood to begin work struck him.

Degreasing compound was apparently necessary, too, which - the label screamed out - was also fatal if swallowed, the warning complete with skull and crossbones in black ink. I began to feel quite nervous. I rang Terry Doe.
"Think yourself lucky he's going to cold-blue it," he cried, waggishly. "There is a method where you have to boil the whole thing up on the cooker to promote chemical rusting. How big is the gun?"
"Do what?" I said.
"Tell you what," he said. "Ring Theoben. Ben Taylor will explain the process to you in glorious detail if you tell him I sent you."

Why do I really want to know these things? That's my trouble; I can't leave well alone. I always have to find out the details of absolutely everything, just in case. As predicted, the lovely Ben launched into glorious detail. He told me about the process of chemical blacking, mentioned things like a hot, caustic soda solution to be applied with a giant cotton bud before the bits to be blued are processed in boiling water, six or seven times. I was fascinated to learn that the ensuing red rust comes off quite easily when wiped with stainless-steel wire fleece, eventually leaving behind a dark blue surface. This process couldn't possibly be done in a kitchen, he said, it was too dangerous. His lecture was interspersed with horrifying words like 'nitric acid' and 'mercuric chloride'. Ben told me that years ago they used to bury gun barrels in wet oak chippings for six months to obtain the same result. That sounded okay to me. I had plenty of patience and I could cope with that, particularly after he told me that mercuric chloride was so noxious that one sniff could kill you within seconds.

Junior couldn't wait for six months, even if I had been able to acquire oak chippings from somewhere, and I should have known that he wouldn't risk experimenting on Webley without first making sure that the cold stuff worked on one of my stainless steel knives. I now have a set of five and a blue one for special occasions.

The instructions seemed to suggest that the whole operation of cold-blueing was dead easy, and would all be over in the matter of an hour or two. It took all day. By the time he'd rubbed the Webley down with a coarse-grade wire wool, then a finer grade and finally used wire wool so delicate that it felt like gritty cotton wool, he was exhausted and inevitably hungry. He took an hour or two off for lunch.

Degreasing was the next step, during which I hovered close by in case he fatally swallowed some of it. This exercise complete, I decided that he was going to be okay, thanked my lucky stars that he hadn't decided on the hot method, and left him to it.

The best bit, carried out in my absence, involved two of my favourite towels, a pair of Marigolds, a bucket of water strategically placed in case he missed with the gel and needed to rinse something off, and several week's newspapers that I insisted he spread over every conceivable surface capable of sustaining acid damage. What did we have at the end of all this? We had a black sack full of used wire wool and crumpled newspaper, a mother with an even more nervous disposition than before, and a Webley Tempest that was only slightly bluer than when he started. The rust had disappeared but there was no startling difference. Maybe that's the general idea, but for all the running about, hard work and bad language, I had expected a complete transformation. I was quite disappointed; now I know why all those great blues songs are so sad.

SQUIRREL AND STUFF

You Can't Eat That! It's Vermin!

There was no word spoken, no intimation of things to come as they prepared themselves for the monthly visit to Farmer Giles' fields and woodland. There may have been just a touch more jauntiness of step and a brighter gleam in the eye, but apart from that, they gave no sign.

To be fair to the boys, they didn't go out expressly for squirrels. They had noted the presence of these creatures during the usual forays for pigeons and rabbits, but hadn't taken too much notice of them. This time, though, they agreed that if they saw one it would be good for the pot and assumed that their mother would be overwhelmed with gratitude. Incidentally, you should always appear to be grateful, whether you are or not, because one fine day they will bring back something you want and if you don't show enough appreciation for the things that you don't want, they won't bother - still with me?

So, they didn't tell me of their intention. They wanted it to be a wonderful surprise. Just what you need after a huge Sunday roast followed by something and custard, to be presented with a small, dead squirrel and a tale of tails that 'come off in your hand' – and that is a tale of tales. I'd like a pound for every time I've heard that one over the years. They had learned, my boys, from my previous life-threatening struggles – their lives, not mine – with the occasional rabbit, not to leave the animal whole and recognisable, so they had dealt with the outside of the squirrel, cut the meat into thinly disguised, jointed pieces, and placed it in the 'fridge until my stomach had settled sufficiently to deal with it.

That same evening, the aforementioned tail was attached to a friend's car radio aerial as a mark of respect for the deceased, they said, and so that they could spot their vehicle more easily in the cinema car-park, providing all the airgunners in town hadn't had the same idea.

The dog always became very enthusiastic when the hunters returned from their jaunts. I know why. He didn't like them any better that the other members of the family, but he knew that whatever they brought home could be leftovers within hours. It was the only time that there were any table scraps worth his consideration, only this time I was determined that there wouldn't be any.

The boys' meagre donation toward the housekeeping languished in the 'fridge for a couple of days while I thought about it. Knowing that my family would not eat it as a fricassee or stewed or in fact, at all, if they knew it was squirrel, I approached my mother for inspiration, but even she, who had been known to eat the most unspeakable things 'during the war', jibbed at the very thought of eating 'vermin.' I had a brilliant idea in the middle of the night - squirrel burgers! That had to be the answer. They would eat anything if it was round, flat, and placed inside a bap with lettuce and mayonnaise.

Almost every weekend there were alien, hungry bodies littering up the floors of my sons' bedrooms as their friends either couldn't be bothered, or were incapable of walking home late at night. They always stayed for breakfast and if they could fry it, they'd eat it.

The small squirrel, combined with breadcrumbs, garlic, onions and a couple of stock cubes made half a dozen burgers which I put in the freezer, in an empty chicken burger box, while I waited for the weekend. When they asked me, panic-stricken and distraught in case I had thrown it away, what I had done with their offering, I told them that I had frozen it until later – well, I had, sort of.

The following Sunday morning, surrounded by several surplus and seriously bleary-eyed young men, my now famous squirrel burgers were removed from the freezer, fried at a hundred miles an hour, together with everything else in the kitchen that didn't move. They were eaten within minutes and pronounced delicious.

There was a stunned silence when I enlightened them all. The temporary lodgers were very polite and apart from gulping a bit, said nothing, apart for one young man who could claim some Romany ancestors. He went into great detail about his grandmother's knack with squirrel stew and dumplings. They all went home shortly afterwards a tad subdued and I suspect, not purely down to the collective hangover. It didn't make them think twice about staying overnight the following weekend, though.

SQUIRREL

Squirrels by Post

Several of my friends and acquaintances recoiled in horror when I mentioned that my next recipe would include squirrel. I'm not judging them, they're entitled to their own opinions but I can't relate to their dismay. After all, squirrels are edible, they have to be culled sometimes, and the average airgunner's bounty is hardly going to wipe out the entire population. I don't understand the 'Squirrel Nutkin' argument. Most of us eat lambs; some eat poussin (month-old chickens), veal, and suckling pig. They're all attractive animals - and practically tasteless, in fact, unless tarted up - so I don't get the aesthetic objection to eating squirrel, or rabbit. 'I couldn't eat them', they say. 'They're all fluffy and cuddly. It'd be like eating Spot or Tibbles. Yik! That's disgusting. You're eating vermin. Tree rats. You are really weird. I couldn't eat anything like that.' I feel like saying, 'Don't eat it then! Stick to your pork chops wrapped in cling film, and next time you make a spag Bol, just remember where the mince comes from!' I'm definitely turning into a grumpy old woman.

Sourcing a squirrel isn't easy. I had already telephoned local butchers and game merchants without success. I even called a Waitrose store in the West End, after being told that they stocked squirrel because it has become quite a popular delicacy in the upper echelons of society. I was treated as a hoax caller and told not to waste their time. I had a brainwave, I made an appeal on t'Internet and was quite overwhelmed by the response from the lads on the BBS forum. They offered words of encouragement and practical help and eventually, airgun writer, Eddie Jones, sent me two fine, plump and 'oven-ready' squirrels by first-class mail. They arrived in a plastic box, complete with one of those blue plastic freezer blocks, and were in perfect condition. I sent the box back with a dozen of my finest sausage rolls and a copy of my latest book as a 'thank you'.

Squirrels need a long cooking time so I braise mine in the oven. Not only does this heat up my kitchen on a cold day and fill the house with delicious aromas, but I can bake muffins and sausage rolls at the same time, which I can swap for squirrels.

INGREDIENTS:

One plump squirrel, portioned
A little flour to coat and oil for frying
Onions, carrots, celery, chopped
A chicken stock pod dissolved in a half a pint each of water and red wine
Garlic clove, squashed, a bay leaf, and seasoning
Half a dozen potatoes cut into quarters
One tin cannellini beans

METHOD:

Pre-heat oven to 180 degrees C
Coat the squirrel pieces with flour and fry gently until browned.
Remove from the pan and place into an ovenproof dish.
Cook the onions, carrots and celery in the same pan and cook for a few minutes, then add garlic, bay leaf, and season to taste, add the chicken stock and wine and bring to the boil.
Add the vegetable mixture to the squirrel pieces and cover the dish with tinfoil or a lid.
Braise for two hours then remove from the oven, then add the cannellini beans and place the potatoes on top. Drizzle a little olive oil over the spuds, sprinkle with salt and return to the oven for a further hour, or until the potatoes are brown and crisp.

You will need ...

Fry floured squirrel pieces.

Fry carrots, onions and celery.

All into an ovenproof dish.

Add cannelloni beans and potatoes.

Roast for one hour.

SQUIRREL

Squirrel Pate

There's not enough meat on a squirrel to feed more than two people, unless you really pad it out with Cumberland sausages and dumplings. I've only just thought of that - now, there's a recipe for a winter's day! Meanwhile, I found a squirrel lurking in my freezer and it needed sorting out.

It was high summer, the picnic/barbecue season was well under way and I always take along small gifts of food when invited to these functions. Come to think of it, I'm invited quite often and probably for that very reason, so I'm always trying out new recipes for portable food.

One afternoon, I went to a friend's house and watched as he knocked up a batch of chicken liver pâté to freeze and after a chat and a cup of coffee, I wandered homeward toward my own kitchen with more than the germ of an idea. Squirrel pâté seemed like a plan. I'd made pâté with trout, mackerel and salmon – so why not squirrel? I had all the ingredients indoors, and I thought I'd surprise some young friends who'd invited me to a summer party at the weekend. They'd be expecting sausage rolls or quiches; I couldn't wait to see their faces when I presented them with rodent pâté.

My conscience wouldn't allow me to turn up without the sausage rolls, though, so I made a batch and trotted off with a full picnic basket. I wouldn't tell them what was in the pâté until they'd tasted it, and nearly all of those who did said it was delicious. I was teased a bit about eating road kill, but if they hadn't taken the mickey I'd have been worried that I'd offended someone.

Only one young woman expressed disgust, and that was only because she's an 'animal lover' - her distaste had nothing to do with the pâté per se. I told her that I was an animal lover, too, if not quite on the same level, because I love a bit of roast lamb on a Sunday. That didn't go down too well. I also pointed out gently that pork liver/chicken/duck pâté was made from animals, and the barbecued chicken drumsticks that she'd just eaten were, in fact, from a chicken. She wasn't having it, though. Apparently, squirrels are cute and should be left alone to bury their nuts in peace. Oh well, you can't please everyone.

INGREDIENTS:

One sad and lonely squirrel
8oz sausage meat – or two sausages, skinned
A few spring onions, finely chopped
An egg, whisked with 2 fl oz cognac
Salt, pepper, one teaspoon of nutmeg
Dried thyme, Four sage leaves – or bay.
A dollop of crème fraîche

METHOD:

Mince the squirrel meat twice – once through a coarse grinder and the second time use the fine attachment. Put the meat into a large bowl and add the sausage meat.
Add all the other ingredients, apart from the sage/bay leaves, and mix.
Spoon into ramekins, place a sage leaf on the top of each, and brush with oil.
Put a piece of foil loosely over each ramekin and then place them in a roasting tin, half full of hot water.
Cook in a medium oven, about 170°C for about 40 mins.
Serve with toast or crackers.

You will need…

Mince the squirrel.

Mix the meats.

Add all other ingredients.

Spoon into ramekins.

Bake until risen and golden.

Squirrel Fantastic

Twenty years ago, we ate squirrel for two main reasons. Firstly, there was a rule that nothing edible was ever wasted in our house, and probably more importantly, so that the boys' cars could be found easily in cinema car parks. A squirrel tail tied to a radio aerial was a sign that the occupants of the vehicle were big, white hunters who'd gone to the pictures, and at the same time, they were showing respect to the animal they had murdered, apparently. None of the creature was wasted. When my boys were at home, I was regularly presented with small gifts of love and expected to conjure up a feast to feed however many bodies had taken part in the shooting/fishing party of the day. I became quite good at padding out meals with vegetables or carbs. There was never enough meat/fish, and teenage boys seem to treat eating as a national sport.

Nowadays, squirrel is eaten in high-class restaurants; minuscule portions from white plates the size of Exmoor, the meat placed at an oblique angle, and accompanied by a tower of other 'exotic' ingredients with a couple of different coloured splodges of jus dripped artistically around it. Not my kind of food, I'm afraid. I prefer the rustic approach but I tried to merge the old with the new and came up with this recipe. It turned out to be surprisingly tasty. When it's blowing a hooli outside and autumn leaves are underfoot, this makes a comforting evening meal for two, or if you're really trendy you can pile all the components on top of each other and make it a 'pièce de résistance' at a dinner party. High-class cuisine, I'm telling you. Maybe not your actual 'haute' but it's close. I've even tried to use the lingo and quenelle-ed' my potatoes.

INGREDIENTS:

Squirrel meat
A very little oil – just to get the lardons going
A small handful of lardons – or chopped streaky bacon
Sliced shallots
Mushrooms
A pint of liquid made up, fifty-fifty, of chicken stock and white wine
A couple of sprigs of fresh thyme – or a teaspoonful of dried
Black pepper
Soured cream to add at the last minute

METHOD:

Add lardons to a pan and fry for a couple of minutes to release the fat, then remove, and set aside. Brown the squirrel meat in the flavoured oil and then place it into an ovenproof dish. Sprinkle the lardons over the top. Add the sliced shallots, thyme, stock, wine and black pepper, then cover tightly with foil and cook in the oven for an hour and a half at 180ºC.

Check that the meat is tender; if it isn't, cook for a further half an hour.

Turn off the oven, remove the dish, and let it cool for five minutes. If you don't do this, it could curdle and you'll have to sieve the gravy – never a great thing to do if anyone's watching. Then mix in a couple of tablespoonsful of soured cream.

Replace the dish into the oven to cook through gently while you add a dollop of soured cream, salt and pepper to drained potoatoes, and pound the living daylights out of them. Place the spuds on a plate and then arrange the braised squirrel mixture. Drizzle the sauce over the top.

You will need ...

Fry lardons to release the fat.

Brown the squirrel meat...

... and into a dish with lardons.

Add veg and stock.

Eddie Jones, squirrel provider!

Let 'em Eat Squirrel

At last, I agreed wholeheartedly with a Government proposal. It was suggested, a while ago, that schools bring back old-fashioned domestic science lessons - now called 'food technology', apparently – seems that everyone's a technician of some description today. This 'new' idea of teaching kids to cook is an attempt to educate the next generation, and beyond, away from the risks of obesity, and short of closing down all the fast-food outlets, and companies that produce prepared food, it seems to me that cookery lessons, starting in infant schools, could be a possible solution.

Too few parents teach their children to cook basic meals from scratch because there are so many families who are too busy, or can't be bothered after a day at work to be messing about with raw meat and vegetables, when they can open a packet, made by someone else in a factory, and bung it in a microwave. I can understand why they do that, but cooking fresh ingredients doesn't have to take hours of prep and long, slow braising. It takes very little time to knock up a curry, or a kebab at home; you can do it in ten minutes, and by the time you've ordered a pizza and had it delivered by a bloke on a bike, you could have cooked a home-made one with as many topping as you like - and you'd know what was in/on it!

I'm not saying give up the take-aways altogether, they're okay now and again, but the 'convenience' food market is beginning to pander to people's laziness and it irritates me beyond belief. I've seen ready-mashed potato, pre-cooked rice, scrambled egg, already-peeled oranges, and more in supermarkets, for heavens sake! There must be a market for it, though.

Teaching our youngsters in schools how to cook basic ingredients, as we were taught years ago, doesn't go far enough, and I'm told this has been recognised and that's why the subject is dubbed 'food technology', rather than just plain home economics. Youngsters are being taught how to budget a meal, and how to 'make something out of nothing' as my mother's generation had to do after the war when every morsel was a struggle to obtain. I know it's a generation thing, but before the advent of freezers and microwaves, and the convenient and mostly unhealthy, expensive take-away and ready meals, all our food had to be shopped for and cooked on a daily basis. There were just no convenience foods or takeaways available; the exception was fish 'n' chips, of course, a childhood treat on a Friday evening - but not every week.

Kids - and some adults - need to know where food comes from and the general lack of knowledge is astounding. Recent surveys have shown that there those who have no idea which vegetables grow under the ground, and the number of youngsters who cannot recognise a stick of celery or name a parsnip, beggars belief - not to mention telling the difference between pork, beef and lamb. I watched a TV cookery programme recently in which a young woman in her 20s asked the assembled company if the lamb she was eating was from a cow or a pig!

When I was growing up there was a cooked meal on the table every night, made from fresh, bought-that-day, ingredients. My mother worked and still managed to produce tasty, satisfying and healthy food. I carried that on when I got married and had children of my own, and so do my sons – and they 'play' in the kitchen with their littl'uns. That's how my boys learned to cook, by joining in and asking questions about where ingredients came from and what they were used for. – "What's the difference between smoked bacon and green bacon, Ma," was one question I was asked by my youngest boy, newly left home and out of his depth in Sainsbury.

Youngsters should be taught how to shop for food; to prepare and cook it, how to budget meals. They should be educated in the science behind it; the constituents of proteins, carbohydrates, fats, and the proportions of each required to maintain a healthy body. There should be school trips to working farms, maybe 'pick your own' fruit and veg afternoons – although these venues are becoming fewer by the year because of the health and safety aspect. When I asked a farmer friend why it wasn't so popular any more, I was told that there are plenty of willing punters, but the majority of farmers are worried that they'll be sued if someone trips over a strawberry, and the public liability insurance premiums are prohibitive, so they just stopped doing it.

School food technology lessons should also include instruction on how not to waste anything in the kitchen. I've seen friends of mine throw perfectly good stuff away because it's past its sell-by date. If it smells and looks okay, then eat it, for goodness sake! I don't waste anything. Even vegetable parings (scrubbed, obviously) with a chopped onion, a few herbs and zapped in a blender are knocked up into soup. With some crusty bread, that's lunch for a couple of days and it costs virtually nothing.

My friends and family shoot grey squirrels, rabbits and pigeons, and often offer them to me for the pot and I'm grateful for everything I'm given; I don't have a problem with preparing and cooking meat so fresh that it was running about in a field that morning. Everything that my boys shot or caught with rod and line had to be cooked as a matter of principle, and they ate it all with relish, both literally and the stuff from a jar – homemade, of course. There was no throwing up of hands or stomach contents when informed of what they'd eaten – that's if they asked; mostly they just ate what was put in front of them. I never asked them 'What do you want for your dinner?' as I've heard parents ask two-year-olds in supermarkets, and then wonder why the infant throws a wobbler when there is too much chance it can't make up its mind.

The definition of 'game' is 'any kind of wild meat, as against the domestic cow, pig or sheep, and tarted up with garlic, herbs or spices, it's delicious, fresher than fresh, cheap and marvellous. There are no preservatives, emulsifiers, E-numbers or other convenience chemicals.

Teach 'em to cook culled squirrel, rabbit and pigeon in their food technology classes – now there's a cost-effective idea! Maybe I'll write to the Minister of Education.

Hare Today

'Ere y'are, Rosie. You like eating road-kill.' I've never eaten road-kill in my life, but I accepted the bag containing a hare, anyway; a reflex action - never turn away free food. It hadn't been killed by a speeding motorist, but shot humanely by an FAC-certificated gun, after a happy life bouncing around in the fields and dancing in the sunshine.

Hare doesn't pose much of a threat to farmland, these days, but if you're offered one, don't turn it down just because it isn't considered to be a major pest.

Sometimes, I'm at a loss with what to do when I'm presented with game that is out of my comfort zone - rabbit, pigeon and squirrel – and end up searching websites or old cookery books for inspiration. The 'accept it gracefully and then bin it' option just doesn't enter my head.

So, there I was, faced with the remains of a hare, grateful that it had already been dressed and prepared for the pot, but still at a loss regarding what to do with the darned thing. I performed my usual trick of standing in front of the open store cupboard and waiting for lightning to strike, and when it didn't I made my way into my library. Since I was a small child, I had dreamed of having a library of my very own, so when my marriage hit the deck 15 years ago, and I managed to get a job and had money for the first time in my life, one of the first purchases was a new kitchen and half a dozen floor-to-ceiling bookcases. Cookery books take up two of them, so I was bound to find a recipe for hare amongst them somewhere. Nope.

Next step was toward my friend, Mike, who is an impressive cook. Mike suggested the recipe below and it turned out to be one of the easiest and tastiest meals I'd had in ages, and had nothing to do with the frequent tastes of the port to make sure it was okay.

INGREDIENTS:

Portioned hare meat, carrots, a white onion, baby red onions, and mushrooms.
Balsamic vinegar, red wine vinegar, Worcestershire sauce and a chicken stock cube.
A good measure of port and a pint of water.

METHOD:

Throw all dry ingredients into a large pan and cook through for a few minutes.
Add the liquid ingredients, including the stock cube and water.
Bring to a boil, lid on, turn down to the heat to a simmer and cook for an hour.
Test the meat with a fork, if it isn't tender enough, cook for a further half an hour.
Fish out the meat and vegetables and place into a serving dish.
Thicken the gravy with a couple of teaspoons of cornflour made into a paste with water, taste it and if necessary add more port.
Serve with the gravy in a separate jug and leave the port on the table.

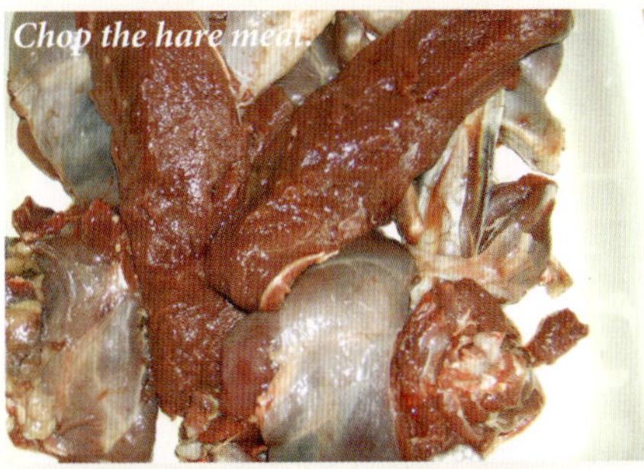

Chop the hare meat.

Prep the veg.

Bung it all in a pot.

Add stock, port and simmer …

…until it looks like this.

Serve gravy separately.

OTHER GAME

Partridges

A friend gave me a couple of partridges.

"A present for you, Rosie," he said, as he offered them to me with a flourish. "I know you eat all this kind of weird stuff. Can't do it meself – too gamey for me."

"Gamey? Have you ever tasted a partridge?" I asked him.

"Not likely," he offered. "Tried a pheasant once. It was 'orrible."

Nothing I could say would convince him that a pheasant or a couple of partridges braised slowly in white wine would make a fine non-gamey meal for anyone, so I thanked him kindly for his present and ran away with them before he could change his mind.

Among my extensive collection of cookery books, mainly due to the 'can't walk past a bookshop without buying a book' syndrome that I seem to suffer from are those that once belonged to my mother. I mention these because within their pages are numerous recipes for all kinds of game; partridge, pheasant, woodcock, ptarmigan, hare, pigeon, snipe, and more. Just a few decades ago, people ate what they could get and game was popular, unlike today, when if it isn't wrapped in Clingfilm and have a bar code, it isn't given a second glance by the majority. That's a shame because so many are missing out on delicious meals for the sake of ten minutes prep time; same old lecture, sorry.

Anyway, back in partridge country, I found a recipe in an old book that I'd bought from a charity shop. The suggestion was to stew the birds 'by the side of a fire until soft'. I already had a stock of the suggested spices and pot-herbs, so I translated the old method and came up with my own modern version. It is very tasty and can be applied to pheasant too, if you're fortunate enough to have a friend who considers anything that isn't chicken to be 'too gamey'.

INGREDIENTS:

Two partridge
Celery
Leek
Shallots
Lardons, or six rashers of streaky bacon, diced
About a pint of chicken stock

METHOD:

Brown the birds on all sides in a little hot oil, then remove from the pan and set aside.
Fry the lardons for a couple of minutes until they release some of the fat.
Add the chopped vegetables to the pan and cook for two minutes.
Add season and stock and simmer, lid off, for ten minutes.
Place half the vegetable mixture into an ovenproof dish.
Lay the partridges on top.
Top with the rest of the vegetables, cover and bake in a medium oven for about an hour.
I served with sweet potato mash and brussel sprouts, but you can serve it with rice, or bung in a few roast potatoes while the partridges are braising in the oven. Whichever way you choose, it's a tasty and filling evening meal – and mine was practically free!

You will need …

Brown birds in hot oil.

Vegetables in a pan.

Add liquid and simmer.

Veg, then partridges …

More veg on top.

Game Pie

I haven't made proper game pies for years. All that mucking about with hot water crust pastry, chopping meat, and stewing pig's trotters to make jelly, slow cooking, nurturing and glazing seems such a lot of effort for something that you can buy in any grocery store. The texture and flavours of a home-produced one, though, far surpasses the mass-produced variety.

I had to buy new game pie tins, because I'd left my grandmother's oval, hinged and decorative moulds behind when I moved, but three non-stick, loose-bottomed pie tins were acquired, and I was off to the kitchen with a plan.

You can use any meat that you happen to have handy for a game pie, providing most of it is game, obviously, otherwise it would just be 'a pie'. I went through my freezer and came up with rabbit, pigeon, pheasant, and some pork belly to provide the fat content. You need some fat because game is always lean meat and fat means flavour. I can never understand the 'you are what you eat' concept of beans, pulses, vegetables and skinless chicken, or fish, as a complete diet. The whole thing is virtually without fat and must be so bland that it's no wonder folk find it so difficult to follow, long term.

INGREDIENTS:

750 grams of mixed meat. I used rabbit, pheasant, pigeon, and diced pork belly.
A couple of rashers of smoked bacon cut into pieces - streaky is best – for added flavour.
A good pinch of mace.
A teaspoonful of dried thyme.
Ground black pepper and a little salt – not too much, there is salt in the bacon.
One clove of garlic – squashed.

METHOD:

Mix all ingredients in a large bowl and leave for an hour so that the flavours can combine.
The hot water crust is so easy that I'm surprised more people don't use it. It's not available ready-made, of course, which might be why. You have to work fairly quickly, while the pastry is warm, but there is no rolling out required. (See page 207)
Use the pastry while it is still warm, bung a handful into a non-stick tin and mould it with your fingers, rotating the tin and gradually pulling up the dough around the edges until it reaches the top.
Then pack the filling into the mould. If you're showing off, you can put the meat in as light/dark layers. Then, shape the lid, crimp the edges, brush with egg, make a hole in the top, and place it into a pre-heated oven - 180°C - for an hour. If it looks too brown, place tinfoil loosely over the top and turn the heat down to 150°C for a further hour.
Prepare the jelly by adding three leaves of gelatine to half a pint of water and a vegetable stock cube. Once the pie has cooled, pour the jelly into the top, using a funnel. Place into a fridge until the jelly has set.
Serve with a green salad, or some piccalilli, or chips - whatever takes your fancy. It sounds really complicated but it isn't. It does take a while to cook but it's worth the wait and you can freeze a couple for a summer picnic.

Chop the meats.

Mix 'em up.

Make the hot water crust.

Mould while warm.

Pull excess over.

Add the jelly.

OTHER GAME

A Cheat's Compendium of Game

Once a year, usually just after Christmas when all the festivities were over, the weather took a downturn, and January stretched far into a 'five-weeks until pay day' lean spell, I used to empty the freezer and make up meals from the bits and pieces that had been put in there and forgotten about for six months. I came up with some pretty good stuff, too; my boys never went hungry.

Nowadays, things are different and I don't have to scrimp so much, but I still do it, and this time I managed to glean small portions of pigeon, rabbit and pheasant, a couple of mouthfuls of venison and a chicken breast. Yes, I know chicken isn't considered game, but this was a case of waste not, want not, so it went in. I did find another use for some dodgy neck of lamb that might have been a leftover step too far for a game pie. I also made an individual game pie for my daughter-in-law's granddad, Alan. He's my biggest fan.

The ready-made puff pastry was also a relic from the summer, and perfectly good to eat. I chose to serve my game pie with creamed spuds and mixed greens because that's what I happened to have handy, but you can even eat it cold with a salad, if you're brave enough on a cold winter's day.

INGREDIENTS:

Any leftover game that you have hanging about.
Two large onions, chopped.
Two carrots, sliced.
A few mushrooms, quartered.
Fresh thyme, if you can get it, or a half a teaspoon of the dried stuff.
Salt and black pepper.
A tin of condensed chicken and white wine soup.
A pint of water
Puff pastry – ready made.

METHOD:

Cut the meat into roughly the same size pieces.
Brown in a little olive oil in a large pan and then remove from the heat.
Fry the onions, carrots, and mushrooms gently for a few minutes, until the onions are softened.
Return the meat to the pan and add seasoning, then the soup and water.
Bring to the boil and then simmer on a very low heat for 45 minutes, lid off so that two-thirds of the liquid reduces.
Put the mixture into a pie dish, roll out the pastry to about a quarter of an inch thick, and drape over the top.
Don't cut off the excess, tuck it in round the edges, then egg wash the top and place into a medium hot oven, about 180° for 40 minutes. Have a look at it after half an hour and if the top is browning too quickly, place a piece of tinfoil loosely over it.

You will need ...

Brown meat in olive oil.

Fry the veg.

Pour into a pie dish.

Tuck it in.

Bake until brown on top.

OTHER GAME

Roe Slo' Good

I often use my slow cooker in the summer, and I know that sounds a bit odd because most people associate slow cooking with comfort food, cold winter days and warm kitchens. I don't know about you, but I often need comforting in the summer too, and there's nothing better on a slightly chilly and wet summer evening - and we've had a few of those in latter years – than a hot and tasty stew or casserole.

This dish is another one courtesy of Norrie and Shiona Southam, my friends in Scotland, who sent me the roe deer meat. Sometimes, in a shooting circle of friends, there is other meat on offer, apart from the more usual rabbit, pigeon and squirrel, and I love it when I'm presented with something like this. In the south-east, we don't get too much fresh roe deer meat, so I hadn't a clue what to do with it and was prepared for an afternoon of Google research, but Shiona also sent me her recipe, which I've tweaked and reproduced for you.

You should seriously consider using the slow cooker for this, although you can bung it into a moderately hot oven for five hours and get a similar result. I don't know why stews seem to be more succulent in a slow cooker, but there's probably a scientific explanation. If you cook this in the winter, by the way, just add potatoes to the holy trinity veg, throw in a few dumplings 20 minutes before you're ready to serve, and you've got a hearty and delicious meal in one pot.

You can use proper venison – or even beef – for this version, if you prefer, but I'm telling you, the roe meat is absolutely divine and so tender that it melts in the mouth, so if you can get hold of some, it's well worth going the extra mile. I accompanied mine with creamed potatoes and broccoli, but you can ring the changes veg-wise – please don't serve it with salad under any circumstances, though!

INGREDIENTS:

Roe deer meat
Olive oil for frying
Onion, carrot and celery – the holy trinity.
A tablespoon of flour
Two teaspoons of English mustard
Small tin of tomato puree
I teaspoon sugar
A bottle of ale
Beef stock cube and water, salt and pepper

METHOD:

Chop up the roe deer meat into 3cm cubes and trim off any fat, roll the pieces in flour, place into a hot pan and brown them in a little olive oil, then set aside.
In the same pan, fry the onion, carrot and celery until the onion is translucent.
Add the meat, along with the mustard, tomato purée and sugar. Give it all a good stir around so the meat is nicely covered and then add the bottle of ale and beef stock cubes.
Season generously with salt and pepper.
Depending on the required thickness of the sauce, you might want to add a touch more flour at this stage, but sprinkle it in so you don't end up with blobs of flour in your stew.
Place it all in the slow cooker on 'low' and then cook for 4-5 hours; three hours if you use the 'high' setting.

You will need …

Brown the meat and set aside.

Fry the holy trinity for a few minutes.

Add the meat.

Add seasoning and ale.

Norrie and Shiona Southam.

From Scotland with Dove

My lovely friends in Scotland, Norrie and Shiona Southam, sent me a parcel. It was still cold because it had been frozen and then securely wrapped; completely covered in silver Gaffa tape, then cardboard, a large plastic box, a waterproof coolbag, and finally, polythene bags – like one of those matryoshka Russian dolls. My reward for hacking my way through the packaging was a box of delights; four plucked and dressed collared doves. I've never cooked collared doves, but I guessed they'd be similar to pigeon, so I stood in front of open cupboards and the fridge to await inspiration, and it came in the form of white wine, warm spices, carrots, onions, celery, and bacon.

The birds were steeped in a marinade for a couple of hours while I went for a walk along the beach, and I know that they should have been left overnight in a fridge, but I was in a hurry to try them. Leave them for at least two hours, though, so that they can absorb the flavours. I've used a bog-standard marinade, but you can experiment with other flavours; honey, ginger and white wine is a good one. Always add a little oil to a game marinade though. You must add some fat because the meat is so lean.

I kept checking them as they cooked, unsure about the timing, and the result was one of the best braised 'pigeon' dishes I've eaten anywhere. You can accompany the doves with any vegetable that you fancy, but I made a one-pot meal and just added baby new potatoes and peas to the pot. This would also be great for a dinner party, as a starter. If you omit the peas and spuds, and blitz the carrots, onions and celery, you'll end up with a thick sauce, which you can call a 'jus'. Some people are impressed by that, apparently.

INGREDIENTS:

Two collared doves per person
Two rashers of bacon
Onion, carrots, celery, chopped
Half a bottle of white wine
A tsp of hot paprika and a half tsp of cinnamon
One chicken stock cube in half a pint of water

For the marinade:
Lemon juice and olive oil – half and half
Garlic, a squashed bay leaf, rosemary

METHOD:

Remove doves from the marinade and wrap each with a rasher of bacon.
Place into an ovenproof dish.
Fry onion, carrots and celery in a little olive oil for two minutes.
Add the paprika and cinnamon and stir into the vegetables.
Add the white wine and cook for a few minutes more.
Dissolve the stock cube in the water and add to the pan.
If you want to add potatoes and peas, now is the time to do it.
Pour the mixture over the doves, seal with foil, place into a moderate oven and cook for about an hour.

For the marinade ...

Marinade your doves.

You will also need ...

Wrap doves in bacon.

Cook mixture for a few minutes.

Add potatoes and peas.

Other Useful Stuff

Croutons:
Always use stale bread. Cut into cubes, and place in a bowl with olive oil, garlic, and a handful of grated parmesan/pecorino.
Spread out on an ovenproof tray and bake for ten minutes in a moderately hot oven.
The croutons will keep for weeks in an airtight tin in the 'fridge.

Dumplings:
4oz self-raising flour
2oz Atora suet – or vegetable suet if you prefer
One teaspoon dried thyme
Pinch of salt
A sprinkling of black pepper
Enough water to make a stiff dough

Place all dry ingredients into a mixing bowl, then add the water and form into eight dumplings.
Add them to your dish about 20 minutes before serving. Cook until a skewer comes out clean from the centre.

Fajitas Spice Mix:
One finely chopped onion.
Half a tsp each of sugar, and chilli powder
One squashed garlic clove
Zest and juice from one lemon.
One tsp each of oregano, coriander, nutmeg and cinnamon

If you can't be bothered with mixing it yourself, buy a packet of Discovery Fajita Spice Mix – it's just as good. I put in about a third of it, but if you like your food so that it blows your head off, add more.

Herb Butters:
You can make herb butters easily, and at a fraction of the price of the stuff that they sell in supermarkets. Make loads at a time and freeze them; they defrost instantly when you add them to hot food anyway.

In a large bowl, cream a pack of unsalted butter until it's soft. Divide it into smaller bowls - one for each herb. Add chopped herb, work it together with a fork and you've got instant herb butter. Repeat with different herbs, and freeze it all for a later date, either in individual pats, or rolled in Clingfilm. Wrap in a cylinder shape and slice bits off when you need them.

Home-made Curry Powder:
Make it in bulk; stored in an airtight container it will keep for about three months.
This is my recipe, but you can adjust it to your own taste:
Two tablespoons coriander seeds, one teaspoon each of fenugreek, fennel, mustard, cumin, cinnamon powder, turmeric, four cloves and half a teaspoon of cayenne pepper.

Zap the seeds in a blender or spice grinder - or pulverize in a mortar if you're feeling energetic - until reduced to a powder for use as and when required.

Hot Water Crust Pastry:
600ml milk
A pound of plain flour
250 grams lard
Melt half the lard into the milk over a low heat and then allow to cool slightly.
Rub the other half into the flour until it resembles breadcrumbs.
Make a well in the centre and pour in the cooled milk/lard mixture.
Mix it into a pliable dough.

Quick Port Wine Gravy:
One stock cube/pod – the chicken variety for rabbit and squirrel dishes, and beef for pigeon
Half a pint of water
Half a glass of port
Two teaspoons of cornflour made into a paste with little of the water
A couple of tablespoons of redcurrant jelly

In a small saucepan, dissolve the stock cube in the water, then add the port and redcurrant jelly and allow to cook, lid off, until reduced by about a third.
Stir in the cornflour mixture which will thicken the sauce, and simmer for a further five minutes to cook out the taste of the flour.

Salsa:
Onion - chopped
Garlic – one clove
Tinned tomatoes - chopped
Tomato puree – one small tin
One small fresh chilli, finely chopped, or dried chilli flakes
One chicken stock cube
400 ml water
Balsamic vinegar – about a tablespoonful
Salt and pepper

Fry chopped onion for a few minutes, until softened, then add garlic and the rest of the ingredients. Bring to the boil and then simmer for about 20 minutes, lid off, or until the liquid has reduced by two thirds. The salsa should be thick.

Satay Sauce
One small onion, very finely chopped or, even better, grated
Half a chilli, finely chopped – or a teaspoonful of 'lazy chilli'
Two tablespoons peanut butter (smooth or crunchy)
One level teaspoonful brown sugar
One tablespoon soy sauce
Couple of dollops of crème fraiche

Fry onion and chilli for a couple of minutes until the onions become translucent. Add peanut butter, sugar and soy sauce. Simmer for three minutes, stirring continuously – otherwise it will become too thick and stick to the pan. Turn off heat and add crème fraîche until the sauce reaches a dipping consistency.

Savoury Rice:
You can use any vegetables that you happen to have handy; onion, a large tomato, a few mushrooms and a couple of broccoli florets, cut down to make very small ones would do, but you can add frozen peas, broad beans, sweetcorn … anything at all.

Put the kettle on to boil. Fry your vegetables of choice in a little olive oil for two minutes only, then add a cupful of rice. Cook for a further one minute, making sure the rice is coated with the oil. Add a vegetable stock pod/cube and two cupfuls of boiling water. Bring to the boil and allow to bubble away for about four minutes, then put the lid on, turn down to barely a simmer and steam for ten minutes. You should have grain separate, fluffy, vegetable rice. Taste it and season with salt and black pepper if required.

Tomato, Apple and Chilli Chutney:
Two kilos of fresh, chopped tomatoes
Four cooking apples, sliced
Half a teaspoonful of chilli flakes
One teaspoonful of mustard seed, cumin seed and salt
One teaspoonful of ground ginger
400ml malt vinegar – or red wine vinegar.
500gms sugar

Bung it all into a large pan, stir until the sugar has dissolved, then bring to the boil, turn down to a low simmer and walk away.
Stir every half an hour for about two hours until the chutney is quite thick.
Pour into hot jars and keep for three weeks before eating, to allow the vinegar to mature. I put my jars into the dishwasher on the longest, hottest cycle to sterilise them before filling with the chutney. It works a treat.

Tomato sauce:
Finely chopped onion
Garlic
Tinned tomatoes
Tomato puree
Dried or fresh basil
A vegetable stock cube and about a pint of water

This is the easiest tomato sauce ever.
Fry onions and garlic for a few minutes.
Add tomatoes, puree and stock.
Bring to the boil and then simmer for 20 minutes, or until the sauce has reduced by half. It should be gloopy.

Yorkshire Puds:
Mike Sully's Yorkshire puddings are the best I've ever had, and this is how he makes them:

Break three eggs into a measuring jug, make a note of the volume, empty the eggs into a large bowl and whisk slightly. Rinse the jug and dry it thoroughly, then add plain flour to the same level as the eggs. Add a pinch of salt and then sift the flour on to the eggs.
Measure the same amount of milk, or milk/water and add gradually to the egg and flour until it resembles single cream.
Make sure that your Yorkshire pud tin is piping hot – Mike cheats and places it hot from the oven onto a gas ring on the hob, to keep the heat intensity.
Pour the mixture as quickly as you can and put into a hot oven – 220C – for between 20 and 30 minutes. Do NOT open the oven door for a look until it has been in the oven for at least 20 minutes.

Join the Club

Eventually, you will get more involved, if only to satisfy yourself that he's going to be safe at the gun club. It's no good imagining that you can stay in obscurity, picking up pellets and repairing the damage caused by 'just testing out the new scope/rangefinder/bean bag'. One Saturday night, in a weak moment after several glasses of something, I allowed myself to be persuaded to accompany my teenager to the gun club the next day. He was very keen that I savour the delights of air-gunning first hand and made me an offer that I couldn't refuse. It was a great honour for me, I had been selected Queen of the May, or in this case March, and it was a privilege, never doubt it.

A strange metamorphosis took place while I prepared myself for this adventure into the unknown. Number one son became almost conciliatory, offering to lend me his cammo trousers and a forage cap. He asked me if I thought I'd be warm enough, told me not to worry, that they are a great bunch of blokes at the club, and no one would take the Mickey because I'd never held a gun before – except to dust it. I wondered if he was going to ask if I was wearing a vest or had a clean handkerchief. At the time, I couldn't understand it but looking back, I realise that he was nervous too but for different reasons. If I approved of the gun club, then I wouldn't worry so much every time he left home with a gun, and that would make his life easier.
"I'm sure you're a good shot, Ma," he said, reassuringly.
What made him so sure? Was he recalling his early childhood and the way I never missed when I clouted him with the child psychology book? Maybe the whole issue is my fault; perhaps I caused irreparable damage to his psyche, and that's why he's so obsessed with guns and shooting.

There's no need to worry, really. On arrival at the club, you'll be met by the 'great bunch of blokes' and be carried off in a wave of enthusiasm and friendliness to the target areas. Don't think you'll just fire off a couple of tentative shots at a series of concentric circles and then be allowed to go home to baste the Sunday roast, though; it doesn't work out quite like that.

My debut as an airgunneress was fraught with mystery and almost total bewilderment, particularly when my 'escort' for the day buggered off because he was there to shoot. He wasn't going to waste time looking after his mother during the safety lectures, especially when there were so many willing and able airgunners prepared to do the job.

Before I was allowed to touch anything at all, I was given in depth safety instruction. You might think that's not necessary; it's only common sense not to point a rifle at anyone, leave it lying around unattended, or to take it indoors while loaded, after all, but you should pay attention. The experts know what they're talking about and unfortunately, there are plenty of folk who do not have a great deal of common sense. There are others who have a surfeit of it but don't listen to the experts because they think they already know it all. Safety is a serious business, though, and deserves respect.
The next talk was on mechanics. I was told how a rifle works, and the functions of all the pokey-out bits. It was all

explained gently and in words of one syllable, though, and I learned that the things that stick up or out from the scope are called 'turrets' and their function is to adjust windage and elevation – whatever that means. A word of advice here: do not show any degree of enthusiasm at this point, or you will be given a mini-lecture on every component both visible and invisible, one at a time and at great length – which is all very well, but you'll want to get stuck into the fun and the targets will be beckoning.

Eventually, they allowed me to approach a lane and someone settled me down on a beanbag – still not holding a rifle, though, they were still not sure I was ready for that yet. There followed another lecture about back-stops, targets, wind speed and direction, and so on, and then number one son was at my side, having taken the edge off his desperate need to shoot something. Lovingly, he placed his 'baby' into my arms with instructions, 'don't touch anything until I tell you.'

He loaded it and suggested that I aim at target number four. Where the hell was target number four? I stared desperately through the scope and could see a darned thing. It turned out that my cheek wasn't in the correct position on the stock, and after a few minor adjustments to my posture, there it was, in full view. I squeezed the trigger gently and the pellet hit the target, not in the middle but at least I hit it. A small crowd gathered and there were muttered words of encouragement as I had another go, and I was hooked.

I demanded more pellets, please, and be quick about it. I could have stayed there all day, given half a chance. Sunday roast? Let 'em eat cake. Number one son tried to retrieve his rifle. I told him to take a hike; it was his idea to bring me here in the first place and he must learn to take the consequences of his actions.

A very nice man, who had witnessed my bad behaviour and number one son's disappointment, approached and offered me a couple of shots from his rifle. A gasp of envy escaped my son's mouth before he grabbed his own gun and wandered off, although I was unaware of the significance of it until afterwards when I was told that the reason for my perfect performance wasn't that 'I'd got the hang of it', but more likely due to the fact that the loaned rifle was a hand-made Ripley which had cost its owner a mere £2000. Thank goodness I'd had no idea of its value when it was handed to me!

The feeling of exhilaration when I hit the target explained to me why airgunners are so devoted to their sport and I was pleasantly surprised at the mature and responsible manners displayed by my teenager, and not quite so pleased with my own attitude when he tried to retrieve his gun. The role-reversal only lasted until we returned home, though, things returned to normal almost as soon as I stepped through the front door. 'When's dinner? Can you lend me a fiver? Where are my clean jeans?' I attended his every need. It was the least I could do in return for a day spent at the air gun club.

SIMPLE PUDS

I asked my friend, Michelle Sully, to scribble down a few easy dessert recipes for me, because I'm not the best pudding cook in the world and she came up with an impressive selection. I do hope you have a go at some of them. They are not for the calorie-conscious, but the double cream can be replaced with yoghurt, or half-fat crème fraîche with a little honey added.

DEL
CHIOSTRO
CHOCOLAT

PUDS

Angel Trifle

This dessert harks back to a 1970's childhood. A time when everything was decorated in orange and brown and every house had a gas fire with holes cut out of the teak surround for a vast array of ornaments - usually kingfishers in our house - and three well-positioned ducks of ascending size on the wall. At the time it was the height of fashion, as was the dodgy photo of me in the latest dungarees and stripy shirt; it makes me shudder just to think of it. Some things, though, just stand the test of time and you can still get away with this recipe and keep your reputation intact, unless you're still driving a Ford Anglia or Austin Allegro and we can no longer save you from the fashion police.

We didn't have the variety of today's ready meals in the '70s; Angel Delight, sago pearls, usually simmered in milk with added sugar (frog spawn), jelly and ice-cream, were among the most popular, along with fruit of some kind. You certainly never saw a freezer full of luxury desserts.

You could buy Swiss rolls and lemon meringue pie was a special-occasion dessert at the time, so the topping idea was stolen from that. Mums cooked everything from scratch back then; steamed puddings, spotted dick, jam roly-poly, and pies which all tool time to prepare, but were a great deal healthier than the convenience foods are now, with so much added salt and sugars.

I have no idea where my mum got this idea from, or even if she made it up herself. There was just Fanny and Johnny Craddock, or the Good Housekeeping guide for inspiration, but this was my mum's quick-and easy-option when we were kids, to keep us quiet on a rainy winter afternoon. She also used it as a blatant attempt at blackmail after putting a load of green vegetables on a plate in front of us, expecting us to eat it and to be happy about it. The only way to get us to eat all the cabbage, broccoli and peas was to put this treat in the middle of the table and wait for the clean plates. We never turned it down. It maybe a cheat, but if you have kids - or you are a big kid yourself - give it a try!

INGREDIENTS:

One shop-bought chocolate swiss roll
One chocolate Angel Delight, mixed with half a pint of milk
Two egg whites
85gms caster sugar

METHOD:

Slice the swiss roll into half-inch slices and arrange them in a suitable round dish.
Whip up the Angel Delight as instructed on the packet.
Pour it over the swiss roll and put into the fridge to set - about ten minutes.
Whisk the egg white until it holds its shape, and then add the sugar, beating until well combined.
Spoon the whipped egg white over the mixture in the bowl, smoothing it into the edges.
Swirl the top with a fork, and put under a hot grill until it just colours the meringue mixture.
This will keep in the fridge for a day or two, so you could make it ahead of time.

PUDS

Banana Soufflé

This is another massive cheaters' recipe; no soaking confusing amounts of gelatine leaves in water, just a packet of jelly and winging it - which tenuously leads us to the RAF who were linked to the Army in which my father was serving at the time of this recipe coming to light – see what I did there?

Dad got posted all over the place, France, Eladem, Cyprus to name just a few, but this recipe hails from good old Sandhurst in Surrey. Andrea was a good friend of my parents, married to a fellow sergeant, a damn good cook, and I owe my middle name to this lady. Her recipe may have morphed a bit, but the basics remain the same; use the jelly to flavour and set your whisked egg white. It's easy, but one word of warning here - whatever you do, don't use strawberry, raspberry or blackcurrant jelly with the bananas. It doesn't work! Some things are just set in stone and this is one of them. Use lime, lemon or orange; they'll go with the bananas like strawberries and cream, and taste wonderful. I have tried the others and it was a disaster - it even cost me a date once. You can make this the day before if you keep it well refrigerated, but the banana will start to discolour after 24 hours, so if you are out to impress a new beau, you have been warned.

This is another recipe you can get away with for the kids; I am yet to meet a child who doesn't like it. If you do insist on leaving the well-trodden road of citrus jelly, do me a favour and change the fruit to go with it; strawberries with strawberry jelly ... you get the idea, or try tinned mandarin segments and tangerine jelly for a real orange hit. The kids will love it!

INGREDIENTS:

Three bananas
Three large free-range eggs
4oz caster sugar
One pineapple or tangerine jelly
Two tablespoons water
Half a pint of double cream

METHOD:

Dissolve the jelly in the water, in a saucepan or use a microwave, and allow to cool.
Separate the egg yolks from the whites and place into two separate bowls.
Add sugar to the egg yolks and beat until light and creamy.
Once the jelly is just warm to the touch, beat well into the egg and sugar mixture.
Beat the egg white until stiff but not dry.
Gently fold in a quarter of the beaten egg white until just combined, to loosen the mixture slightly. This makes it easier to add the rest without knocking all the air out of the mixture.
Add the remainder of the egg white and mix well.
Slice two bananas and stir through lightly, spoon into a serving dish and put into the fridge to chill.
Lightly whip the double cream and smooth over the banana mousse. Add the remaining sliced banana to decorate.

PUDS

Blackcurrant Fool

Traditionally, a fool - or in old English, 'foole' - is made with gooseberries, but you don't have to stick to tradition; you can change it a bit and use pretty much any fruit that will mulch or stew down. The French word 'fouler' meaning 'to tread' has been linked to the origins of the recipe, possibly a grape-treading connection, but while that argument could drag on about who named it, what, when and how, why worry? Just enjoy it.

I make my own custard but for the 'don't have the times' out there among you I've used a good-quality, refrigerated vanilla custard, which you will find in the cream section in a supermarket. If you want this fool to taste half decent, stay clear of the bright-yellow powder variety of custard that we used to carve up with a spoon at school dinners – remember that? They ruined many a good pudding with that stuff, and we didn't have a choice. The pudding was served with it whether you wanted it or not. Don't have nightmares!

If you want to adjust this dish to make it a bit more grown-up, invest in a nice bottle of crème de cassis. This blackcurrant liqueur adds a certain something to any fruit sauce or syrup, but obviously, in a blackcurrant sauce, it's ideal. Just add a glug or two to the syrup to bring it up a notch. Cassis is also great when reduced within a sugar syrup (equal parts water and sugar, boiled until it's reduced by half), then cooled and poured over ice-cream on a hot summer day.

INGREDIENTS:

200g blackcurrants
Half a pint of whipping/double cream
Half a pint of good-quality vanilla custard
Two tablespoons caster sugar
Half a lemon

You can make this fool with gooseberries, strawberries, rhubarb … any fruit that you can mash.

METHOD:

First, wash and strig the blackcurrants.
Put the blackcurrants, lemon, and sugar into a saucepan over a low heat, stirring until the blackcurrants burst and all the sugar has disappeared. Cook for a further two minutes and then leave to cool.
You can separate the blackcurrants from the syrup or leave intact. I separate them because I like to pour the syrup over the finished dessert.
Whip the cream until it resembles whippy ice cream.
Fold the blackcurrants into the custard until well combined, and then gently fold the custard and blackcurrant mixture into the cream, leaving it marbled. Don't go mad with it; you don't want a solid mass.
Spoon into dessert dishes and chill until needed.
If you have reserved the syrup, chill it alongside the fool and pour over just before serving.

You will need …

Stew blackcurrants.

Retain the juice.

Combine custard and blackcurrants.

Add to whipped cream.

Glass 'em up.

PUDS

Mariner's Chocolate Mousse

Rosie is well known for her love of cocoa products and her eyes went the size of saucers the first time she tried this mousse. From her reaction, and those I have had since from others, I took it that this is a winner. I named it Mariners' Chocolate Mousse as a nod to the added rum, but you can use whisky or brandy in its place if you like, and you'll have to call it something else!

I've tried all manner of chocolate mousses and this is the one I like best. It's much richer than just chocolate and egg white, or chocolate and cream, and it hits a spot that other desserts just fail to. It may take a little while to prepare, but it's worth it. Decant this mousse into wine or martini glasses to set if you want it to look pretty, but if you don't care, then it can go into one large dish and be spooned into bowls.

To get a really great chocolate hit, you really must use one with high cocoa solid content - at least 70%. Using a chocolate bar that you grab with a newspaper on the way home just won't cut the mustard. This recipe, like many of them that I've done for Rosie in this book, requires some whipping, so do invest in a food mixer if you haven't already got one. It will make life a whole lot easier, unless you want the work-out and arms like tree trunks!

I've used a shot glass as a rough measurement because it's easy to grab from the cupboard - and I can refill it as a cook's perk - but if you really want to measure everything out exactly, then a regular shot glass holds around 2fl oz.

INGREDIENTS:

8 oz/227g good-quality dark chocolate (min 70% cocoa solids)
Four large eggs
4oz/113g caster sugar
Half a pint/8fl double cream
Two tablespoons of cooled espresso coffee (80ml)
A shot-glass of rum (80ml)
1 teaspoon vanilla extract

METHOD:

Melt the chocolate in a bowl over a pan of barely simmering water. Don't let the bottom of the bowl touch the water or the chocolate will burn.
Next separate egg whites from the yolks, putting the whites to one side.
Add the sugar to the yolks and beat until creamy, then add the chocolate while still just warm. Beat well. The gentle heat from the chocolate will help the egg yolks to cook slightly; the mixture should be quite stiff.
Add the coffee, rum and vanilla, mix well.
Add the double cream slowly, a little at a time, combining well.
Whip the egg whites to firm peaks - they should just hold their shape.
With a metal spoon add one spoonful of the egg white into the mixture, folding gently to start it off. Then add the rest, combining well but taking care not to beat out too much of the air in the egg white.
Divide between six glasses. Chill for at least 30 minutes to allow the mixture to thicken.
Serve with soft fruit such as raspberries, a chocolate twist or just a spoon!

You will need ...

Beat sugar and yolks.

Melt chocolate.

Add flavourings.

Combine with cream.

Fold in egg whites.

PUDS

Meringue Gateau

I know this looks scary but it really is very easy to make. You can let this languish on a low heat in the oven and confidently disappear down the pub for a while - I don't mean four hours though, lads. This dessert dresses to impress, and it's one to attempt when feeling brave and fearless although when you've done it once you'll get all blasé about it. When it has sat in the oven, served its time and is ready to come out, you will need to find the 'gentle' in you - easy does it, it's delicate. Leave it to cool and then carefully turn it over in your hand and peel away the paper; if it cracks slightly, don't panic, the cream will cover a multitude of sins. Use any soft fruit you like in this, raspberries, strawberries, banana, passion fruit, peaches ... the list is endless.

So that you know a bit about meringue - and I bet you can hardly wait - let me enlighten you. In this recipe, I've used French meringue, which is egg white with two types of sugar gently added, and then beaten until thick and glossy, but there are two other types of meringue out there; Italian - used in mousses and the like, is sugar and water melted together in a pan until it reaches 250F and then slowly drizzled into the beaten egg white and then left beating on a low speed until cool. This is used for desserts like baked Alaska too, because it is safe to use uncooked.

Swiss meringue is egg whites and sugar whisked over a bain-marie until warm, and then beaten until cooled. This one is usually baked and used like French meringue, although it has a bit more of a marshmallow feel to it and is considered to be less likely to collapse. There you go - now you can appear knowledgeable on the subject while prancing around the kitchen in your pinny. Don't worry, I won't tell a soul.

INGREDIENTS:

Six eggs
6oz/180g caster sugar
6oz/180g icing sugar
One pint double or whipping cream
Soft fruits of your choice – you can include tinned mandarin oranges.

METHOD:

Pre-heat the oven to 110°C.
Cut two pieces of greaseproof paper to the approximate size of your oven shelves.
Separate the eggs and whisk the whites on full pelt until they are stiff.
Add half the caster sugar and whizz gently for a few seconds, then add the other half.
Do the same with the icing sugar, then turn the speed to high and beat for about five minutes. The meringue mixture is ready when it is thick and glossy and holds its shape.
Divide onto two pieces of greaseproof, and smooth into equal rounds approx 7 inches across.
Pick up the edges of the paper and lay the meringue directly onto the oven shelf.
Bake for 1hr 50mins/2 hrs, then remove and leave to cool on wire racks.
Whip the cream until thick, slather over the bottom half, top with the fruit, lay the second meringue on top and repeat.

You will need ...

Whisk egg whites ...

... then add sugar.

Divide equally.

Slide on to oven shelf.

Perfect meringue!

PUDS

Peach Upside-down Cake

Everyone is use to pineapple upside-down cake, this is just a variation on that classic we know from our childhood. Like the blackcurrant fool recipe, you can change your fruit as you see fit, but with this one steer clear of anything too soft. Soft fruit, such as raspberries, will go a bit mushy in the bottom of the cake tin and will sometimes stick to it, so try your hand at pears, apples or nectarines, for example. Tinned are okay to use, but drain them well or the sponge will turn soggy.

If you decide to use apples, stop the fruit from discolouring by squeezing lemon juice over them once they are peeled and chopped. Cooking apples are more tart than the dessert varieties and usually require added sugar to sweeten them up, so you might want to avoid using those, too. Dessert apples, such as Braeburns or pippins are sweeter and hold their shape well during cooking.

When making any sponge, make sure that you beat the butter and sugar together well. It should completely change colour when it is well mixed, almost to a cream in appearance. Butter gives a richer flavour than margarine and makes the mix a bit denser, but use what you prefer, or have to hand.

This pudding will keep, covered, for a couple of days, but it is really at its best eaten on the day it is made, warm, with lashings of custard or cream.

INGREDIENTS:

Four fresh peaches
(or a tin of peach halves)
6oz self-raising flour
6oz caster sugar
6oz butter or margarine
Three eggs
One teaspoon vanilla essence

METHOD:

You will need an 8-inch, spring-sided or loose-bottomed cake tin.
Pre-heat the oven to 160°C.
Boil a kettle. Ready two bowls, one with cold water and one with the boiling water.
Drop the peaches into the boiling water and leave for a couple of minutes, then fish them out and plunge them into the cold water.
Peel away the skin with a knife and then halve the peaches and arrange around the bottom of the tin.
Next, using a mixer, cream together the sugar and butter until light in colour, beat the egg and vanilla together until it runs off the whisk like water.
Gradually add the egg mixture, along with spoonfuls of the flour, to the butter and sugar mixture until it's all combined.
Smooth the mixture over the peaches, covering completely.
Bake in a pre-heated oven for 35/40 minutes, until golden brown and springy to the touch.
Leave the cake to cool in the tin for ten minutes, then remove the sides and invert onto a plate, using a flat knife to remove the bottom. The peach slices will now be on the top.
Serve with vanilla custard, cream or ice cream.

You will need.

Remove skins.

Remove stones and halve.

Arrange in a pan.

Cover with mixture.

Turn out on a plate.

PUDS

Pears in Pear Cider

Personally, I can't stand cider in a glass, but I do like to cook with it; apologies to my lovely friends in Cornwall who might now shoot me on sight for hating the Scrumpy, but it wouldn't do for us to all be the same, I say.Cider (or apple wine) is made from fermented apple juice, apparently mostly from concentrate these days, which seems a bit of a shame for the traditionalists, but there are still cider farms in Somerset that stick with the old methods.

Any apple can be used, but a lot of artisan makers of fine cider use only one type, or recipe, so I am told by a lover of the stuff, and I shall take his word for it. The same deal applies to pears, of course, for pear cider, which has a long tradition, despite becoming popular relatively recently. A name change caused the rebirth of interest; it was always 'perry', and was marketed as Babycham in the 50s and 60s as a 'champagne perry' aimed at women, but considered naff in today's sophisticated drinks market. 'Pear cider', on the other hand, is trendy – apparently. However they label it, I'm not drinking it!

Pears cope well with being poached, they hold their shape and don't have to be fully ripe for this recipe, but steer clear of them being rock hard; too under-ripe and this won't work, and besides I don't think that is being too kind to your belly either. I wouldn't want anyone getting sick.

Try to leave the stalk in place on the pears when you peel them. There are two reasons for this; firstly, it looks pretty when you dish it up, and secondly, you have something to grab hold of when removing them from the saucepan - no burned fingers here, please!

You can serve your poached pears with a large blob of whipped double cream, or a slug of crème fraîche or yoghurt for a healthier version. You really can't get easier than this!

INGREDIENTS:

Six pears
150g caster sugar
One bottle of pear cider

METHOD:

Peel the pears and slice off the bottoms so that they will stand upright.
Put the sugar and cider into a saucepan and bring to a simmer.
Place the pears into the simmering sugar syrup mixture and pop on a lid.
Simmer for about 35 minutes. If you are using very ripe pears they may only need about 20 minutes. The pears are done when you can pierce with a fork and they feel soft.
Remove the pears from the sugar mixture and place on a plate to drain.
Turn up the heat until the sugar mixture thickens and turns a golden colour
Turn off the heat and allow to cool.
Place the pears into serving dishes and spoon over the syrup.
Serve as they are or with ice cream, or cream.

You will need ...

Peel pears.

Sugar and cider ...

... brought to a simmer.

Poach pears.

Reduce syrup.

Pecan and Treacle Tart

Pecans liven up this treacle tart and add some crunch. Walnuts and hazelnuts work well too, but there is something about pecans that seems to suit the sweetness of this dish. I love the American pecan pie, and this tart has a similar flavour, but it's much lighter because of the addition of breadcrumbs, and is less sweet than the US version – they use sugar and golden syrup!

Try to roll out the pastry as thinly as you can. You want a crisp texture rather than thick lumps of pastry in your mouth. It really is important to rest pastry, so don't be tempted to skip it or you'll have shrinkage as it cooks, and a mess at the bottom of the oven when your mixture overflows.

When buying sweet, ready-made pastry (if you're not making your own) choose the all-butter type if your local shop stocks it. It tastes far better than the regular one and is worth spending a few more pennies.

Bake it in a loose bottomed tin, if you can, because a regular pie dish will cause you some difficultly when trying to remove it in one piece. Rub the surface of the tin with butter, and lightly dust with flour to prevent it sticking.Don't remove it too soon from the tin, but leave it to cool a little and firm up.

The filling holds its heat well, so handle with care when removing from the oven and tin.

INGREDIENTS:

1 pack ready-rolled sweet pastry
4½oz fresh breadcrumbs
Eight tablespoons golden syrup (approx half a tin)
One lemon
Four tablespoons double cream
4oz pecan nuts (optional)

METHOD:

Pre-heat the oven to 160°F.
Butter and flour an 8-inch, loose-bottomed flan tin, line with your ready-rolled sweet pastry, prick all over with a fork and put into the fridge to rest.
After ten minutes, cover the pastry with some greaseproof paper and fill with baking beans, rice or lentils, and bake for ten mins.
Remove from the oven and take out the baking paper carefully, return the empty pastry case to the oven and cook for another five minutes.
Use a food processor or grater to make fine breadcrumbs.
Chop the nuts and add to the breadcrumbs, reserving a few whole ones to decorate the top.
Measure out your golden syrup and add the finely-grated rind and juice of one lemon. Stir in well, and then add to the breadcrumbs along with the cream.
Blend well; the mixture should be very moist. If it seems at all dry add more syrup.
Fill the pastry case with the mixture, pressing down lightly and evenly.
Add pastry strips and whole pecans to decorate, or leave it plain.
Put it back into the oven and bake for 35 minutes or until golden brown.
Serve with ice cream or cream.

You will need ...

Bake blind.

Blitz breadcrumbs.

Combine filling ingredients.

Decorate with pastry strips.

Bake until golden.

PUDS

Rhubarb and Apple Crumble

Crumble is a very British dish, usually spread over stewed fruit and topped with lashings of double cream - or custard, for the traditionalists. My gran was a bit of a character, and as she can't be punished for any misdemeanours now because she's long since departed, I can see no harm in telling you what I know. My grandmother spent the Second World War years living a quiet life in the Kent countryside, and like most people she was committed to the war effort so she became a land girl at a local farm. He was bringing up three daughters and she made it her mission to see them well fed, so as she went along digging up potatoes for the masses, who's to say if the odd good one got dumped on the edge of the field, partially hidden by a well-placed foot, and picked up after dark - or the odd cabbage disappeared from the middle of the farmer's field so it wasn't missed? That was my gran for you! She also kept chickens, well fed from the corn the farmer let them keep once they had cleared a field after a harvest. She didn't bat an eyelid over where meat for the pot came from, and nor should we. Rabbits generally came from her own backyard, may they rest in carrots … and as for apples; where do you think the term 'scrumpy' comes from? She'd 'scrump' pears and rhubarb too, if truth be known.

Anyway, back to the humble crumble; during those war years, flour, fat and sugar was rationed heavily, something we can barely comprehend these days. Gran told me they would replace the flour with stale bread crumbs and use local honey to sweeten the mix. They had to make the best of what they had. These days crumble is still as popular as it ever was, but we have the luxury of adding whatever we like. Throw in some crushed hazelnuts for crunch, or coconut as they did back in the 16th century. Let your imagination run wild.

INGREDIENTS:

1lb rhubarb
Four dessert or two large cooking apples
4oz light brown sugar
4oz caster sugar
4oz porridge oats
2oz chopped walnuts (optional)
8oz plain flour
4oz salted butter, cubed
One teaspoon of ground ginger
A lemon - or bottled lemon juice

METHOD:

Pre-heat the oven to 170°C
Wash and cut the rhubarb into approx two-inch pieces and put into a saucepan with 2oz of the caster sugar and about four tablespoons of water.
If you're using cooking apples, peel and slice the apples and add them to the pan.
Simmer the rhubarb on a slow heat until it softens slightly and begins to break up.
Remove from heat and reserve.
Peel and core the dessert apples then slice.
When the rhubarb has cooled slightly, put into an ovenproof dish along with the apples, and combine.
Make the crumble topping by rubbing together the flour, butter and sugars until the butter has broken down to a rough crumb.
Add the nuts (if used), porridge oats and ginger, stirring to combine.
Scatter this mixture over the rhubarb and apple, making sure all the fruit is covered.
Sprinkle with Demerara sugar and place in the oven for about 40 minutes.

You will need ...

Stew rhubarb.

Add apples.

Combine dry ingredients.

Fruit into dish.

Top with crumble and Demerara.

PUDS

Strawberry & Mandarin Syllabub

Syllabub is a very old English dessert that goes back to Tudor times when it was made from milk still warm from the cow, but Health and Safety will have put the block on that, so you'll have to use a less traditional method. The sugar is steeped overnight in wine, lemon juice or cider, and then the mixture is added to milk or cream and whipped until light and soft. I've used lemon juice and brandy because I prefer the taste, but like all recipes, this is just a guide, so you can use what you like and play with different flavours.

Now, here's the thing with syllabub; if you over-beat the mixture, it will stiffen hard and there is no way to recover it, so don't be too heavy-handed. As soon as it starts to thicken, turn off your beaters and stir by hand until it just holds its shape. The acid in the lemon juice, cider or wine curdles it naturally so it really doesn't need a lot of help. If you have a balloon whisk now is the time to use it; hand whisking is a bit easier to predict than an electric beater, but it's your choice.

Taste as you go. If your lemons have made the mixture too tart, add a tablespoon of sugar and mix until just blended, like I said, don't over-beat, though. You can also replace the brandy or sherry with an orange liqueur or Limoncello. I've used strawberries and mandarins here, but if you can get them, tinned guava work very well at the bottom of the glass and add a flavour that is a bit different. In fact, you can use any fruit you happen to have around.

Mrs Beeton didn't use fruit at all, by the way, just white wine, sugar and milk - and grated nutmeg on top - but it's a tad more interesting with fruit underneth it.

There's an old legend, and I'm totally not convinced, that syllabub came about by a milkmaid milking a cow straight into a container of cider. That seems a bit odd to me, but romantic all at the same time. I'll leave it to you to believe it or not - we all like to spin a good yarn don't we!

INGREDIENTS:

One can of mandarin oranges
One punnet of strawberries
Two medium unwaxed lemons
4oz caster sugar
½ pint double cream
A shot glass of either brandy or sherry

METHOD:

Divide the fruit evenly between four wine glasses or dessert dishes.
Reserve four strawberries for decoration.
Finely grate the rind from the lemons onto the sugar in a large bowl. Be careful not to add any of the pith.
Juice the lemons and add to the rind and sugar.
Leave for about 60 minutes, to allow for the sugar to dissolve in the lemon juice.
Add the cream and beat to a soft, dropping consistency - similar to thick yogurt.
Spoon over the fruit evenly, top with a strawberry and refrigerate until needed.

You will need ...

Fruit into glasses.

Sugar into lemon juice.

Leave to infuse.

Whisk in cream.

Pour over fruit.

Top Tips

To prevent rice from sticking together, rinse it until the water runs clear. This removes the starch and helps the grains to remain separate.

When making meringue, use eggs that are a few days old and are at room temperature. They whisk up with more volume than those straight from the fridge.

When peeling fresh ginger, always use a teaspoon, lightly scraping the skin away. You won't lose as much as when using a knife, and it's safer!

Freeze whole chillies when you buy them; that way, none are wasted if you don't get around to using the whole bag … and they're easier to chop when frozen and firm.

Almost all herbs can be frozen. Harvest what you grow and seal them in plastic boxes or freezer bags to use in the winter months. Chopping and then freezing them in ice-cube trays with a little water will give you perfect measures every time, too.

To get the most out of a lemon or a lime, roll the fruit firmly with the palm of your hand, backwards and forwards on a work top, to bruise the innards before you cut and juice it - you'll get a load more out of it.

After you have rolled out homemade or shop-brought pastry, put it into your pie dish and allow it to relax for ten minutes, or so, before you fill or blind bake it. This helps to prevent shrinkage from the edges.

If you don't have baking beans to use when blind baking, just line your pastry shell with greaseproof paper and use rice, dried lentils or dried peas as a substitute. Keep them in a jar and re-use up to a dozen times for baking.

To keep game fresh while on a shoot, or transporting home, freeze water in used soft drinks bottles and add them to a supermarket freezer bag before you go. This will act in a similar way to a freezer box but is less bulky and easier to carry.

Before plucking a bird try plunging it into cold water, weighed down for ten minutes. This moistens the feathers and keeps them together, preventing too much mess.

Always pull feathers out in the opposite direction from their growth pattern by pinching a few feathers between your thumb and forefinger. Done on the same day as they are shot makes this job slightly easier

After plucking game birds, if you find you are left with a lot of pin feathers, try using a domestic kitchen blowtorch to singe away the remains. The fluffy down should disappear easily.

Wild rabbit has a slightly darker, stronger meat than farm-reared rabbit, so will be slightly tougher when cooked. Keep the rabbit tender by cooking in a sauce, in wine or a good stock; remember - fluid is good!

For quick vegetable rice: Fry any chopped vegetables that you happen to have handy with a crumbled vegetable stock cube for a couple of minutes, and then add pre-cooked, boiled rice, salt, and pepper. Heat through. Easy-peasy.

My grandmother taught me that the combination of carrots, onions, and celery should always be the basis of beef stews. The mixture also works well, placed underneath a roasting chicken, pheasant, or pigeon.

A quick note about small pickling onions: they are very useful items to have in your vegetable tray. They will keep for weeks and will add flavour to roasted roots either on their own, or when placed under a joint. Use them whole and eat when slightly caramelised. Delicious!

I roll homemade burgers/rissoles/meatballs/fishcakes in semolina before frying because it gives a satisfying crunch to the outside. You can achieve a similar effect with seasoned flour, egg and breadcrumbs but it takes longer and is much more hassle.

To make use of leftover egg yolks, why not make a mayonnaise? Simply, beat the egg yolks in a bowl. Keep the mixer beating and very slowly, in a fine stream, pour olive oil - or a mixture of vegetable and olive oil - into the eggs until the mixture becomes thick and creamy. This will take a lot of oil! Then add a spoonful of mustard, salt, pepper and a squeeze of lemon to taste. Add three cloves of squashed garlic for an aioli.

Crumble topping is so versatile. You can use it to top any fruit - pear, simple apple, or peach and plum. Let your imagination roam free! You can add walnuts, almonds or hazelnuts for crunch and a drizzle of honey or a sprinkling of Demerara sugar gives a lovely golden top when cooked.

To remove tomato skins: Lower tomatoes carefully into a large saucepan of boiling water and cook for one minute, then plunge the fruits into cold water. The skins will peel off easily.

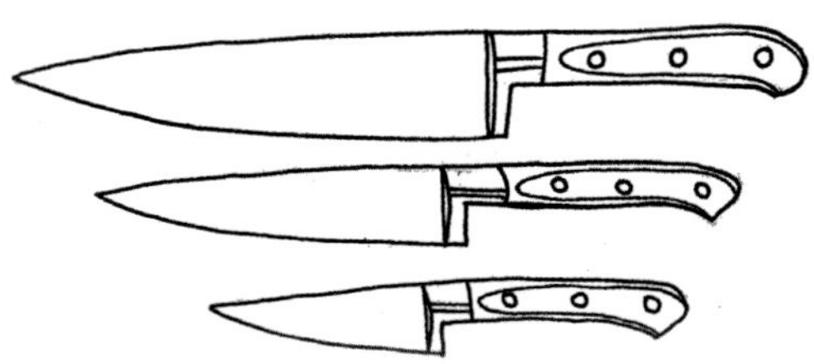

Son and Heir ... Gunner

In the beginning...

Home from school he came, one summer afternoon in '85.
'I need to eat,' he begged, 'so I can stay alive.
'Make cups of tea, and sandwiches, please do.
'That orange juice looks nice. The tea's for you.

'Sweet tea is good for shock. Drink more than one,
'For in my schoolbag, here, I have a gun.'
Fighting down a surge of dread, 'How nice,
how quaint; to whom does it belong?' I quietly said.

'Tis mine,' quoth he. 'To me it does belong.
'A kid at school's got two. I had it for a song.
'I swapped it for my Guns 'n' Roses album, 'Lies'.
'With this, I'll get those bunnies right between the eyes.'

'It's nothing special, really, just a Gat.
'Now I can shoot at things, but not the cat.'
'You will not shoot at living things,' I said.
'Or prey may not be all that winds up dead!'

We made a target out of wood and tin,
So he'd be safe. I knew I couldn't win.
A love of shooting took a hold that day.
Soon, targets, rats and pigeons were his prey.

Not with the Gat, of course, that's just for fun.
More powerful means were needed, not a gun.
A proper rifle did the job, his pride and joy.
Huntin', shootin', fishin' - that's my boy!

Gathering Friends

Hunting animals for food goes hand in hand with foraging for wild plants, berries, nuts and so on, so when it was suggested that I attend one of Ronnie Sunshines' foraging days, I jumped at the chance. I'm always on the lookout for 'free' food and couldn't wait to learn how to identify mushrooms, which was what the day would be about, or so I thought. In my ignorance, I had no idea of the bounty that might be on offer in our woodlands. I conned number two son into being my cameraman for the day, and set off to meet him at the Bourne End services on the A41. I had a phone call from Simon as I approached our rendezvous to tell me that I could turn back home because he had already done his 'foraging' for the day. He'd found a Maccy D's and had gathered himself a Breakfast McMuffin and a Fanta. I wasn't entirely sure that he was taking this foraging lark seriously.

We arrived at our destination, eventually after a few wrong turns. At one point Simon, who was following me, indicated for me to pull over, overtook me and led us to our journey's end. Even with a sat nav I'm still direction dyslexic, and I was impressed with my son's navigational skills without one. We pulled into a field and awaited developments.

Kevin and Ruth were our guides for the day and they gave the assembled company a ten-minute talk on safety. Very sound advice, it was, too! They told us where to pick our wild plants from; to avoid anything rare or unusual - which it all was to me, I didn't have a clue what I was looking at; don't gather berries that grow low enough for a dog to pee on, and much more. The most important phrase was, 'if you can't identify it, don't eat it!'

The common or garden weeds that most of us take for granted, and compost when they grow in our gardens, are what our ancestors used on a daily basis, not only to supplement their diets but also to heal various ailments. Many of these wild plants have analgesic or anti-bacterial properties as well as, or instead of, a culinary value and I was captivated by the thought of a great x 10 grandmother of mine having had that knowledge. My father's ancestry goes back hundreds of years in rural Somerset, and many were reliant on the farming industry, from agricultural labourers to yeoman farmers, so there was a good chance that more than one great-grandmother gathered plants for medicine as well as for the pot. I was determined to find out some of what they had known.

I discovered that the 'dock leaf on a nettle sting' ploy didn't work for me because I'd been doing it wrongly. For years, I've been slapping a single leaf directly over the stings, as directed by my father, who clearly hadn't listened to his grandmother. We were told that you must pick several dock leaves, squash them together to get some juice and apply that. At least I could recognise them without being shown – and I knew what a nettle looked like. I began to feel quite smug, until Kevin expanded on the nettle lecture and I realised how little I knew, really.

There are 101 uses for nettles, apparently, including the making of string and fishing line. They've been used as an arthritis therapy, and if you approach the plant with purpose, hence the phrase 'grasp the nettle', there is no sting. The humble stinging nettle contains more iron, magnesium, potassium and vitamins than spinach, so a bowl of nettle soup, or even a cup of nettle tea, can be beneficial providing you pick the young tips. We were told to be careful, though; the older leaves contain silica which is a stomach irritant.

The whole day was a wonderful experience. The musty dampness of the woods on a boiling hot day was pleasantly cool, and it seemed that we'd gone back in time a couple of hundred years. It was so peaceful, apart from the harsh, parrot-like call of a jay, and the rustling sound of small animals as we tramped our way through their territory, and we learned a great deal. How to pick blackberries, for a start! That seemed a tad pointless, until we were enlightened on the nature of these small, succulent fruits. My usual method is to grab handfuls of blackberries, shove them into a container and carry them home for a jam-making session. In future though, I shall be a little more discerning and follow Kevin's advice. "Eat the ones on the end," he said. "They're the sweetest. Then use the ones a little further up the stem for crumbles and pies, and the berries further back are for jam. Oh, and an infusion of blackberry leaves is a cure for diarrhoea, if you eat too many of the fresh berries." There's nature's yin yang at its finest.

I'm not sure about doing this.

We were shown dozens more plants, trees and shrubs that had culinary, medicinal or practical uses and I don't have room to tell you about all them here, but I was amazed at the amount of 'weeds' that are edible, and actually taste pretty good. Chickweed, for example, used to grow at an alarming rate when I had a garden and I was always ripping it out and throwing it on the compost heap. If only I'd known! I could have put some of it into a quiche, or a salad – not too much, though, that'll give you diarrhoea, too, apparently ... although next door did have a bramble bush that was forever growing through the fence, so I could have made blackberry tea from the leaves as a cure – if only I'd known about that, too.

We were shown where to find beech nuts, sweet chestnuts, wild sorrel, hedge garlic and the inevitable mushrooms. It's advisable to leave the fungi well alone, though, unless you are absolutely certain of your subject. At the end of our day, when the fruits of our foraging bounty were assessed for suitability for the pot, a resident mushroom expert was busily employed sifting through the specimens on offer, discarding the ones that were a bit suspect. He looked up a couple of them in a mushroom 'can we eat these?' book, which didn't inspire confidence in the onlookers, but he clearly knew what he was doing, and no one died.

When we were told that the properties of the foxglove included caffeine, nicotine and digitalis, Simon became quite animated until told that although used as a base for digoxin to treat heart patients, the whole plant was in fact a bit dodgy and out of bounds. I have to say that there does seem to be ample opportunity in our woodland for self-inflicted injury or suicide should you be so inclined. It takes just seven yew berries to kill you, and even inhaling the smoke from burning yew logs can make you feel a bit iffy.

I had a thoroughly enjoyable day, and learned a great deal, not least how to rip the breast meat from a pigeon with just my hands as tools. I didn't think I'd be able to do it because of a hand injury, but I donned a rubber glove to protect the dressing and went for it. The feeling of achievement was immense and although it was only a small victory, I was delighted, despite the grimaces of horror from my youngest son, who was my photographer for the day, and had no idea that his mother could be quite so bloodthirsty. I don't know who he thought cut up the meat and fish he used to eat at home!

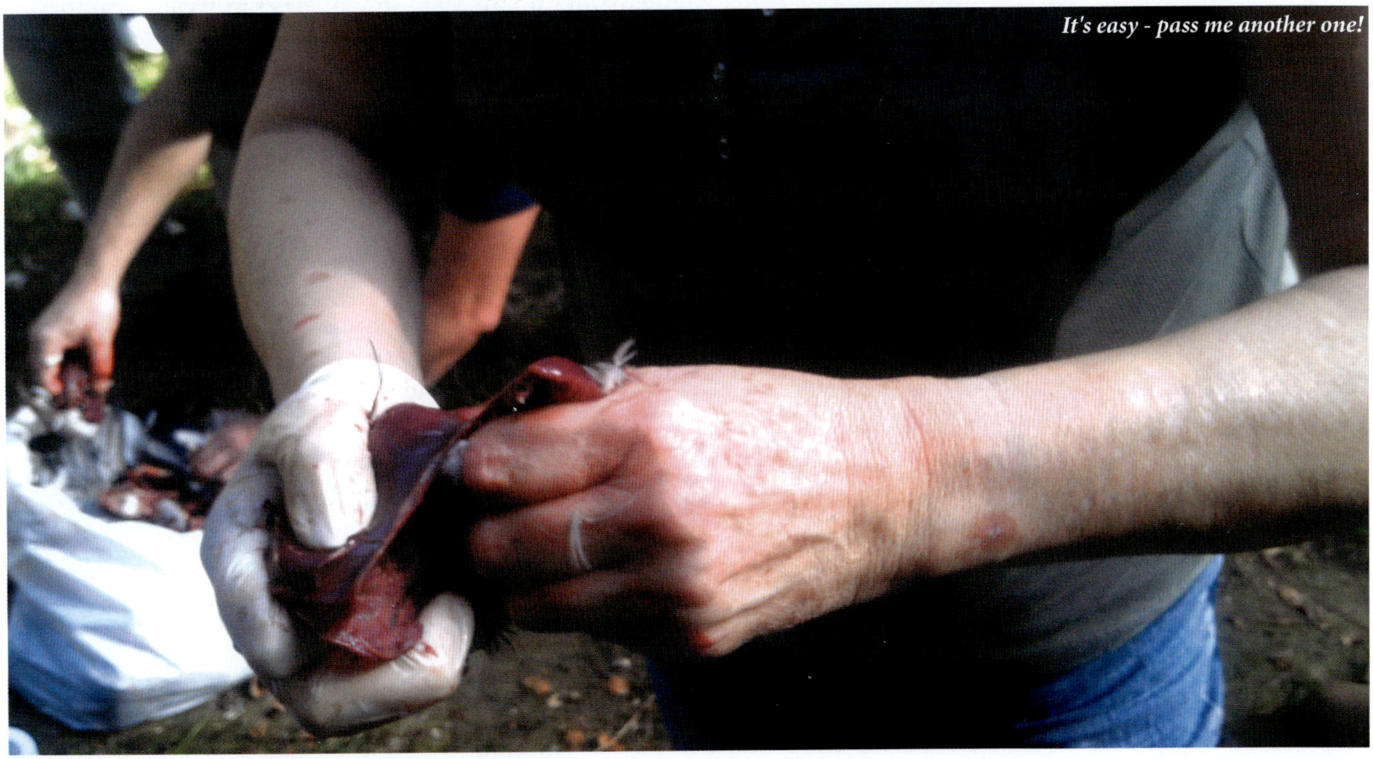
It's easy - pass me another one!

I met some great fellow foragers, too, and that's one of the great benefits of what I do for a living. I am privileged to know some fine people who I've met through being on the periphery of the airgunning/shooting scene, and I can now call many of them friends. Airgunners, in particular, are a friendly bunch and there's a great camaraderie between them, especially at airgun club meetings. Youngsters should be encouraged to join a shooting club if they are just starting out. It's a great sport for young folk, as I've already mentioned within these pages, and at a club, their activities can be monitored, and the correct advice and training given if need be.

Shooting, in any form these days, gets a bad press, but the vast majority of shooters are responsible, safety-conscious and thoroughly decent human beings. There will always be one lunatic, of course, but that's going to happen in any aspect of society; any group of people, regardless of race, colour, creed or ambition. It's a great shame that the very few ruin it for everyone else.

So, if you already have a 'hunter' in the household who will provide you with fresh game, you'll need something 'gathered' to go with it, and while you can forage in a supermarket, if that's your preference, I would still recommend a foraging trip as a great family day out. I wish I'd had the forethought to take my grandchildren along. Kids should be educated into the ways of the countryside anyway, and they would have loved it; maybe next time. Oh yes, did I forget to mention that I'll be going back for more?

Woodland fare in a Dutch oven - fantastic!